DARK HORIZON

THE WITCHING HOUR

THE CHILDREN OF THE GODS
BOOK EIGHTY-TWO

I. T. LUCAS

Published by Evening Star Press

EveningStarPress.com

ISBN: 978-1-962067-37-9

NEGAL

Outside the panoramic windows of the ship's converted dining hall, the moon spilled its silver light across the waves, its reflection creating a shimmering path of luminescence that moved with the gentle swell of the water.

As Negal led Margo through the crowded dance floor, the ship's swaying felt like its own dance, a slow, rhythmic motion that didn't match the cadence of the lively Latin piece blasting through the loudspeakers.

"Are you up for it?" Negal extended his hand to Margo.

She cast him a challenging smile. "I am if you are. Do you know how to salsa?"

He snorted. "I carry a Portuguese passport. Mastery of mambo and salsa was a requirement for obtaining citizenship."

Margo laughed. "Salsa didn't originate in Portugal. It was invented in New York."

"I didn't know that, but I do know how to dance it."

"Then lead on because I'm rusty."

Negal might have exaggerated his mastery of the dance, but watching the other couples was enough to refresh his memory, and he guided Margo effortlessly through the steps. Following his lead she quickly found her rhythm, with her body responding naturally to the beat. As she gained confidence, so did he, and he spun her out and then back into his arms.

Her dress flaring with every turn, her smile broad and her eyes shimmering with excitement, she looked so lovely, so joyful, that his heart swelled with emotion.

Was this love?

It had to be.

He'd never been in love before, but he couldn't imagine a stronger emotion than what he was feeling for Margo. It was as if the world had narrowed down to the space they occupied, creating a bubble in which only they existed.

As the song reached its climax, Negal executed a final, daring spin, bending Margo over his arm in a graceful arch.

The room erupted into applause, and as Margo curtsied gracefully, he bowed to their audience.

When the next piece started playing, Negal was grateful that it was a slower, less demanding dance.

The immortals were still going just as strong as they had before dinner, but Margo was human, and it had been a long day for her. The salsa had drained her, and he noticed that she was growing fatigued even though she tried to hide it.

Her steps were no longer as sure as they had been during the previous dance, and her movements were becoming slightly sluggish, but her eyes were so full of joy and her smile so bright that it would pain him to suggest she should rest.

Besides, he didn't want to let go of her just yet.

The clarity that had begun to crystallize in his mind was like the afterglow of a supernova—blinding in its intensity and too grand to settle comfortably.

He'd always considered himself a creature of duty, and the concept of finding a mate and intertwining his life with another's had seemed almost alien to him.

Yet, here he was, on the cusp of a revelation that threatened to redefine his very existence.

The realization that he desired Margo not just for a few fleeting moments of passion, but at all times and in every conceivable way, was exhilarating and terrifying at the same time.

The possibility that Margo could be his fated one was a concept he might have scoffed at in another life, but now it held a weight of truth he could not ignore. The fact that Aru and Dagor had found their fated mates on

Earth hinted at a design rather than a coincidence—a thread in the Fates' intricate tapestry of destinies.

Against the backdrop of the brewing rebellion on Anumati and their discovery of the heir to the Anumati throne on Earth, the personal destinies of Negal and his teammates seemed to be somehow intertwined with the Fates' grand design.

The question was how he would navigate the complexities of being bound by the duties of his post while also fulfilling his duty to his mate.

Right now, it seemed as if the two would be difficult to reconcile, maybe even impossible. At some point in the future his time on Earth would come to an end, and he wouldn't be able to take Margo with him.

There was also the question of whether Margo was indeed his mate.

If it turned out that she wasn't a Dormant and had no godly genes in her, there was no way she was his one and only. He could still love her, but it wouldn't be the unbreakable bond of fated mates.

The old Negal would have prayed that she had no godly genes so he wouldn't be bound to her, but the new Negal was allowing himself to hope for a miracle and possibly opening himself up to a world of hurt should that miracle not come to pass.

When the song ended, he leaned closer to whisper in her ear. "You seem tired. Ready to call it a night?"

"What makes you think that I'm tired?"

He chuckled. "You are swaying on your feet, and it's not because of the ship."

Margo sighed, a reluctant smile playing on her lips. "I don't want the magic to end." She took a step away from him and twirled in place. "This dress makes me feel like a fairy-tale princess, dancing with the prince on an enchanted voyage."

Her eyes sparkled with joy, but there were dark shadows under them, and even though Negal wished he could prolong the enchantment for Margo, he couldn't ignore the physical toll the long day and night had taken on her.

Taking her hand, he led her away from the dance floor. "The magic doesn't end with the night. To me, you are always a princess, and it has nothing to do with the dress."

"Men are so literal." She rolled her eyes for effect. "It has everything to do with the dress. I don't feel like this every day."

Had he said something wrong?

He was experienced enough to know to avoid most of the usual landmines that females liked to plant in front of males to test them, and he was sure that telling a female that she was always a princess to him regardless of her attire had been the right response.

Margo laughed. "You look so confused."

"I am," he admitted as he pulled out a chair for her. "You look offended, and I can't understand why."

"Oh, my sweet Negal." She leaned her head against his bicep. "I'm not offended. I just feel that once I leave this ballroom, the magic will disappear, and I'll turn back into Cinderella minus the glass slipper." She lifted her head and looked at him. "I keep forgetting that you are not from around here and that you might not know what I'm talking about." She snorted. "That was a major understatement. How many light years away from Earth is your home planet?"

"Hundreds, but I'm familiar with the Cinderella fairy tale, and I know that you have nothing in common with her."

Margo frowned. "You are right. In my case, the prince got me the beautiful evening gown, not the fairy godmother, and he doesn't need a glass slipper to find me."

"You are also not a timid girl who needs a prince to rescue her."

"But you did."

"First of all, I'm not a prince. I'm more of a cinders guy, just without the mean family. Secondly, I can't take credit for your rescue because it was a team effort, and most of the credit belongs to Kalugal. Thirdly, you get to keep the dress, and fourthly, tomorrow we will dance at yet another wedding, and you will be wearing yet another beautiful dress."

She let out a tired laugh, leaning more heavily against him. "You're right. My fairy tale started the moment you caught me when I fainted, and it will probably end when the ship docks in Long Beach. I have four more nights of magic to enjoy, and then my memories of it will be erased, and I will not remember that it ever happened."

Negal's chest tightened despite him feeling confident that their story would have a much happier ending.

Even if he didn't manage to induce Margo's transition before the end of the cruise, he would find a way to do it after. Aru hadn't answered him yet about the possibility of delaying their departure for Tibet, but even if their commander didn't approve a delay, Aru and Dagor could go ahead while Negal stayed behind for a few more weeks to induce Margo. Once that was achieved and she transitioned, they could join the expedition.

Aru might object, but he would cave.

As someone who had just found his mate, Aru knew how impossible it was to deny the call of one's fated partner and leave her for any reason.

"That's not how our story is going to end, and you know it. You're just tired, so everything seems gloomy to you."

She lifted a pair of sad eyes to him. "I'm not a guaranteed Dormant, Negal. I don't have any special paranormal talents, and I'm not related to any immortals. If the induction doesn't work, I can't stay with you or even work for Perfect Match with Frankie. Toven might arrange a job for me in the company's offices in the city, and I might even become a beta tester, just not in the immortals' village. They will thrall me to forget everything I know about them."

He wrapped his arm around her shoulders. "That's a worst-case scenario, Margo. And I refuse to be a pessimist. I believe that you are a Dormant and that you will transition, and so should you."

2

MARGO

Platitudes usually did nothing for Margo. She was too cynical and practical to feel encouraged by empty words of comfort. And yet, Negal's confidence in her ability to turn immortal was welcomed, and it made her feel all warm and fuzzy inside.

She hadn't intended to voice her fears and insecurities, especially not during the party, but Negal had been so sweet and said such nice things that it had all felt too good to be true, which meant that it couldn't be.

She was no princess, and Negal was not her prince.

He was amazing, not just because he was a god, but that only diminished the probability of him being hers. She was just an average woman, a nobody, and she didn't believe in fairy tales.

Then again, she wasn't any less worthy than Mia or Frankie, so why not?

Margo sighed. "As much as I want to continue the fairy tale, I don't want to fall on my face when the clock strikes midnight either, so I should get going while I can still walk."

"The last thing I want is for my princess to wear out her slippers." Negal rose to his feet and offered her a hand up.

Margo laughed. "That was a good one." She took his offered hand. "But you don't have to leave just because your feeble human date is exhausted. You should stay and have fun. I can find my way back to my cabin by myself."

His lips thinned out, and his brows dipped in an affronted expression. "First of all, escorting you to your cabin is my privilege and my duty. And secondly, I won't have any fun without you, so there is no reason for me to stay."

Her heart happily somersaulting in her chest, Margo lifted on her toes and kissed Negal's cheek. "You are adorable."

What she really wanted to say was that she loved him, but she still wasn't ready to make such a declaration. They had just met two days ago, for goodness' sake, and she didn't really know him well enough to have strong feelings for him. It was an infatuation, and surprisingly, for her, lust.

The kiss they had shared earlier had been like no kiss she'd ever experienced, but it had probably been nothing special for Negal. He was an exceptionally good kisser, which was one hell of an achievement given that his fangs elongated when he was aroused, and he had definitely been aroused by their kiss.

Was she ready to take it to the next level, though?

She should be if she was like any other twenty-seven-year-old who wasn't a virgin, but she needed a little more time. Negal was hot, had the face of an angel, and on top of that, he was also smart and kind, but getting naked with a male and allowing him into her body required a deeper emotional connection, and that couldn't happen overnight.

Negal looked at her with amusement in his eyes. "Adorable is not the adjective a male wants to hear from a female he desires." He took her hand and brought it to his lips for a soft kiss.

"How about sweet?" she teased.

"No, not sweet either."

"Handsome?"

"Getting close. But no. I was thinking along the lines of irresistibly sexy, devastatingly attractive, etc."

"You are all that and more." She averted her gaze. "We should congratulate the newlyweds and say goodbye before we leave."

"Sharon and Robert are on the dance floor." Negal wrapped an arm around her waist. "But if you want, we can say hello to Kian and Syssi. You said that you wanted to meet them, and I see them walking toward their table."

Margo swallowed. "Perhaps not tonight."

He leaned down and whispered in her ear, "Don't feel intimidated. Kian is a little gruff but he's a good guy, and if you want to catch him in a good mood, this is the best time. He's with his wife and the rest of his family, and he's having fun."

That was true. Besides, she would be less intimidated by the guy while looking her best and with Negal by her side than if she was summoned to his office or cabin during the day and on her own.

Still, Margo wanted Mia and Toven to be there when the introductions were made. After all, she and Frankie had gotten invited to the cruise only because Mia had insisted, and Toven had backed her up.

"Let's find Mia and Toven first. I want them to introduce me to Kian and his wife."

Negal regarded her for a moment before nodding. "I don't see why you need them, but if their presence will make you more comfortable, then why not?"

"I'm here thanks to Mia and Toven. I mean, I'm here because you saved me from the Modanas, but if I hadn't gotten in trouble and needed rescuing, I would have waited in the resort to be picked up as Mia had arranged."

Negal's arm around her waist tightened. "But then we might never have met. I'm sorry that you had such a scare, so I can't say that I'm happy you got kidnapped by the cartel, but I believe that everything had to happen the way it did so we would find each other."

3

KIAN

Kian noticed Toven and Mia heading his way with Negal and Margo. He hadn't been introduced to her yet, but he'd seen her dancing with Negal last night, and then the two had gone outside and hadn't returned. Today though, they had put on a show, and he had gotten a good look at her.

She was very pretty, but that wasn't what had impressed him about her. What warmed Kian's heart was the way she looked at Negal. It was obvious that she was smitten by the god, which wasn't surprising, and the feeling seemed mutual.

Hopefully, the Fates would be merciful and grant the two a happy ending. It would be a shame if Margo turned out to be just a plain mortal.

Had they begun the process?

Getting induced by a god was Margo's best bet, and if it didn't work, there would be no point trying with anyone else. They would get their answer about her sooner rather than later, which was good. The fewer memories she accumulated of their world, which would have to be later thralled away, the better.

"Margo is beautiful," Syssi said. "Mia and Frankie didn't mention how gorgeous their friend is."

"Her friends are both attractive females." Amanda plucked a chocolate-covered strawberry off the platter. "So, they probably didn't even see that." She took a bite of the strawberry and moaned. "This is so good. I need Onidu to get the recipe from the dessert chef." She looked at Kian. "Is there a chance we can lure the kitchen crew to move to the village?"

He shrugged. "We can try, although I had a different proposition for them in mind."

"Do tell." Amanda took another strawberry.

"I'll tell you about it later." He rose to his feet and waited for the group to reach the table before offering his hand to Margo. "Welcome aboard, Margo."

She took his hand and dipped her head. "Thank you for having me, and an even bigger thank you for saving me and my friend from the cartel."

"You're welcome." He let go of her hand. "How are you doing? I bet your head is spinning from all you've learned."

"It is, but at least it's all good." She offered him a bright smile. "I'm so glad to finally be proven right. For years,

I've been telling everyone who cared to listen that the governments of the world are hiding contact with aliens from the public. And now I know it's true."

Kian chuckled. "I hate to disappoint you, but the governments don't know about us, and if they have contact with some other aliens, we don't know about them."

Margo's face fell. "Well, at least I have proof that aliens exist." She turned to look at Negal. "I'm dating one."

"Yay!" Amanda clapped her hands. "That's wonderful. A god is your best chance of successful transition."

"My thoughts exactly," Toven said.

Margo's cheeks turned crimson. "If you don't mind, I would rather change the subject."

"Sorry," Amanda said with a smirk. "I didn't know that you were bashful."

Margo frowned. "I prefer to describe myself as reserved."

"Same here." Syssi lifted her hand. "Amanda makes me blush about twenty times a day every day, and I've known her for years."

Amanda pretended to pout. "You make me sound so bad."

"That's because you are bad." Syssi mock-glared at her.

Kian realized that he hadn't introduced his table companions yet. "This is my sister Amanda, next to her is her husband Dalhu, and this lovely lady is my wife, Syssi."

"Nice to meet you all." Margo put a hand over her chest. "I just hope that I won't have to forget you soon. I would very much like to become part of your world, and not just to become immortal. I would love to become part of the biggest conspiracy on the planet."

As everyone laughed, Kian regarded the young woman with curiosity. He found her likable and wondered whether it was just that he enjoyed her unconventional personality or if there was an affinity at play.

He could never tell the difference between normal feelings of friendliness toward people and affinity for Dormants.

"I wish we were the biggest conspiracy on the planet," Syssi murmured. "We also thought that we were the biggest deal around until not too long ago, but now we've discovered conspiracies so big that they dwarf our secretive existence."

Margo's eyes sparkled with interest. "What could be bigger than the existence of the gods and their descendants among humans?"

Evidently, Negal hadn't told her about the threat of the Eternal King, and Kian appreciated that. The council had been informed, but he had asked them not to spread the news. There was no reason to alarm the entire clan. But that wasn't even the biggest secret. The Anumati queen communicating with Annani with the help of the telepathic twins was the biggest one of all, but Negal didn't know about it, and he was not going to find out.

Kian still hadn't told Syssi about the first session being tomorrow after the wedding ceremony. The queen could only hold the telepathic meeting at one o'clock in the morning local time, which meant that he and Aru would have to sneak away while everyone else was still celebrating. Perhaps Syssi could advise him on how to excuse his and Aru's absence so it wouldn't look suspicious.

"There is always a bigger fish," Syssi said with a smile.

"Indeed." He nodded and added, "Enjoy the rest of your night."

Thankfully, Margo understood from his tone of voice that no further questions should be asked about the subject.

"Thank you." She returned his smile. "I'm afraid that this feeble human is tired and needs to go to bed. It was very nice to meet all of you." She dipped her head. "Good night and thank you again for saving me and hosting me aboard this lovely ship."

4

NEGAL

"That wasn't so bad," Margo said as she walked into the elevator. "Kian was a little intimidating, but I've met worse in the advertising agency I work for." She pressed the button for her deck. "Do you think he was trying to be nice for the poor human's sake?"

"I told you that he was a good guy. I don't know why he has such a reputation."

They were alone in the elevator, and Negal considered pulling Margo into his arms for a quick kiss, but the ride was too short, and by the time he completed the thought, the automated voice announced the third deck.

"Perhaps he was nice to me because of you." She took his hand. "After all, you are a visiting god, right? A dignitary of sorts."

He shook his head. "Not a dignitary. We are not here in any official capacity. The people back home don't even know that immortals exist."

They had spent a lot of time together today, and yet there hadn't been enough of it for him to tell her anything significant about himself or to learn more about her. It was impossible to cram everything there was to know about a person into a few hours, and on top of that, he knew that she might be made to forget everything he told her, so what was the point?

Margo stopped in front of her cabin and pulled out her phone from her purse. "Tomorrow, we are going to sit down somewhere, and you are going to tell me about yourself."

He chuckled. "Is that an order?"

"Yes."

As she lifted her phone to open the door, he put his hand over hers. "Not yet."

She lifted a pair of questioning eyes to him. "We don't have to say good night out here. You can come in and we can have a quiet cup of tea together."

If the invitation had come from any other female, he would have assumed that tea meant something else, but in Margo's case, tea meant tea.

Still, he would take whatever she was willing to give him, including sharing a cup of tea, but he needed to kiss her, and he wouldn't be able to do that with Dagor and Frankie inside. They hadn't attended the wedding, and they would probably be in their bedroom with the door closed, making up for lost time during Frankie's transition, but they might be taking a break from their marathon lovemaking, and he didn't want to take the chance.

He cupped her cheek and lowered his head, so their lips were almost touching. "Frankie and Dagor might be in there, and I want to kiss you good night."

He waited for her to close the fraction-of-an-inch distance between their lips.

Mischief dancing in her eyes, she wound her arms around his neck and teased his lips with hers. "Like this?" she whispered.

"Yes, but I need a little more."

Gripping her hips, he pulled her closer to him and took over the kiss. She tasted of the sweets she'd eaten for dessert and the vermouth she'd drunk and her own unique taste, which was sweeter than both.

Delicious. Addictive.

She moaned, and as her fingers threaded through his short hair, he regretted it not being longer so she could tug on the strands, claiming him as he was claiming her with this kiss.

Hoisting her up, Negal hooked one of Margo's legs around his waist and ground his erection against her center. Despite the layers of clothing between them, he could feel her heat and imagine how wet she was for him.

A groan escaped his throat, and in answer, she rubbed back against him. Wanton, uninhibited. He had a feeling that if there was no one in the cabin behind the door he was pressing her against, she wouldn't have objected to him taking her to bed.

"Margo," he breathed as he propped her up with one hand so he could free the other one to smooth over her exposed thigh.

Her heated core was like a magnet to his roaming fingers, but as he got so close that he could actually feel the heat radiating from her, she stiffened, and he immediately retracted his hand.

"I apologize," he murmured. "I got carried away." Gently, he eased her back down to the ground, taking a moment to carefully adjust her dress, ensuring everything was properly in place.

"Don't be." She smoothed two shaky fingers over her puffy lips. "I'm the one who should be sorry."

She was panting, a beautiful blush painting her cheeks crimson.

"Never." He cupped the back of her head and pressed a soft kiss to her forehead. "I shouldn't have rushed you when you weren't ready. I want it to be perfect between us, and that can only happen when you are fully ready for me."

"Thank you." Her shoulders relaxed, and a teasing smile lifted her lips. "Tea?" she asked.

"I would love some."

As Margo opened the door, Frankie and Dagor looked up at them from the couch with twin fake-innocent expressions.

Negal stifled a chuckle as he took in their languid state. They looked like a couple of satisfied cats, lounging lazily on the sofa after making love for hours.

They hadn't attended the wedding because Frankie was supposedly still recovering from her transition, but anyone could have guessed the real reason.

"How was the wedding?" Frankie asked.

"Beautiful." Margo put her purse on the bar and filled the kettle with water. "Such heartfelt vows." She shook her head. "You could see the love shining through their eyes."

"We saw it on the ship's channel," Dagor said. "Not live, but the rerun is already available. You can watch all the previous weddings as well."

"That's so cool." Margo pulled two mugs out of the cabinet. "Do you want tea? I'm making some for Negal and me."

"No, thank you." Frankie lifted her half-empty cup of coffee. "We are good."

"Do you need help?" Negal asked.

Margo eyed him from under lowered lashes. "I'm tired, but I'm not dead. I can still make tea."

Touchy female. The funny part was that she was touchy about things no other female he knew cared about.

He lifted his hands in surrender. "Just asking."

"Come, take a seat." Frankie beckoned with a wave of her hand.

Negal unbuttoned his tux and sat down on one of the armchairs. "Can I ask you a favor?"

"Of course," Frankie said.

"I need you to keep an eye on Margo. Can you leave your bedroom door ajar so you can hear her and check on her from time to time?"

"Sure thing," Frankie said with not much enthusiasm, and he could understand why. She and Dagor probably planned to continue their lovefest, and they wouldn't be able to do that with the door open.

"I'm fine." Margo put down two teacups on the coffee table. "I don't need babysitting." She sat on the other armchair. "Frankie is fresh out of her transition and needs rest."

"Bridget said that you need to be watched for reaction to the drugs for seventy-two hours, and it hasn't been that long yet. You are still mortal, and I'm worried about you."

Negal was also worried about Karen and how her transition was progressing. Once he was done here, he planned on going down to the clinic and checking up on her.

"I have no problem keeping an eye on you." Frankie leaned on Dagor's shoulder. "I'll check on you during the night."

"I will do that," Dagor said. "You need to rest." He looked at Negal. "If that's okay with you."

"Hey." Margo snapped her fingers. "I thought that gods were an advanced species, not cavemen. You should ask me if I'm okay with that, not Negal."

Dagor dipped his head. "Apologies. Are you okay with me checking up on you?"

"Although it is not necessary, yes, and thank you."

Negal was glad that the nightgown she'd gotten at the boutique earlier that day was not as revealing as the one she had borrowed from Frankie the night before. He would have definitely had an issue with Dagor checking up on her if she was sleeping with that flimsy thing on.

Margo cast him a sidelong glance. "Does that meet with your approval?"

"Of course." He reached over the armrests of both chairs and took her hand. "I just want to make sure that you are okay."

Her eyes softened. "Thank you for worrying about me."

"Always." He leaned over and kissed her knuckles. "Sleep well and dream sweet dreams." *Naughty ones of me*, he wanted to add.

5

MARGO

When the door closed behind Negal, Margo's heart was still racing, and her core still throbbing with need. If she weren't so damn repressed, the kiss they had shared outside the door would have ended with them naked in bed, and Margo had a feeling that she would have been just fine with that.

Why the hell had she frozen when Negal's fingers got close to where she had so desperately needed them?

She was still so wet that she worried about the evidence of her arousal showing on her dress, which would be mortifying on several counts. First of all, she didn't want to soil the magnificent gown, and secondly, she didn't want Frankie and Dagor to see it.

Dagor cleared his throat. "I'm going to watch some television in bed." He smiled at Frankie. "You can stay with Margo until she's ready to retire for the night."

Some sort of silent communication passed between the two of them, and then Frankie nodded. "I'm going to make more coffee. Do you want me to bring you some to bed?"

"Thank you, but I'm all coffeed out." He winked at her before ducking into the bedroom and closing the door behind him.

Frankie rose to her feet and walked over to the kitchenette. "Do you want coffee or another cup of tea?"

"I'll have tea," Margo said.

"Why didn't you invite Negal to spend the night with you?"

That was so direct and so like Frankie. The girl had no filter and just blurted out anything that went through her head.

"It's a bit early for that." Margo crossed her legs, hoping to ease the itch in her center that was growing uncomfortable. "I'm not ready to take it to the next level yet."

Frankie lifted a brow. "You seem very ready to me."

Margo was sure that she'd done a good job of keeping her expression schooled, not panting like a cat in heat or devouring Negal with her eyes.

"What do you mean?"

Frankie chuckled. "Did you forget already what I told you about immortals' enhanced sense of smell? Poor

Dagor had to escape to the bedroom not to react to that."

As a wave of mortification washed over Margo, she closed her eyes.

"Oh, my God. I did forget about that. I'm so embarrassed."

"Don't be. It's natural, and both of us are happy that the two of you are drawn to each other. That's precisely what I wanted and hoped for. I just don't understand what you are waiting for."

Damn.

Neither Frankie nor Mia knew about Margo's problems with intimacy, and she needed it to stay that way. If she told them, they would immediately start offering her unsolicited advice on how she could overcome her problem, and worse, they would pity her.

"You heard Negal. I'm still not out of the woods with the drug I was injected with. I feel fine, but I want to be absolutely sure that I'm sober before I let myself be intimate with anyone. I don't want to do anything under the influence of drugs and regret it later."

Frankie surprised her with a hearty laugh. "Believe me, you will not regret this even if you decide that Negal is not for you. Words cannot describe what sex with a god or an immortal is like. Think multiple earth-shattering orgasms, euphoria, and an unrivaled psychedelic trip all combined into an unparalleled pleasure package. And that's not all. The next morning, you will feel like you've just been through a rejuvenating spa instead of feeling like you were hit by a freight train. The venom contains healing properties, so even the most intense session won't leave you with bruises and sore lady bits."

"That sounds incredible, but I still prefer to take it slow and savor the buildup. You know what I think about hookups."

Frankie returned with their drinks and set them down on the coffee table. "Negal doesn't think of you as a hookup. I've seen him around other females, and he never looked at any of them the way he looks at you."

Margo's heart fluttered. "And how is that?"

"Like you are precious to him." Frankie sat down next to her on the couch. "Besides, you don't have time to play it safe, Margo. Negal is your best chance for a successful transition, and he's leaving shortly."

"He said that he would talk with Aru about postponing the mission to Tibet by a few weeks."

Frankie shook her head. "Aru is not going to agree to that. He's already postponed it so he and his team could be on this cruise. He won't ask for another delay. The only exception might be if you are already transitioning. He might let Negal stay behind until you are out of danger, and then he would have to join us with you or without you. Negal is a trooper, and he has to obey orders. He doesn't have a choice."

6

NEGAL

T t was late, or rather early, since it was about two o'clock in the morning, and the smart thing to do would be to head back to his cabin and go to sleep, but Negal was still buzzed from being around Margo most of the day and the two kisses they had shared.

Negal shook his head.

He'd bedded hundreds of females, goddesses, and those of created species, but here he was, excited about sharing two kisses with a female and counting himself lucky and blessed for the privilege.

If he went to his cabin right now, he knew what he would be doing. He would get in the shower and repeat what he had done the day before. It wasn't a bad idea, and it would definitely ease some of the pressure building up inside of him, but it would also leave a bad taste in his mouth, and not because of his venom or the towel he would have to bite.

On some level, it was disrespectful to Margo.

Not that he would mind in the slightest if she pleasured herself while thinking about him. He would be the smuggest guy on this ship if she did. But he had a feeling she wouldn't, and therefore, he shouldn't either.

Besides, he needed to check on Karen.

He hadn't heard anything about how her transition was progressing, and since she wasn't young in human terms, the process was supposedly dangerous for her, and she might need a blood transfusion from him.

The question was how to do it without anyone knowing. Kian was adamant about keeping the power of a god's blood a secret, so it would have to be done in a way that wouldn't arouse suspicion.

Gilbert was no doubt sitting by his mate's side, and Negal was sure that the guy wouldn't agree to leave her alone with him no matter what.

He could get into Gilbert's mind and thrall him to forget that he was there, but then he would also need to do something about the security camera, and he wasn't an expert on that like Dagor.

Well, the obvious solution was to ask Dagor for help.

When he arrived at the clinic level, Negal was relieved to see Gilbert outside by the coffee machine.

He hadn't texted the guy to ask for permission to visit his mate, and knocking on her patient's room in the middle of the night was not really appropriate for someone who wasn't an immediate family member.

Hearing his approaching footsteps, Gilbert turned to look at him. "Negal. What brings you here?"

"I'm worried about Karen. How is she doing?"

"Bridget says that she's doing fine. She's sleeping, but she's conscious. I wake her up from time to time to make sure."

"That's good news." Negal took Gilbert's place in front of the machine, put a cup under the nozzle, and pressed the button for an Americano. "Do me a favor." He removed the paper cup and lifted it to his lips for a quick sip. "Let me know if anything changes."

Gilbert nodded. "I will. Thanks for checking up on Karen."

Negal smiled. "For better or worse, I'm in part responsible for what she's going through."

"I know what you mean." Gilbert chuckled. "When Karen gave birth to Idina and then to the twins, I felt guilty for getting her pregnant. It was absurd since we both wanted to have those children, and Karen didn't blame me, but I couldn't help it." He took a sip from his coffee. "Nothing worth having comes without a struggle, though. So, there is that."

Negal understood what Gilbert was trying to say. "With a few exceptions, that's mostly true. You didn't have to struggle to bring the children into the world like your mate did, but I'm sure you faced other struggles while raising them."

Gilbert huffed out a laugh. "They are a daily challenge but also the joy of my life."

"I believe you." Negal clapped him on the back. "Text me if Karen's situation changes."

Gilbert frowned. "I get it that you feel responsible, but what can you do for her if she gets worse? You'll just join me in worrying."

"Not knowing will make me worry all of the time, but as long as I don't get a text from you, I will know that Karen is okay."

7

MARGO

Margo showered, got dressed in the nightgown she'd bought earlier that day, and climbed into bed, all while Frankie was watching over her from the living room through her bedroom's open door.

"Are you going to stay out there all night?" Margo asked.

"No, I'm going to bed, but I will leave our bedroom door open so I can hear you."

"There is really no need. I'm feeling fine."

Except for the throbbing in her center and the disquiet in her chest, but neither had anything to do with the drug and everything to do with Negal and the fire he'd ignited in her with that kiss that had been more than a kiss.

"I know," Frankie said. "But I promised Negal." She peeked into the bedroom. "Good night, Margo."

"Good night. Can you close the door just a little bit? I feel exposed with it wide open."

"Sure thing." Frankie closed it almost all the way, and a moment later, the lights in the living room went off.

Margo let out a breath.

Solitude at last.

If she had one of her books with her, she could've scratched that itch, just to make sure that everything still worked. It had been a while since she'd pleasured herself, and as the saying went, you had to use it or lose it, and Margo wanted to make sure that she hadn't lost it.

The good news was that it had taken very little for Negal to ignite the fire within her, which was unusual for her, but getting from there to a climax was a different story. She had trouble achieving that even when self-pleasuring, and never with a man.

With a sigh, Margo closed her eyes and tried to remember one of the hotter stories she'd read recently, but it wasn't the same as reading. She liked the slow buildup of a good story, but she lacked the imagination to create it in her head.

What if she fantasized about Negal, though? She could start with the kiss they had shared outside the door, but in her fantasy, she wouldn't freeze up, Frankie and Dagor wouldn't be in the cabin, and things would progress as they should have. Maybe she could even give it a Perfect Match twist and make Negal a dragon shifter.

Nibbling on her lower lip, Margo pulled up her night-gown under the blanket and feathered her fingers over the gusset of her panties. The movement was so minimal that there was no way Frankie and Dagor could hear her all the way in their room, even with their supernatural hearing, and if her arousal intensified, the scent would hopefully stay trapped under the blanket.

Perhaps she could also add a little magic to her fantasy.

Instead of stiffening when Negal's fingers grazed her panties, she would moan and grind herself against him. He would magically get the door open and, with a partial shift, get his wings up and fly them both to the bed.

Naturally, he would also remove their clothing with his magic while flying them so they would both be naked when they reached the bed.

Margo chuckled.

It was such an absurd fantasy that it was amusing instead of arousing. Hopefully, Frankie and Dagor hadn't heard her chuckle, but if they did, they wouldn't know what had caused it.

Taking a deep breath, she tried to concentrate.

Negal opens the door and strides into my bedroom. He's cradling me to him as if I'm precious to him, and I'm a little scared, but I don't stop him because I want him so much.

I burn for him.

He gently lays me on the bed and then takes a step back to look at me.

"Do you want me?" he asks.

"More than anything," I admit as I scoot back and lie against a stack of pillows. "I want to see you. All of you."

Margo chuckled again. She'd never said those words to a man, but she'd read them so many times in romance novels that they almost didn't sound ridiculous to her.

With a cocky smile, he takes off his tux jacket and then starts unbuttoning his shirt slowly, teasingly, one button at a time. Forget about being undressed by magic, this was going to be a lot more fun. *I watch him with hooded eyes, but I don't make a move.*

He shrugs the shirt off and toes off his shoes, but he leaves the pants on as he prowls toward me. "Your turn, love."

Would he call her his love? Or would he have some other term of endearment for her?

Beautiful? Gorgeous? Sweet?

Maybe they had some other terms of endearment where he came from, and he would say a sexy-sounding foreign word that she wouldn't understand the meaning of.

As he carefully removes my dress, I help him so it won't tear, and as I'm left with only the sexy bra and panties set that's also brand new, he sucks in a breath.

"I wanted to see these things on you from the moment the saleslady brought them to the changing room."

"And I wanted you to see me in them from that same moment. That's why I got them."

Margo had gotten them because she'd needed under-things, and in reality, Negal probably wouldn't even remember that she'd bought several sexy sets. All he would care about would be how fast he could take them off her. In her fantasy, though, he would appreciate the lingerie.

He trails his fingers up my calf, my thighs, and as they brush against the lacy trim of my panties, I suck in a breath, but I don't freeze.

Negal looks into my eyes for a long moment and then dips his head, and I suck in another breath as I guess what he's going to do next.

Margo was never a fan of oral pleasuring, not on the receiving end and not on the giving end. It was just too intimate, too personal, and she'd never felt comfortable enough to do that, even with boyfriends she'd been having sex with for a while. But this was a fantasy, and she could be as wild as she pleased, and surprisingly, the prospect of such intimacy with Negal didn't turn her off.

As he presses a soft kiss to my moist folds through the lacy fabric of my panties, I moan and thread my fingers through his hair to encourage him to keep going.

A hungry look taking over his eyes, he hooks his fingers in the elastic of my panties and slides them down my legs.

At that point, Negal's eyes would no doubt be glowing, and his fangs would elongate, but Margo was okay with leaving those parts out of her fantasy for now.

My bra is next, and then his mouth is on my breast. I hiss at the wet heat of his mouth, the rolling of his tongue. He repeats the same with the other breast, and I'm on fire.

Margo pressed her fingers to the needy bundle of nerves at the apex of her thighs, but she still did it over her panties, not ready for full contact. With her other hand, she cupped her breast over her nightgown and pressed her lips tightly shut to prevent a moan from escaping.

Negal lets go of my nipples and looks at me with hunger in his glowing eyes. "I need to taste you. Will you allow it?"

"Yes," I whisper.

And then his mouth is on me, with his lips and tongue setting me on fire. I'm not climbing. I'm shooting up like a rocket.

Margo's hand snaked into her panties, and as she dipped her fingers to coat them in her wetness, she had to turn her head into the pillow to muffle the groan that was forcing its way out of her throat.

Negal devours me with his mouth, sucking and licking, and I spread my thighs even wider like some wanton woman from a romance story to allow him better access. My fingers claw into his hair, and I shamelessly grind myself against his mouth.

"Negal," I whisper as he flicks his tongue over the most sensitive part of me, and then I shatter into a million pieces, with his name still on my lips.

But he's not done with me. Slipping a finger into my wet heat and then another, he stretches me wider to prepare me for his erection, and the anticipation tightens the coil that sprang loose only a moment ago.

He's in no rush, though. He hooks his long fingers and touches a spot I've only read about but never found before, and the coil releases again with an intense wave of pleasure washing over me.

I'm so ready for him to take me.

With a satisfied smile on his glistening lips, he rears on his knees and pushes his pants down.

I gasp.

I imagined him being generously endowed, and he is mouthwateringly so, and for the first time in my life, I want to pleasure a male with my mouth.

"I want to taste you." I reach for him...

"Margo? Are you alright?"

With a start, Margo turned her head and opened her eyes to see Frankie standing in her doorway with a worried expression on her face.

The worry in her friend's eyes was a relief. It meant that she hadn't smelled the arousal that was trapped under the blanket. She must have heard Margo moaning or groaning and had come to check up on her.

"I'm fine. It was just a dream."

Frankie made a sad face. "A nightmare?"

Margo hoped it was dark enough to hide her blush, even from Frankie's new and enhanced vision.

"No. Just a very vivid dream."

"Okay then." Frankie released a breath. "I'm going back to bed. Try to get some sleep."

"Good night, Frankie. And thanks for checking up on me."

8

KIAN

Syssi took off her shoes as soon as they reached the door to their cabin. "I know that I say this about every wedding, but tonight was magical."

Kian smiled. "I agree. I love weddings." He opened the door.

Parker rose to his feet as they walked in.

"Allegra slept the entire time." He sounded disappointed.

"Good." Syssi put a hand on the boy's shoulder. "It means that you have a peaceful aura, and she felt safe with you."

He pursed his lips. "Is that a real thing? I mean, auras?"

"Of course. Babies and animals are more attuned to them than adults. If you were emitting nervous energy, Allegra would have been restless or fussy."

"I was a little nervous," Parker admitted. "I watched over Cheryl's brothers, but they are older, and she was there to help."

"You would have been fine." Kian pulled out his wallet, took out a hundred-dollar bill, folded it, and put it in Parker's hand. "Okidu was here in case you needed help, so there was no reason to be anxious."

Hearing his name, Okidu poked his head out of his bedroom. "Is there anything I can do for you, master?"

"No, thank you. You can close the door now."

"As you wish, master." Okidu dipped his head before doing as Kian instructed.

"Thank you." Parker put the folded bill in his pocket. "I'm available whenever you need a babysitter."

"Good. We will probably be using your services again tomorrow." Kian opened the door for him. "Good night, Parker."

"Awesome." The kid flashed them one last smile before walking out. "Good night."

Syssi shook her head as Kian closed the door. "You practically threw Parker out."

"It's almost morning, and I want to get in bed." He pulled her into his arms.

She laughed. "I guessed as much." She unbuttoned his tuxedo jacket and put her hands on his chest. "You look devastatingly handsome in the tux but even better with nothing at all."

"Ditto, my ravishing beauty."

Perhaps telling Syssi about his problem with Aru could wait for the morning?

Narrowing her eyes, she patted his chest before removing her hands. "Okay, big guy. Out with it."

"Out with what?"

"You were frowning throughout the evening, so I know something is troubling you." She walked over to the kitchenette and popped a pod into the coffeemaker. "Talk to me."

With a sigh, he pulled out a stool and sat down. "It's about my mother speaking with the queen through Aru and his sister. The queen scheduled the first telepathic meeting for tomorrow night after Kri and Michael's wedding, and the following sessions will be at the same time each night, or rather at one o'clock in the morning of the following day."

Syssi tilted her head. "Your mother leaves right after the ceremonies conclude, so that's not a problem."

"Right, but Aru and I will need to be there, and people will notice that we are leaving. My mother offered to invoke her diva status and demand that Aru show up at her cabin each night to tell her about Anumati's history before she goes to bed, and naturally, I would need to be there as well, but that's not a good enough excuse. My mother never issues such unreasonable demands, and people will get suspicious, and by people, I mean my sisters."

Syssi removed the two cups from under the twin spouts of the coffeemaker and put them on the counter. "Maybe we can use Allegra as your excuse. We can transfer her to your mother's cabin and have Parker babysit while she's presiding over the ceremony, and then when the time comes, your mother can call you and say that Allegra is fussy. I will come with you because everyone knows that I wouldn't send you alone to deal with our daughter."

He frowned. "I'm perfectly capable of calming Allegra without your help."

"I know, love." Syssi sat next to him and cradled the coffee mug in her hands. "But someone needs to transcribe what the queen is telling your mother. It's too important to just commit to memory."

He hadn't thought about that, but Syssi was absolutely right. They needed to record the sessions and keep the recordings safe, using the same security protocol as they had for Okidu's journals.

"You are right. I can use my phone to record everything Aru says, and we can transcribe it later. But the excuse of a fussy baby might work once, not every night, and it doesn't solve the problem of Aru leaving at the same time as we do."

Syssi sighed. "I still think that I should be there, taking notes in real time. There is no substitute for that. Transcribing recorded audio is time-consuming, often requiring several hours to transcribe one hour of speech. Live transcribing will eliminate the delay, allowing us to discuss what was learned immediately following the conversation and enabling better absorption of the material and deeper understanding." She pushed a strand of hair behind her ear. "It's like taking notes during class and reviewing them right after as compared to copying the notes someone else made. It's not the same, and the first method is much better."

Kian nodded. "In a way, it will be like attending a lecture, and the information dump will not be easy to absorb. That still leaves the problem of secrecy. How are we going to excuse our early departure?"

"The easiest solution is to tell the family what's going on. It's not like any of us can tell anyone from Anumati about the communication, but if Aru is so concerned, you can ask your mother or Toven to compel everyone to keep Aria and Aru's telepathic connection a secret."

Kian shook his head. "Negal and Dagor don't know about it, and it's crucial to Aru that they don't find out. He doesn't even know that I told you, and he will be furious when he finds out. He didn't even tell Gabi."

"I'm sure he told her."

"He did not. His sister's life is on the line. He wouldn't risk it for anything other than a direct command from his queen."

9

GILBERT

Gilbert leaned over the bed and kissed his wife's cheek. "Karen, honey, wake up."

It was early morning, and they had been doing it all through the night to make sure that she was sleeping and not unconscious.

There was no response.

Panic rising, he shook her shoulder. "Karen?"

Still no response.

"Crap." He ran out of the room, frantic to find Bridget or one of the nurses, but there was no one in there. It was still too early.

Pulling out his phone, he dialed Bridget's number, which he'd programmed in his short favorites list.

"Hello," she answered after several rings, sounding like he'd woken her up from sleep, which he probably had.

"Karen lost consciousness," Gilbert said without bothering with any preamble.

"That's no reason to panic, Gilbert," she said in a much more alert tone. "I'll be there in half an hour."

Half an hour was an eternity, but there wasn't much he could do about that.

"Can you send one of the nurses over? There is no one here."

"Karen is fine, Gilbert. I can see her stats on my phone. I'm coming over more for your sake than hers."

Some of his panic abated, but not all. "I appreciate that, I truly do, but I would feel better if there was a medical professional here to watch over her."

"Gertrude and Hildegard are asleep, and it will take them as long as it will take me to get ready. Do you prefer one of them to come over instead of me?"

He closed his eyes. "I want you."

"I thought so." She ended the call.

"Damn it." Walking back into Karen's room, he scrolled down to another number on his favorites list.

"Gilbert?" Kaia answered almost immediately. "What's happening?"

"Your mother lost consciousness. I called Bridget, and she said that her stats looked okay. She's coming over in half an hour."

"I'll get Darlene to watch over the kids and come down. I'll bring Cheryl with me."

"Good. I want you to take a look at the stats. I don't know if Bridget's telling me the truth, and I don't know what those readouts mean."

"I'll take a look. Hang in there, Gilbert. She's going to be fine. We have to believe it."

"I know." He sighed. "See you in a bit." He ended the call.

Twenty-five minutes later, Bridget arrived and got busy checking Karen's vitals. "She's doing okay." She smiled at Gilbert, but the smile looked forced.

She also hadn't said that Karen was doing great.

"What are you not telling me?" he asked.

Bridget released a breath. "Her blood pressure is a little elevated."

She'd told him before that it would happen as the transition got in full swing.

"Isn't that normal during transition?"

"It's a little higher than what is normal at this stage."

His heart started pounding. "Can't you give her something to lower it?"

Bridget shook her head. "Not unless it reaches critical levels. The best thing for her is to let her body do what it needs to do without interfering." She pulled out her phone. "I'm calling Gertrude. Karen will need round-the-clock supervision until her vitals level out."

So, he hadn't been panicking for nothing, and she'd lied about looking at the readouts on her phone. If she'd seen that Karen's blood pressure was higher than was normal for a transitioning Dormant, she should have told him that.

"Why did you tell me that her vitals were okay when they weren't?"

She gave him a frosty look. "They were fine when I checked half an hour ago. The elevated readout is the most recent one. The blood pressure monitoring is not continuous. The machine was programmed to measure it once every two hours, but I've changed it now to every half an hour."

"I see." That sounded reasonable, and he believed her. "I'm sorry for questioning you."

She lifted a hand. "That's okay. Doctors are not infallible, and it's the duty of family members to remain vigilant and watch over their loved ones. It's especially true when it comes to children. Parents and grandparents know them much better than the doctor who might be seeing them for the first time. If their response to whatever is done to them is atypical, it's important to bring it to the physician's attention."

He nodded. "Thanks for the advice, doc, but since my family is going to be in your care for the foreseeable future, I don't need to remember it. I'm sure you will remind us."

That seemed to placate her, and she gave him a genuine smile. "You have a very nice family, Gilbert, and it's my pleasure to take care of them."

"Thank you."

As Bridget walked out and sat behind the desk in the front room, Gilbert sat on the chair he'd been sitting on throughout the night, took Karen's hand, and kissed the back of it.

"You are going to be okay, my love. You are a fighter." He repeated the same sentence several more times in his head until he started to actually believe it.

When Kaia and Cheryl arrived, he pulled them both into his arms. "Your mother is going to be okay. She's a fighter." He said it with newfound conviction.

PETER

Marina stirred in Peter's arms. "What time is it?"

"Seven-fifteen." He kissed the tip of her nose.

She groaned. "I need to get up. I'm on breakfast cleanup, and I'm also working the lunch and dinner shifts today."

"You were supposed to get the night off yesterday and didn't. Are you telling me that you and Larissa are stranding me and Jay tonight as well?"

One of the human servers had sprained her wrist, and the other was suffering from an upset stomach, but Peter had hoped they would both feel better today so he could have Marina to himself the entire evening and night.

"I'm sorry, but with two staff members still out of commission, no one can take time off." She kissed the underside of his jaw. "I'll come to your cabin after I'm done in the kitchen tonight." She smiled. "Anyway, that's the best part, right?"

Peter couldn't argue with that, but as much as he loved Marina in his bed, he also loved seeing her having fun with him outside of it.

"Not good enough," he said, cupping her lush bottom. "Be prepared to be whisked away for a dance or two. I'm sure you are allowed breaks."

"I can't." Marina pulled out of his arms and rose to her feet. She was gloriously naked save for the long blue hair cascading down her front and covering one of her breasts. "We are short-staffed, and I will be running around like crazy. I also need to collect Jasmine's dress from the laundry and return it to her. I should have done it yesterday, but there was no time." She walked into the bathroom but didn't close the door behind her and continued talking to him.

Peter listened with only half an ear to her prattle. Not surprisingly, he was hard again, and all he could think about was getting her back under him.

They hadn't done anything overly naughty last night because Marina had been exhausted after the long day she'd had at work, and she probably wouldn't be up to anything overly strenuous before her shift, but he could think of a few things he could do to her in the shower that would keep her humming with arousal for the rest of the day until she came back to his bed again.

Ah, good times.

Peter's hand wrapped around his arousal, and he gave it a few lazy strokes. He would need to refrain from biting her, but since he had bitten her last night, that shouldn't be too difficult.

When he heard the shower faucet turn on, Peter released his shaft and got out of bed. In the bathroom, steam rose in the shower, and Marina hummed a tune he wasn't familiar with. After emptying his bladder and brushing his teeth, he walked into the small enclosure, positioned himself behind her, and cupped her breasts.

She leaned into him. "That's nice."

"Nice? I don't do nice." He turned her around, clasped her wrists, and lifted her hands over her head.

Marina's eyes became hooded, and as he bent down and twirled his tongue over her right nipple, her breath hitched.

"I don't have much time," she whispered.

"I'm going to be quick." He moved his mouth to her other nipple and licked it before giving it a hard suck.

Marina hissed, but it wasn't in pain, it was in anticipation, and when he nipped it with his front blunt teeth, she jerked even though she must have known what he'd been planning.

It was amazing how quickly they had learned each other's bodies and how to deliver them the most pleasure.

He licked it, coating it with his healing saliva, as she'd known he would.

Immortal males were uniquely well suited for the intricate dance of providing just the right sprinkling of pain to enhance a female's pleasure.

Letting go of Marina's wrists and her nipple at the same time, Peter straightened up and took a step back. "Turn around and put your hands against the wall."

She hesitated. "What are you going to do to me?"

"Something you were craving. Now, do as you're told." He laced his tone with command.

She spun around, braced her hands against the wall as he'd told her, and pushed her ass out.

The vixen had guessed what he had in mind.

"Excellent." He rubbed a hand over her round bottom. "You've earned a spanking for pleasuring yourself without my permission yesterday."

"But I didn't know that I wasn't supposed to," she protested, as the scent of her arousal flared.

"Ignorance of the law is no excuse." He delivered a sharp smack to her left cheek and another one to her right. "But I'll take into account the extenuating circumstances." He massaged her beautiful bottom before delivering two more smacks.

She emitted a sound that was part groan, part moan, and as he slid his fingers over her wet folds, she stuck her bottom out even more and threw her head back.

He pressed his body to hers and nipped her ear. "Do you want me to continue?"

Her answer was immediate. "Yes, please."

"That was the right answer." He took a step back and delivered several smacks to each cheek.

He would have loved to prolong the play, but given the ferocity of Marina's scent, she was about to come, and he wanted all that delicious nectar on his tongue.

Going down to his knees, he lifted one of her legs and licked into her from behind.

"Fuck!" Marina exclaimed.

He chuckled. "Not yet, but soon." He speared his tongue into her wet entrance and wrapped an arm around her to keep her from collapsing in a heap when she climaxed.

Pushing two fingers into her, he sucked and licked on her petals, and when he pressed his palm to her clit, she exploded, and he got to lick up all the bounty.

When he'd had his fill, he rose to his feet and aligned his erection with her entrance. With his arm still wrapped around her waist to brace her, he surged all the way inside of her in one hard thrust.

Marina climaxed again almost immediately, her sheath gripping and squeezing his shaft. Peter tried to prolong the pleasure, but he didn't last more than a few more thrusts before tumbling over the edge after her.

"Marina," he roared as he came, his seed shooting into her and filling her with his essence.

The urge to bite her again was strong, but he somehow managed to keep his wits about him and refrained from sinking his fangs into her neck. Instead, he licked and sucked the spot, which was sure to leave a hickey, but at least it wouldn't make her black out when she needed to report to work.

He was still hard when he brushed her wet hair aside and turned her head to him so he could take her lips in a soft kiss. "Was that quick enough for you?"

She laughed. "It was perfect."

"Yes, it was, and so are you." He withdrew, immediately missing the connection. "Finish washing up. I'll make us breakfast."

11

NEGAL

Negal dropped another pod into the coffeemaker and glanced at the door to Aru and Gabi's room.

It was after eight in the morning, and his commander should have been awake already. On second thought, Aru and Gabi might have been up for a while and were engaging in some morning fun.

The soundproofing on the damn ship was so good that he couldn't hear them, even with his superior hearing. Not unless they got really loud, which they hadn't so far.

When the door finally opened, he cast a smile at the emerging couple. "Good morning. Can I interest you in coffee?"

"Yes, please." Gabi tightened the tie around her short robe and sat down at the dining table. "Did you sleep here last night?"

He pulled out two mugs and put them under the twin spouts of the coffeemaker. "Frankie is back in her room with Dagor, so Margo was not left alone, and I had no excuse to stay."

Gabi's brows furrowed. "I thought things were going well with the two of you. Why is she still playing hard to get?"

Negal's shoulders stiffened. "Margo is not playing any games." He took the two full mugs and placed them in front of Gabi and Aru. "She just needs more time to feel comfortable with me."

"You don't have time," Aru said.

"Then I will make time." Negal popped another pod into the machine. "I like it that we are taking it slow. It allows us time to get to know each other, and there is also something to be said for delayed gratification."

Given the doubtful expressions on Gabi and Aru's faces, they didn't share his opinion, but that was their prerogative. Each couple had its own dynamic, and what was good for one wasn't necessarily good for another.

"I can't delay our departure." Aru took a sip from his coffee. "We've already pushed it with the commander."

"You said that you would try if Margo started transitioning. That means that you've thought of a way to convince the commander why we need to stay in the area for longer."

"I've thought of many things, but none of them are very convincing."

Gabi took her mug and rose to her feet. "I'll leave you two to talk while I get dressed." She leaned down to kiss Aru on his cheek before turning around and padding to their room.

When the door closed behind her, Aru turned to Negal. "Did you talk with Margo about coming with us?"

"I did." Negal took his mug and joined Aru at the table. "Her main objection is that she would need medical supervision while transitioning, and her second objection is about the job Toven promised her if she joined the clan."

Aru leaned back in his chair, holding his mug. "The truth is that Margo can go without medical supervision. Your blood can ensure that she makes it."

It had occurred to Negal that he could give Margo a boost with a transfusion of his blood, but that still didn't make it acceptable for her to transition without Bridget or one of the clan's other doctors watching over her.

"Your blood helped Gabi, and Dagor's helped Frankie, but they still needed a doctor's supervision."

Aru sighed. "What do you suggest we do then?"

"You, Dagor, and your mates can go ahead while I stay behind to be with Margo and join you later. It will be easier to come up with a good excuse for why only I stayed behind."

"Like what?"

Negal rubbed a hand over his jaw. "Now that we need our resources to last much longer than was originally planned, we need to find a way to supplement our allowance. I think it can be an excellent excuse to give the commander. You can tell him that I stayed behind to work on a deal. He knows that we are using the flea market trading as a cover and as a way to refill our coffers."

"That's a possibility." Aru put his mug on the table. "But again, I would rather do it only if we know for sure that Margo is transitioning. We can use that excuse once, but not over and over again."

"Agreed. Although I can think up more plausible excuses. We could have gotten a lead about something suspicious in the Los Angeles area that we need to investigate."

Aru chuckled. "We used that one to explain our prolonged stay in California and our trip down to Mexico. I'm surprised the commander didn't realize that it was highly unlikely for us to find any clues so far from the crash site. There is no way any of the pods landed in this area."

"True." Negal took a sip of his coffee, giving himself time to collect his thoughts. "But information about the pods could have traveled elsewhere. Perhaps we found someone who knew something that could point us in the right direction. Or maybe a pod was taken to a facility for investigation. The commander is well aware that humans are not as primitive now as they were the last time gods visited this planet."

Aru sighed. "And that's another reason for worry. How long do you think he would be able to hide this knowledge from the king?"

"He won't be able to hide it at all, but he can downplay it. As long as humans don't have interstellar travel capability or even communication, he won't consider them a threat."

His words didn't seem to reassure Aru. "Once the Eternal King finds out how close they are to achieving these benchmarks, he will be watching them much more closely. I hope the heir and her clan can do something about it and thwart human advancement in that area."

Negal shrugged. "Humans would also need to come up with a way to keep their travelers in stasis so they could traverse hundreds of light years, and that's an even more advanced technology than traveling at the necessary speed."

12

MARGO

"Good morning," Frankie said as Margo emerged from her bedroom. "Did you sleep well?"

"Yes. Thanks for checking up on me."

"It was our pleasure," Dagor said. "Are you feeling okay?"

"Of course." She forced a smile. "I was fine yesterday, too. Negal was worried for no reason."

"Perhaps," Frankie said. "But it's better to be vigilant, right?"

Nodding, Margo sat down at the breakfast table and accepted the cup of coffee from Frankie.

The truth was that it had been a miserable night. After getting interrupted during her attempt at self-pleasuring, Margo couldn't summon the energy to try again and had fallen asleep, but each time Dagor had peeked

64

into her room to check up on her, she'd woken up and then had trouble falling asleep because her mind had been racing.

"You seem to be doing great." She smiled at Frankie. "From what you've told me, I expected the recovery from transition to be much longer, but you seem to be ready to trek through Tibet."

She wondered if Frankie really wanted to do that. Her friend wasn't fond of camping or hiking. She was a city girl through and through.

The thing was, Aru and his teammates didn't have a choice. They were soldiers, and they had to follow their orders. So, if Frankie wanted to be with Dagor, she had to follow him, and if things went well with Negal, Margo would have to do the same.

She loved the idea of the six of them going on an adventure together, but she wasn't looking forward to roughing it out in nature. She also wasn't happy about passing on the opportunity to be part of Perfect Match, but she wasn't naive enough to believe that she could have everything she wanted.

"I'm not a hundred percent okay to go yet, but I will be by the end of the cruise." Frankie sat next to her with a cup of coffee cradled in her hands. "What are your plans for today?"

"I don't have any."

Frankie regarded her new sundress with a little smirk. "All dressed up with nowhere to go?"

"I thought I'd call Negal and have him meet me at the Lido deck."

Frankie's smirk turned into a grin. "That's a very good plan. Call him right now."

Margo chuckled. "Give me a moment to wake up. I can't call him before I've had my first cup of coffee of the day. I sound like a zombie." She exaggerated slurring her words.

"You can finish your coffee and then call him." Frankie rose to her feet with her coffee cup in hand. "I should get dressed and plan the rest of my day." She sauntered toward her bedroom with Dagor happily trotting behind her.

Margo had a feeling that they wouldn't be emerging anytime soon.

They were probably hopping back in bed to make up for all the sex they had missed last night because they were watching over her.

It would be so nice to be in that stage of her relationship with Negal.

No more awkwardness, no more uncertainty.

To think that Frankie had reached that stage in only a few days was mind-blowing. She'd bedded Dagor the same day they met, or the next, Margo wasn't sure, and then she started transitioning, and now it was all behind them, and they were bonded for eternity.

Even the couples in the romance books she read did not progress so fast from initial meeting to everlasting commitment. If she hadn't seen Frankie with Dagor, Margo would have thought it was just an infatuation, or that her bestie had fallen in lust, not in love, but their feelings for each other were so evident that the air around them sizzled with their love.

Lucky.

They were so incredibly lucky.

With a sigh, she pulled out her fancy new phone and called Negal.

He answered on the second ring. "Good morning. How was your night?"

"Good. And yours?"

"Lonely," he said, melting her heart a little. "I would have loved to sleep on your couch again, but with Frankie and Dagor there, I knew that you wouldn't feel comfortable."

"Are you sure that you would have wanted to spend another night on the couch?"

"I would have loved much more spending it with you in bed, but since that wasn't on the menu, the next best thing was the couch. At least I would have been close to you."

He sounded so sincere. There hadn't been even a tiny note of artifice in his tone, and if that was how Dagor had talked to Frankie, Margo could understand why her bestie had fallen in love with him so quickly.

"That's so sweet of you to say, Negal. To tell you the truth, I would have loved that too."

"Which part? Me on the couch or me in your bed?"

He'd been so truthful, so open, and he deserved no less from her. "The couch, for starters, and then my bed."

It had been on the tip of her tongue to tell him what she'd done last night, but she didn't have the guts. Besides, it had been a failure because she hadn't climaxed, and even if Frankie hadn't interrupted her, she didn't know whether she would have succeeded in reaching that peak.

Usually, Margo needed a steamy book to get in the mood, and she'd never been able to bring herself to completion without one. And it wasn't just the steamy parts. She needed the whole story, and it had to be good and believable for her to be able to enjoy it.

The irony wasn't lost on her.

Here she was, falling for her supernatural hero in a matter of days while she'd sneered at insta-love stories as unrealistic and cheesy.

As the saying went, reality was stranger than fiction, and unbelievably, it could also be better.

Negal cleared his throat. "I've never thought I would enjoy a slow buildup, but here I am, more aroused than I ever was by the prospect of sleeping on your couch."

Margo laughed. "That's desperation talking, and I'm really sorry for that."

"Don't be sorry. I mean it. I enjoy the torture. It's only going to be so much more epic when it finally happens."

What was she supposed to say to that?

What if all this anticipation culminated in a grand disappointment?

Margo wasn't some great seductress, and her former lovers hadn't praised her bedroom prowess.

Instead of responding to his statement, she chose to change the subject. "Would you like to meet me on the Lido deck for a cup of coffee?"

He chuckled. "I made you uncomfortable. I apologize. I would love to meet you on the Lido deck. Do you want me to come get you, or do you want to meet up there?"

"I'll meet you there. How about an hour from now?"

Would an hour suffice to calm the churning butterflies in her stomach? Perhaps she could watch some television. The weddings she'd missed could be a nice distraction.

"Perfect. I'll see you there." Negal ended the call.

Taking a deep breath, Margo rose to her feet, walked back into her bedroom, reached for the remote, and clicked the television on.

13

MARINA

"Is it ready?" Marina asked the woman in charge of the laundry.

Thankfully, the ship was equipped with dry cleaning equipment because Marina wouldn't have entrusted Jasmine's beautiful dress to regular washing even though the label said that it could be handwashed. The dress probably cost a fortune, and if it got ruined in the laundry, Marina would have to pay Jasmine back. Not that she was destitute now that she was earning a decent salary for her work at Safe Haven, but it would be a shame to deplete her savings for something as stupid as not being careful with a loaned dress.

"It is." Aina turned around and took one of the hangers off the rod. "Good as new." She handed the plastic-covered garment to Marina.

"Thank you."

Aina smiled. "You're most welcome. Are you going to be dancing with your immortal at the wedding tonight?"

"No, not tonight. I'm working."

"That's a shame. Your immortal is so handsome, but then they all are. So much nicer than the Kra-ell." Aina leaned closer. "Are they good in bed?"

Marina snorted. "I don't know about all of them, but mine is."

"I thought so." Aina sighed with a dreamy expression on her lined face. "If only I was ten years younger." She laughed. "Make that twenty."

"You are a married woman." Marina playfully punched her bicep. "You don't want Boris to hear you talking like that."

"Boris is not here." Aina waggled her brows. "But I'm just kidding. Even if I was young and pretty like you, I wouldn't have chosen one of them over my Boris. I can look, though, right?"

"You can look as much as you want, just not at my guy."

The smile slid off Aina's face. "Be careful, Marina. You can have fun with the immortal, but don't let him into your heart. Once this job is over, it's back to Safe Haven and bye-bye hunky immortals."

Marina shrugged. "Some of them are stationed at Safe Haven. Peter might ask his chief to send him to me." Or even better, Peter would invite her to live with him in the village.

Aina shook her head. "Don't get your hopes up."

"I'll try." Marina lifted the hanger so the dress wouldn't drag on the floor. "I'd better get this back to its owner. Thanks again." She turned around before Aina could give her more useless advice.

What did all of them think? That she didn't know how unlikely a happy ending with Peter was?

She wasn't dumb, but she was an optimist, and she had a few more days to get Peter to fall in love with her.

In a way, it was good that she couldn't accompany him to last night's wedding or tonight's. The less his mother and his other relatives saw him with her, the less pressure they would put on him to end things between them.

It wasn't hard to guess that Peter's mother was not happy about him spending time with the blue-haired vixen, and hopefully, she didn't know that they were spending their nights together as well.

When Marina reached Jasmine's cabin, she knocked on the door but wasn't surprised that there was no answer. The woman spent most of her time in the staff's lounge, playing cards, talking with everyone who knew a few words in English, or watching television.

Marina knocked again, just in case, and when there was still no answer, she turned around and headed to the lounge.

This time, however, she found Jasmine playing cards not with one of her friends but with Amanda, the gorgeous immortal lady who had been the second bride to get married on the ship and who supervised the decorating of the dining room for all the weddings.

She stopped by their table. "Hello. I'm just returning the dress." She draped it over the back of a chair. "Thank you so much for loaning it to me."

Jasmine frowned. "I didn't expect you to return it until the end of the cruise, and you didn't need to dry clean it either."

"I wanted to bring it back in the same pristine condition I got it."

Amanda regarded her with a small smile playing on her full, red lips. "I expected you to dance at Sharon and Robert's wedding last night. Is everything alright between you and Peter?"

Marina didn't detect any derision in Amanda's tone, and the immortal seemed like she didn't object to Peter's interest in the human serving girl.

"Peter and I are fine. I just needed to work because two servers were out of commission, and we were short-staffed."

Amanda frowned. "What happened to them?"

Did she really care?

"Nothing serious. One slipped, fell, and sprained her wrist, and the other had stomach cramps. The doctor gave her painkillers, but they made her dizzy and sleepy, so she couldn't work."

"That's a shame. You created quite a stir, and it was fun to watch."

Marina's gut twisted, and she swallowed. "A stir?"

"Quite. Everyone was whispering about the beautiful blue-haired girl dancing with Peter."

Right. Maybe a few of the males had said that, but she very much doubted it had been everyone.

"I'm sure many didn't approve of Peter inviting a servant to the wedding as a guest."

Mischief danced in Amanda's deep blue eyes. "Perhaps some did not, but is it important what they think? Many did not approve of my husband either, and some still do not, but it's their problem, not mine."

14

AMANDA

Marina's face brightened. "Is your husband like me?"

The humans working on the ship were compelled to keep the identity of immortals a secret, and since Jasmine was there, Marina couldn't say anything that would indicate they were different in any way.

Amanda laughed. "No, he's not a cute blue-haired young woman. He used to be the antagonist in our story, but he switched sides, and now he's devoted not only to me but to everyone I care for as well, and he will fight his former brothers with everything he has to protect me and mine."

"I see." Marina's eyes dimmed. "So, he's like you."

Amanda nodded. "Fierce and protective," she added for Jasmine's benefit.

The woman had been watching their exchange with curiosity in her strangely colored eyes, and Amanda had a feeling she knew more than she was letting on.

Jasmine's talent with card games was uncanny.

So far, she had beaten Amanda in every game, and Amanda was starting to get suspicious. She had an excellent poker face, with even other immortals having a hard time guessing the strength of her hand, let alone humans.

"You both look formidable," Marina said. "It was nice chatting with you, ladies, but I need to go." She turned to Jasmine. "Thanks again for the dress."

"No problem. If you need another outfit, come see me. I don't have any more evening gowns, but I have a couple of short, fancy dresses that will look great on you."

"Thank you." Marina smiled. "I might take you up on that offer."

After the girl left, Amanda turned back to Jasmine. "It's so sweet of you to offer Marina your clothing."

Jasmine shrugged. "I'm not invited to the weddings, so all my party dresses are going to waste. I'm glad someone gets to enjoy them."

"I'm sorry about that." Amanda lifted her cards. "I wish I could invite you, but the amount of paperwork you would have to sign wouldn't be worth it. Confidentiality is paramount in our business."

Jasmine believed that the cruise was a Perfect Match company retreat and that the couples getting married were success stories of the company's matchmaking algorithm. It was a good cover story, and Amanda had no problem using it. As someone who worked in the human world, she had to lie more than she cared to, but at least it came easy to her.

"Did you meet your husband in a Perfect Match adventure?" Jasmine asked.

Amanda smiled behind her cards. "I'm not at liberty to say, but I can tell you that the circumstances of our first meeting were extraordinary. Dalhu kidnapped me."

Horror filled Jasmine's eyes. "He did what?"

Damn. Amanda had forgotten what had almost happened to the woman. Her so-called boyfriend had sold her to a cartel boss, and if not for Margo and the clan's intervention, she would now be in the scumbag's bed, probably drugged within an inch of her life.

"It wasn't like that. Dalhu was very respectful, and he didn't do anything I didn't agree to. He just wanted me to give him a chance, and since I considered him my enemy, I wouldn't have given it to him under normal circumstances."

"What kind of enemy? Was he working for a competitor?"

"Yes, but I really can't say more about it without revealing things I'm not allowed to."

In a way, it was true. Navuh and the Brotherhood were competing with Annani and the clan for control of all humans, so technically, they were a competitor.

Jasmine pursed her lips. "All this confidentiality business is so frustrating." She looked at the back of Amanda's cards. "Are you going to make a move?"

"I thought it was your turn?"

"No, it's yours."

Amanda looked at the cards on the table, back at the ones she was holding, and then sighed. "I can only add this one here." She put the card down.

Jasmine smiled. "I win again." She put down a series of three and added two after the one Amanda had just added to the series.

Jasmine won just as easily playing rummy as she won playing poker. With her skills, she should have been loaded, but she didn't strike Amanda as rich. She was down to earth, laughed easily, and was friendly with everyone.

"What a surprise." Amanda put the rest of her cards down and leaned back in her chair. "Have you ever been tested for paranormal abilities?"

As Jasmine's smile turned into a grimace, the golden flakes in her eyes started swirling. "The fact that I'm good at card games doesn't mean that I'm using any unnatural means to win."

Amanda let out a breath. "There is nothing unnatural about extrasensory abilities. They are rare, and those who are not gifted are sometimes jealous or afraid of those who are, but that's like vilifying people for being extraordinarily good at math and science or sports."

The flakes in Jasmine's eyes stopped swirling, and her smile returned. "The problem is that there are many people who are good at sports or science, but as you've said, freaks are rare."

Amanda huffed. "I object to that term. I happen to be a neuroscientist, and I research paranormal abilities. I would like to test you for telepathy and precognition."

Usually, people were excited when she told them what she did and that she suspected they had hidden talents, but Jasmine looked like she'd bitten on a lemon.

"How do you perform your tests?"

"At my lab, I have equipment that projects random images, but I can do it here with these cards. If you correctly guess which card I'm holding more times than is statistically expected, that will indicate that you have precognition ability. The more correct guesses, the stronger the ability. As for telepathy, I will hold an image in my head and have you guess what it is. Both are simple tests that can be performed anywhere."

Jasmine leaned back and crossed her arms over her chest. "What happens if you confirm your suspicion that I have some paranormal ability?"

It could mean that she was a Dormant, and Amanda would send immortal males her way to assess affinity. She would also get Lisa to sniff her out and maybe even Syssi to see if her foresight would kick in. If Jasmine's abilities were marginal, she could also bring Mia over and ask her to sit near the woman to enhance her performance and make sure that the test results hadn't been a fluke. But all of that needed to happen without Jasmine being aware of the others' role in her testing.

"I will invite you to come to my laboratory in the university and test you further. I've been researching the subject for many years."

Jasmine was still regarding her with suspicion in her eyes. "And what then? You'll report me to the government so they can use my so-called talents to spy on their enemies?"

Aha, so that was why Jasmine was so skittish about admitting paranormal abilities, and it also reinforced Amanda's conviction that she had paranormal talents and was afraid of the implications.

"I assure you that I will never report you to the government or any other organization that might want to exploit your talents. You will appear in my research as subject number X, and your name will not be mentioned."

Jasmine still didn't look reassured. "I will want that in writing before I agree to participate in any test."

"No problem. You can draft an agreement, and I'll sign it."

"Not good enough. I'm not a lawyer, and I won't know how to close all the loopholes. But since you are working for Perfect Match, you must have access to their nondisclosure paperwork, true?"

Amanda nodded.

"Can you get me a copy?"

Toven could probably print it out for her, but it was no doubt specific to the Perfect Match experience and would not assuage Jasmine's fears.

"I can, but I doubt it's generic enough to cover what you need."

"I'll just use it as a base." Jasmine shrugged. "Or we can scrap the whole idea and just keep playing cards." She collected the discarded cards and started reshuffling them. "For every time you win, I will perform one test. Deal?"

It could be so easy to get into Jasmine's head and win every time, but that would be unethical. Amanda wanted to win the woman's trust the normal way.

"I'll play another game with you, but since we both know you will win, I will not make that deal with you. I'll get you the paperwork you asked for, you will craft an agreement you are comfortable with, and I'll sign it, provided that you don't ask for anything crazy."

Jasmine arched a brow. "Like what?"

"No clue, but I've learned from my brother to read the small print of every contract I sign."

"That's good advice." Jasmine shuffled the cards with a professional magician's flair. "Let's play."

NEGAL

egal arrived at the Lido deck half an hour early, ordered a drink, and secured a table. Margo had said coffee, but if he ordered it now, it would be cold by the time she arrived.

Did Bob even serve coffee?

As Negal looked around to check if anyone was drinking hot beverages, he saw Karen's twins and her little girl arrive at the pool deck with Darlene and Eric, who were carrying a bunch of pool toys.

Why were the kids with their aunt and uncle? Gilbert had said that Kaia was watching them.

He rose to his feet and walked over to where the family had settled down by the pool.

"Good morning." He smiled at the little ones, who were peering at him with curiosity in their eyes. "Are you going swimming?"

"I am." The little girl lifted her arms to show him the pink floating devices she was wearing. "Uncle Eric is going swimming with me." She waved a dismissive hand at her brothers. "They don't know how to swim. They can only float on their ducks."

Negal shifted his gaze to Eric. "You're a brave male taking on these three." Instead of asking if everything was okay, he asked, "Where are their older sisters?"

"With Karen," Darlene said quietly. "Gilbert is freaking out, and they are keeping him company."

Negal's gut twisted. "Is something wrong with their mother?" he asked in a whisper that was audible only to immortals.

"Karen lost consciousness early this morning," Eric whispered just as quietly. "Her blood pressure is elevated more than it normally would be for this stage of transition, and Bridget is a little worried."

Gilbert was probably too distraught to remember that he'd promised to contact Negal if Karen's situation changed.

"She's going to be fine," Darlene said. "Bridget is watching over her. Besides, she was given the best kind of venom." She winked at Negal. "Premium stuff. Not the diluted kind that I got. Still, I made it just fine despite that."

Negal was sure that Darlene's grandfather had something to do with her successful and easy transition. Toven had given her a transfusion of his blood, which compensated for Max's weaker venom.

Then again, Darlene was close to the godly source, and she would have probably made it just fine even without the god's intervention.

"I should go visit her," he said.

Eric clapped him on the back. "Maybe later. Right now, it's pretty crowded down there."

"Right." Gilbert and Karen's older daughters were there, and the ship's clinic was small.

Negal's main reason for visiting was to give Karen a boost with an injection of his blood, and he couldn't do that while she was surrounded by her family. Not unless he thralled all of them, and he would rather not do that if he didn't have to.

"Uncle Eric." The little girl tugged on Eric's hand. "Come to the pool with me."

"Yes, munchkin." Eric bent down, lifted the child, and put her on his shoulders. "See you later, Negal." He walked over to the shallow end of the pool, where he could wade in without having to jump or use the stairs.

When Darlene led the little boys and their floating ducks to the water, Negal turned around and walked back to his table.

A few minutes later Margo arrived, looking fresh and beautiful in the colorful sundress she'd gotten the day before.

He got up and greeted her. "You look lovely this morning." He kissed her cheek.

"Thank you." Her gaze roamed over him. "So do you."

He'd put on his best pair of jeans and a white, button-down short-sleeved shirt. After all, this could count as a date, and he'd dressed with care to honor his partner.

He pulled out a chair for her. "I'm not sure Bob is serving coffee, but I'll ask."

"It's okay if he isn't." She smiled up at him. "I just want to be with you. It doesn't matter what beverage we consume."

"What would you like if coffee is not an option?"

"A ginger ale would be refreshing. In fact, I prefer it to coffee."

"Coming up."

When Negal returned a moment later with a frosty can of ginger ale and two packs of pretzels, he saw Margo watching the children playing in the pool with a smile on her beautiful face.

"Do you like children?" He put the can in front of her.

"Who doesn't?"

He chuckled. "You'd be surprised how many people don't want children around. They are messy and noisy."

Shrugging, she popped the lid and took a small sip. "I love the sounds of children playing, but I have to admit that I hate it when they cry or whine. Whose are they?"

"These are Karen's kids."

Her eyes widened. "The Dormant who's transitioning right now?"

"She lost consciousness this morning, and her older daughters are with her and Gilbert, so their aunt and uncle are taking care of the little ones." Negal raked his fingers through his short hair. "I plan to visit her later. Would you like to join me?"

Perhaps he could somehow use Margo to distract the family while he gave Karen the blood transfusion.

Probably not a good idea since he couldn't tell her why he needed her to distract them. Dagor would be a better choice, and he also knew where to get syringes.

He needed to call him.

Margo frowned. "Are you close friends with Karen?"

Was there a note of jealousy in her tone?

He was Karen's inducer, which was more than a friend, and yet he didn't know the woman well. At some point, he would have to tell Margo about what he had done, but not yet.

"I'm a friend of her mate, Gilbert, and his brother Eric, who is the one playing with the little girl in the pool."

"He seems good with kids." Margo opened the bag of pretzels. "If you want me to accompany you, and if that's okay with Karen's family, I'll go with you to visit her. They might not want strangers to hang around her during a time like this."

"I'm sure it's okay with them." Negal needed to tell Dagor to get a syringe for him and to come over as well, and he didn't want to do that in front of Margo.

She was sharp and observant, and she might put two and two together.

He rose to his feet. "If you'll excuse me, I need to visit the bathroom."

"Of course." Margo smiled up at him. "When do you want to go visit Karen?"

Eric had said that he should wait, but Negal didn't want to take the risk of delaying the blood transfusion. If he waited for the right moment, he might be too late.

"When I get back if that's alright with you."

"Of course, it is."

16

MARGO

A soft smile played on Margo's lips as she watched Karen's brother-in-law playing with his little niece. The child was squealing with glee, and Eric was grinning so broadly that it threatened to split his face.

As her mind substituted Negal for Eric, and a little blond-haired girl who looked like Negal for the dark-haired child in the pool, Margo stifled a chuckle.

That was one hell of a leap. If she didn't find a way to quickly overcome her intimacy problem, and Negal's commander refused to let him stay around for a little longer, Negal would have to leave, and there would be no future for them.

She couldn't go with him because she couldn't keep up with five immortals, and she couldn't expect them to slow down for her. She also couldn't risk transitioning on a trail with no medical facilities for miles around.

Ugh. If she wasn't such a coward, she would have just taken the dive and hoped for the best. She could imagine that it was an arranged marriage and that she was no different from millions of women who had barely any contact with their husbands before their wedding night.

They had survived, and so would she.

Or even better, she could convince her brain that she was in a Perfect Match adventure with Negal and that none of it was real.

With a sigh, Margo pulled out her phone and texted Frankie. *Are you busy?*

Her phone rang a moment later. "For you, never."

Margo laughed. "I wasn't sure you and Dagor were out of bed."

"I'm still in bed, and Dagor is ordering room service."

"I didn't know that was an option. I was under the impression that the staff couldn't handle orders."

"They usually don't, but they don't mind if you call to request a meal and then come get it yourself. He's going to pick it up when it's ready."

"That's good to know." She looked around to make sure that no one was paying her attention and lowered her voice. "Did you bring any romance novels with you on the cruise? Mine are on my phone, which is probably at the bottom of the ocean, and I need something to read to relax."

Frankie chuckled. "You have a real romance going on. What do you need a book for?"

"Reading helps me fall asleep, and I need something sweet and silly that will not make me anxious." It was the truth, just not the whole truth.

"Yeah, I like reading before bed, too, but only if I don't have something better to do to relax me." She laughed. "I have some e-books on my phone, but I can't give that to you for obvious reasons."

Damn. "What about Mia? Do you think she might have brought some paperbacks with her?"

"I don't think she reads romance novels now that she has Toven. But maybe he has some. He writes under several pen names, and the dude is an old-fashioned romantic, so maybe he has a completed manuscript that he needs someone to beta read for him."

"Right, I forgot that he's a writer. But it would be super awkward to read sex scenes written by Mia's fiancé. Do you know what I mean?"

She wouldn't be able to keep from imagining that he was describing making love to Mia.

"Yeah, I totally do. I can ask around for you, but the truth is that the only one I've seen with a paperback book on board was Kaia, and knowing her, it was a science book. Most everyone reads on their phone these days. Come to think of it, they should have a library on this ship."

"That would be wonderful if they do. Is there a suggestion box somewhere? Not that it's going to help me right now, but it could benefit future passengers."

"We should tell Mia. She knows everyone by now, and as Toven's mate, she can talk to the bosses whenever she wants."

"You mean Kian and his wife?"

"Yeah. Anyway, Dagor is back, and I need to go."

Lucky girl.

"Have fun. We'll talk later." Margo ended the call.

Perhaps Jasmine had brought with her some of those historical romance novels she'd talked about. But if she was like Margo, she'd left the paperbacks at home and only read e-books while on vacation.

Some of the covers of romance novels were so racy that reading them in public was embarrassing. Then again, Jasmine didn't seem like the type who got embarrassed about stuff like that. The woman was an extrovert and a flirt, and there was a small chance that she had what Margo needed.

If not for her promise to accompany Negal to the clinic, Margo would have gone to see Jasmine right away, but it would have to wait. Perhaps she could leave Negal with Karen and her family and excuse herself to go see Jasmine.

SYSSI

"So, what exactly do you want me to do?" Syssi followed Amanda into the elevator.

"As I said, Jasmine might need a demonstration of precognition and how it works. Did you bring a coin to toss?"

Syssi patted her pocket. "It's right here."

"Good. I also want you to get an impression of her." Amanda tucked a stack of papers under her arm and pressed the button for the staff level. "Maybe she will trigger a vision."

Syssi frowned. "Why would she do that? I've never had a person trigger a vision before. They either come on their own, or I ask for them and actively try to induce them. Do you want me to do that?"

"No way." Amanda leaned against the elevator wall. "It's not important enough to find out what she's about. If it were, I would have an excuse to probe her mind, but it's not. I'm just curious. She's an odd bird."

"In what way?"

"She appears friendly and open, the kind of woman you want in your social circle because she's fun to be around—not stuck up, not timid, quick to smile, and easy on the eyes." Amanda smiled. "I know that's incredibly shallow of me, but I can't help it. It gives me pleasure to gaze upon beauty even if she gives me a run for my money."

Syssi gaped. "No way. No mere human can do that."

Amanda smirked just as the elevator door opened. "Bingo. Things just don't add up. Even if she's had tons of plastic surgery, which I don't think she has, I have to wonder why a beauty like her is not on the covers of magazines or playing in movies. She says she's an actress, so she's putting herself out there. Why hasn't she landed any roles?"

"Now I'm really curious."

"I had Lisa sniff her." Amanda headed down the corridor to the staff lounge.

"What did she say?"

"She wasn't sure."

"So, you think Jasmine is a Dormant."

Amanda nodded. "Everyone who's met her so far has liked her, including me. I just have this itchy feeling that there is more to her than meets the eye, and I'm not talking about the possibility of dormant godly genes."

They were about to enter the lounge when Syssi stopped and put a hand on Amanda's arm. "If you have a bad feeling about her, that's a good enough excuse to enter her mind. After all, she's on our turf, and if she's up to no good, we need to know."

"But that's the thing. I don't have a bad feeling. I like the woman." Amanda shrugged. "I'm just curious, and you know me. I won't rest until I get to the bottom of things."

"Yeah. That's what makes you such a good researcher."

As they entered the lounge, Syssi had no trouble identifying Jasmine from Amanda's description. She was indeed beautiful, but Amanda had exaggerated. Jasmine wasn't in the same league as her sister-in-law.

Jasmine sat on the couch between two men who were practically drooling over her, but she seemed oblivious to their lustful glances and looked completely absorbed in the sitcom she was watching.

It was an old *Big Bang Theory* episode that was playing in English with subtitles in Russian.

"Hello, Jasmine," Amanda said. "I'm back."

The woman turned to look at them, and a bright smile spread over her face. "Awesome." She rose to her feet and offered Syssi her hand. "You must be the sister-in-law Amanda mentioned. The one who works with her in the university."

"That's me." Syssi took the woman's hand. "Nice to meet you, Jasmine. I'm Syssi."

"The pleasure is all mine." Jasmine gifted her with another dazzling smile.

Unless the woman was a superb actress, the warm smile was genuine. Syssi felt as if she was truly glad to meet her and wanted to get to know her, and since Jasmine wasn't a movie star, she probably wasn't such a great performer.

"Let's sit over there." Amanda pointed to the table. "I printed out the Perfect Match nondisclosure agreement for you, and I also drafted a one-page agreement between us that I think will satisfy your needs."

Jasmine eyed the big stack of papers under Amanda's arm. "Do you expect me to read all of that right now?"

"I highlighted the relevant passages." Amanda put the stack of papers on the table. "Does anyone want something to drink?"

Syssi shook her head. "I just had coffee, so I'm good for now."

"Diet Coke for me, please." Jasmine sat down.

Syssi suppressed a chuckle. Evidently, Jasmine had no idea how important Amanda was, or she would have never asked her to serve her.

Perhaps that was precisely what endeared her to Amanda. Jasmine treated her just like she would any other person she befriended. No special treatment.

Watching her read through the document gave Syssi the opportunity to observe the woman without having to hide her interest. She was nearly as tall as Amanda, but she had curves. Where Amanda appeared slim and athletic, Jasmine had large breasts, rounded hips, and a lush bottom. Maybe that was why she hadn't made it big in movies. Supposedly, the camera added at least fifteen pounds to a person's appearance, and actresses had to be super-slim to look good on the screen.

Still, her face was so gorgeous that it was hard to look away from her. Jasmine's eyes had the most unusual ring of floating gold flakes around the pupils, and the irises were chocolate brown with some amber hues. Her hair was wavy, thick, long, and almost black, with a few golden strands that were probably not natural. Her skin looked perfect even though she didn't have much makeup on.

"Here is your Coke." Amanda put a cold can in front of Jasmine and sat across from her. "If you need me to explain anything, let me know."

"No, I'm good." Jasmine sighed. "I read the one you wrote, and I think it's good enough." She lifted her eyes to Amanda. "If you wanted to sell me to the government, no paper would protect me anyway."

"True." Amanda popped the lid on her can of soda. "But you can take my word to the bank, and I vow to protect your identity and never sell you out to the government or any other agency who might be interested in your talent."

"I can vouch for Amanda," Syssi said. "When she tested me and saw that my scores were off the charts, she hired me, and we're still working together. If she was a recruiter for the government, I wouldn't be here."

That got Jasmine's attention. "What's your talent?"

"Precognition." Syssi smiled and pulled out the coin from her pocket. "I brought this to demonstrate and also to test you. Do you know the statistical probability of guessing heads or tails correctly?"

"Fifty-fifty?"

"Correct." Syssi flipped the quarter in the air.

18

AMANDA

When Syssi guessed the first four tosses correctly, Jasmine's eyes widened, and when she continued guessing the next ten, she gaped.

"Unbelievable." Jasmine shook her head. "You could make a killing at poker."

Syssi chuckled. "I never tried applying my precognition in a card game. With my luck, it wouldn't work. Besides, it would be cheating."

A blush tinted Jasmine's cheeks. "I'm just good at reading people's responses, and that's a legitimate part of the game, so it's not cheating."

"It might also be precognition, and that's what I want to test." Amanda reached for the card deck. "To eliminate the possibility that you are reading my responses, I will turn my back on you so that you won't see my face when I lift a card and ask you what it is. Or better yet, close your eyes and try to guess."

"I'm curious to see what my results will be." Jasmine glanced at the printed page Amanda had prepared. "Would you mind signing this before we start? I know that it's probably worthless, but I will still feel better having a signed document from you."

"No problem." Amanda whipped out the tiny pen she'd stashed in the pocket of her leggings just for that purpose and signed the page. "I don't even know your last name, so I really can't sell the information to anyone."

Jasmine cast her an amused look. "Kevin had my pass-port in his hands. I'm sure he took a peek."

"Probably," Amanda admitted. "But I promise you that you have nothing to fear from me or any of us. We are not in cahoots with the government or anyone else."

Jasmine let out a breath. "I'm too curious to keep objecting. Let's start with me closing my eyes while guessing which card you are looking at."

"Good idea." Amanda cast a sidelong glance at Syssi. "Your job is to write down the results." She handed her the pen and a clean page.

When Jasmine closed her eyes, Amanda pulled out a random card from the pack. It was the four of spades.

"What card am I looking at?" she asked in her best neutral tone.

Jasmine's forehead furrowed. "It's a numbers card, and it's black, which means that it's either spades or clubs, but I can't guess the number."

"That's very good. It's four of spades." Amanda put the card on the table. "For some reason, colors are easier to guess, and not just in the case of cards where there are only two. Perhaps they make a bigger impression on our brains."

Jasmine opened her eyes. "Do you want to repeat the test the same way, or do you want to try it while my eyes are open, and you are with your back to me?"

"Let's try it a few more times this way."

Jasmine guessed the color of the next two cards correctly, but she said that one of them was a face card when it was another number card, and she was completely off for the next five.

"I guess I don't have precognition talent." She shrugged. "Oh, well. I told you that's not the reason I'm good at card games."

"It's not unusual for the results to diminish after several tries," Syssi said. "Normally, I start guessing wrong after ten correct guesses. It's like the brain becomes tired."

Amanda nodded. "We have observed that happening with all our test subjects that had some talent. You can improve with practice and keep guessing accurately for longer, but eventually, you will start guessing wrong."

Jasmine pursed her lips. "You are the expert, so I have to take your word for it. Do you want to try the other methods?"

"Not yet. I want you to rest. But we can test other abilities that require different mental muscles. This time, I will think about an object, and you will try to guess what it is."

"Do I need to close my eyes?"

"No. I want you to look into mine and try to catch what I'm thinking. It's going to be an object, but it can be anything from a lemon to a spaceship. Ready?"

Jasmine nodded.

Amanda thought of a red rose, which was easy to visualize, and those with even weak telepathic ability could sense the bold color.

"What am I thinking of?"

Jasmine scrunched her nose. "A flower."

"Good. What kind of flower?"

"I don't know."

"What color is the flower?"

Jasmine closed one eye and pursed her lips. "White?"

"No." Amanda was disappointed. "It was a red rose."

"Damn." Jasmine grimaced. "I was close."

"What made you think that it was a flower?" Syssi asked.

Jasmine smirked. "Amanda's nostrils flared a little like she was imagining smelling something, and I knew it was something good because her eyes widened a tiny bit, and her forehead remained smooth."

"Those are exceptional observational skills." Syssi looked at Amanda. "True?"

"Indeed. It's not a paranormal talent, but it's a useful one. Can you tell when people are lying?"

Jasmine huffed out a laugh. "If I could, would I have believed Alberto when he told me that he loved me? But you are right. If I knew for a fact when people lied, I could learn the tells. My observational skills are good because of my acting background. Mimicking behavior is a very important aspect of acting, so I trained myself to pay attention to body language and facial expressions."

Syssi tilted her head. "Were you good at poker before you studied acting?"

"I joined the drama program in middle school, and I didn't play poker back then, so I don't know how good I would have been at poker without the training that started in that program."

Amanda had a strong urge to delve into Jasmine's head and find out if she was telling the truth.

She didn't emit any scents that would indicate it, but it was possible that she was a method actress, capable of convincing herself that she was telling the truth.

"Let's try another object." Amanda thought of a chair. A simple wooden chair that didn't evoke any emotions in her. "Well?" she asked.

Jasmine lifted her hands in surrender. "No clue. You must have thought about something very mundane and boring."

"That's correct. I thought of a chair."

"Does that count as a good guess?" Syssi asked.

"It's not a paranormally good guess, but it's not bad. With proper training, Jasmine could become an excellent interrogator."

The woman recoiled. "No way. I would never do something like that."

"Why not?" Amanda asked.

"I don't want to deal with the ugly underbelly of society. I want to be surrounded by pretty things and good people."

Amanda snorted. "Then you've chosen the wrong profession. The movie industry is a nest of vipers."

"I know." Jasmine sighed. "When I started acting in middle school, it was great because everyone in the acting club was like me. It was the first time I felt comfortable in my own skin. No one thought that I was overdramatic or that I was an attention seeker." She chuckled. "Well, I was, but so was everyone else in the club. Actors like attention. Anyway, it got even better in high school, but then the real world was a different story. Instead of well-meaning drama teachers, I was suddenly dealing with people who thought they could exploit my ambition to get me to do things I would never do otherwise, and I realized how naive I was when I dreamt of a career on the big or small screen. Still, I love acting too much to do anything else. I might be only getting small parts and playing in commercials, but it's better than nothing."

19

KIAN

Kian stood on the top deck, watching the harbor crew at work preparing the ship for departure.

The pilot's boat approached, carrying the harbor pilot tasked with guiding the cruise liner out of the seaport. Kian didn't like an outsider boarding his ship, but harbor pilots were experts in local water conditions and port intricacies, and they were essential for the safe exit of the ship from the congested seaport area.

Once onboard, the pilot would collaborate with the captain and the bridge team, helping them navigate the ship out safely, and after it was done, he would depart on the small boat that was trailing the ship out to sea.

Kian had learned a lot about the operations of cruise ships on this voyage, and it was much more complicated than running hotels, but Shai had run the numbers, and it was a profitable business, provided of course that the passengers were the paying kind, and not his family.

He contemplated purchasing two more ships for the clan, and if that operation proved successful, to keep adding more. He needed to put someone in charge of the operations, though, and he was not happy with the shortlist of candidates he'd compiled. None had experience in the cruise line industry, and Ragnar, who was the most knowledgeable and experienced in the hospitality business, had enough on his plate with running the clan's hotels.

The human staff that used to serve the Kra-ell were doing a remarkable job, given that they had no prior experience save for the voyage that had taken them out of captivity. Kian planned on visiting Safe Haven and offering them the option of permanent employment in the clan's cruise liner business.

Amanda wouldn't be happy because she'd hoped he would invite some of them to work in the village, especially the talented cooks, but he believed that they would be better off traveling the world and seeing places they wouldn't otherwise get the chance to visit.

It had never sat well with him that they had to be confined to Safe Haven after spending their lives in captivity, but for now, it was the best option for them and for the immortals. The humans were not ready to live independently, and their knowledge of aliens had to be protected. Working on a cruise line could solve both issues.

"I thought I would find you here." Onegus leaned against the railing next to Kian. "Edgar called. He inspected the helicopter and confirmed that we got all we were promised." He chuckled. "He's as excited as a kid with a new puppy. When should I tell him to fly the craft over?"

"I want us to be far enough from the shore so that no one sees the helicopter landing on the ship." Kian cast Onegus a sidelong glance. "He should take off in about two hours unless that will be too far for its range?"

"This bird has great range, so it's fine even with Ed making a detour and flying south before heading out to sea from an unpopulated spot."

"Good plan."

"I'm glad we finally got the helicopter," Onegus said. "With the Clan Mother on board, it's crucial that we have an escape vehicle."

Kian crossed his arms over his chest. "If we are under attack, evacuating her with the helicopter is not a good move. I prefer to have her where I can protect her. But it's good to have an aircraft for other emergencies."

"It depends on the situation." Onegus rubbed a hand over the back of his neck. "The helicopter can seat twelve, which is plenty of Guardian power to protect the Clan Mother, but if the enemy has missiles, then the helicopter will become a death trap."

"True," Kian agreed.

The best option was to remain hidden, but the unexpected encounter with the cartel and then the Doomers in Acapulco had undermined the secrecy of their location. They'd managed to salvage the situation by altering the ship's travel plan, but it was still possible for the Brotherhood to deduce where the adversaries who'd annihilated the Acapulco cell had come from.

"Are you coming to Michael's bachelor party?" Onegus asked.

"I wasn't invited." Kian cast him a smile. "Which I'm thankful for. I don't want to spend every afternoon at a different bachelor party. I want to spend as much of my vacation time as possible with my wife and daughter."

As if talking about them had summoned them, Syssi walked over with Allegra in her arms. "Allegra wants her daddy." She handed him their daughter.

As Kian took her and hugged her to his chest, his heart swelled with love. "Did you miss me, sweetie?"

"Daddy." She lifted her arms, cupped his cheeks, and planted a slobbery kiss on his lips before turning to watch the activity taking place below.

"I'll see you at the wedding," Onegus said before turning on his heel and walking away.

"Look, Daddy." Allegra pointed at one of the other cruise ships. "Big."

"Yes, it's big." Smiling, he shifted his gaze to Syssi. "Her vocabulary is growing by the day. Is that normal for a child her age?"

She chuckled. "Not at all. But we know that Allegra is special." She leaned and kissed their daughter's cheek. "Right, sweetheart?"

"Mama," Allegra said in a tone that conveyed her amusement.

"She says even more with tonality than with words, and right now, she's communicating that she thinks you are being silly, but she likes it."

Syssi laughed. "I know." She took Onegus's spot, leaning against the railing and crossing her arms over her chest. "Amanda and I visited Jasmine earlier, and Amanda tested her paranormal abilities."

For some reason, apprehension flickered through him. "And?"

"Her results were interesting. She guessed the first few cards correctly, which was impressive, but then her accuracy diminished, which is common even for those who have a smidgen of real paranormal ability. But that wasn't the interesting part. Her observational skills are phenomenal. She noticed subtle changes in Amanda's expressions, tiny cues that even I missed. It's not a paranormal ability, but it's an important talent."

Kian mulled over her words, the wheels in his mind turning. Jasmine's unique skill set could be an asset, but only if she proved to be a Dormant. Otherwise, she would need to find a use for her unique skill set in the human world.

"What about affinity? Did you feel any toward her?"

Syssi hesitated. "Jasmine is friendly, upbeat, and very likable. She's also not easily impressed or intimidated by others, which I admire. On the flip side, she's very hesitant about referring to her abilities as extrasensory. I have a feeling that she's had bad experiences with people who caught her doing things she shouldn't have been able to do, and that's why she's hiding what she's actually capable of." Syssi canted her head. "I keep wondering whether her small oddities justify a thrall to find out what she's hiding."

Kian shrugged. "We will thrall her before we let her off the ship, so if she's hiding something that we should be aware of, we will find out then. In the meantime, I'm not worried about her, even if she has some nefarious plans. She's just a human, and she's being watched."

"Jasmine doesn't have nefarious intentions," Syssi said. "At least, I don't think she does. But maybe we should ask Edna to probe her. Her probe is not a thrall, so it's not considered breaking the rules." She shifted closer to him. "After all, Edna probed me when she first met me, making sure that I wasn't taking advantage of you."

Kian wrapped his arm around her shoulders. "You are welcome to take advantage of me any time you want, my love."

NEGAL

As Negal walked toward the clinic with Margo at his side, he was running through different scenarios in his head for a way to administer a blood transfusion to Karen without anyone being any the wiser.

Through the open door of the clinic's front room, Negal saw Karen's older daughters standing next to the nurse's desk. Kaia looked distraught, her eyes wide and darting around the room as if seeking some anchor in the storm of her thoughts. Her younger sister looked worried but calm and collected.

Raking her fingers through her long blond hair, Kaia mumbled under her breath, "I need to crack the code. I'm so close, but I don't have it yet, and I need it. What am I missing?"

Negal exchanged a quick glance with Margo before returning his attention to Kaia. He had no idea what she was talking about.

What was the code she believed she had deciphered?

"You will find the answer." Cheryl, her younger sister, moved closer and wrapped her arms around Kaia in a tight hug. "You always do."

The words of comfort seemed to pierce through the haze of the young woman's distress. "Yes, I know. It's just that I'm almost there, and once I get it..." She finally noticed Negal and Margo standing outside the door and stopped. "Hi." She forced a smile. "If you are here to ask about my mother, there is no change. She is still unconscious."

The door to the inner room opened, and Doctor Bridget stepped out, her gaze sweeping over the small crowd before settling on Karen's oldest daughter. "Kaia, you need to calm down. Your mother is not dying. She's stable and doing just as well as most of the other Dormants in this stage of transition. There is no need for alarm. An easy and straightforward transition like Frankie's is the exception, not the norm."

The tension slowly dissipated from Kaia's expression, and she took a deep breath. "What about her blood pressure? You said that it was elevated more than it was for other Dormants during this stage."

"It's stable," Bridget said. "There is no need for you to be hovering around here. Go inside, talk to your mother for a little bit, and then go take care of your brothers and sister. They need you more than your mother does right now."

Kaia's thunderous expression indicated that she didn't like getting lectured by Bridget, but her only response was a nod.

Negal was glad that the doctor was sending Kaia away. It would be great if she did the same to the younger sister. With only Gilbert remaining, it would be easier to execute his plan.

Where was Dagor, though?

He needed the guy to get him a syringe and to create a distraction.

"Can we see Karen?" he asked the doctor.

"Perhaps a little later." She cast him an apologetic smile. "I don't allow more than two visitors at a time. After Kaia and Cheryl are done, you can go in and keep Gilbert company for a little bit." She looked at Margo. "I'm sorry, but you'll have to wait outside."

Margo looked disappointed, but she nodded. "I understand. I don't really know Karen, but I'm curious about the process."

"When Negal goes into Karen's room, I'll answer any questions you might have."

Negal needed to get Gilbert out of the room as well, but first, he needed the damn syringe.

"Hello," Dagor said from behind him. "I was looking for you." He signaled with his eyes that he wanted Negal to follow him.

Negal let go of Margo's hand. "I need to have a word with Dagor. I will be right back."

She smiled. "I'll stay here and talk with the doctor."

Negal followed Dagor to the coffee station. "Do you have it?" he asked quietly.

"I do." Dagor took a paper cup, put it under the coffeemaker spout, and dropped a pod into the slot. "Do you want coffee?"

"I don't, but Margo might want some."

He felt Dagor's hand slide into his pocket and deposit his loot.

"I have more. I'll leave them in your bathroom in one of the drawers."

"Thank you."

When the machine stopped brewing, Dagor removed his cup and placed a new empty one under the spout. "How are you going to do it?"

"I'm not sure yet. Do you have any ideas?"

Dagor looked around to make sure that no one was within hearing distance. "I was thinking about delivering a cup to Gilbert and *accidentally* spilling it on him, but I'll wait for it to cool down."

"That's a good plan. Make another one, and I'll pretend to drink it when I go into Karen's room. I'll spill it over Gilbert."

Dagor nodded. "That's a better plan. You have a good reason to visit them. I don't."

Negal hadn't told Dagor about his role in Karen's transition, but his friend had probably guessed it, and Negal wasn't going to bother with denials.

When the elevator dinged at the end of the corridor, Negal looked in the direction of the sound. "More visitors will make this more complicated."

His eyes widened when he saw Toven striding down the corridor with a determined expression on his face and his glow on full display.

"What's going on with him?" Dagor asked in a whisper. "He never glows."

"I'm wondering the same thing."

"The Clan Mother asked me to perform the blessing ritual in her name," Toven announced, sweeping into the clinic's front room with a flourish Negal had never seen him show before.

Dagor leaned closer to Negal. "Are you thinking the same thing I'm thinking?"

"Yeah, I think he's about to do what I had in mind." Negal walked over to watch the performance from the opened door with Dagor right behind him.

Bridget eyed Toven with skeptical eyes. "Karen is not in critical condition."

"I thank the merciful Fates for that, but why wait? Karen is like family to me, and it's my privilege and duty to bless her."

"How are they related?" Dagor whispered in Negal's ear.

"No clue, but we need to support him."

"I wish I could bless Karen," Negal said out loud. "But only those with royal blood can do that. It's a sacred ritual that no one else is allowed to witness."

Margo turned to him with questioning eyes. "You didn't tell me about a blessing and neither did Frankie."

"Frankie didn't need it, and I didn't know whether either of the gods would volunteer to bless Karen. It's not as if I can speak in their name."

Bridget rose to her feet. "Very well. I'll let Gilbert know."

"Can Cheryl and I stay here?" Kaia asked Toven.

"I prefer for everyone to stay outside. My full concentration is needed for the ritual, and I don't want to get distracted."

Kaia nodded. "Thank you for doing this for our mother."

Toven's eyes softened. "I'm glad to help in any way I can."

As Bridget entered Karen's room and everyone other than Toven left the clinic, Toven snuck a quick look at

Negal and dipped his head in acknowledgment. "I entrust you two with guarding the door." He shifted his gaze to Karen's bewildered daughters. "It's part of the ritual. It needs to be done in total secrecy."

Negal bowed to the royal. "Dagor and I are honored to be the guardians of the blessing."

Once Bridget and Gilbert joined them out in the corridor, Negal closed the door, and he and Dagor stationed themselves in front of it.

"The Clan Mother and Toven have performed the ritual for several of the transitioning Dormants," Bridget said. "I don't know what she did, but it seemed to help. They all did better after that."

Gilbert wrapped an arm around each of Karen's daughters. "We are grateful for any help we can get."

21

KIAN

Kian hopped into the cabin of the newly acquired helicopter. "It's much more luxurious than I expected."

"It's not just about the fancy leather seats," Edgar said. "It's also about the performance and safety. Compared to the one we have in the village, this one provides a remarkably smooth and quiet ride thanks to the advanced technological innovations."

As Edgar continued to list all the marvelous avionic features, Kian understood only a fraction of what he was talking about, but the pilot was so excited that he felt bad about stopping him and pretended to listen with interest.

When he was finally done, Kian thanked him and stepped out of the craft. All that had interested him was that the copter could transport up to twelve passengers, had an average cruising speed of approximately 138 knots, could travel a maximum range of 475 nautical miles with standard fuel tanks, and had a maximum endurance of about four hours and thirty minutes, ensuring that it could stay airborne for extended periods when needed. It could also reach a maximum flight altitude of 20,000 feet. Those were impressive specs that made it a valuable asset, and it had certainly cost accordingly.

The truth was that the clan needed to upgrade its fleet, and Kian had no intention of leaving the helicopter with the ship. It was coming home with them.

He should call Aru to invite him to see the helicopter and use the opportunity to tell him about Syssi joining them for tonight's session with the queen. Except, it didn't look like Edgar would be leaving his new baby anytime soon, and the conversation Kian needed to have with Aru had to be private.

Instead, Kian headed back to his cabin and sent the god a text message, asking Aru to join him.

When the doorbell rang a short while later, Kian opened the door and motioned for Aru to enter. "Thank you for coming on such short notice."

Aru looked worried. "I knew you wouldn't ask me to come if it wasn't important. I assume that this is not a social meeting." He glanced around the cabin. "Otherwise, you would have invited me together with my mate, and yours would be here."

"Syssi took Allegra to see her grandparents, so we have the place to ourselves." Kian motioned to the couch.

"Please, take a seat. Can I offer you a drink?"

"Sure. I'll have whatever you are having."

Kian walked over to the bar and pulled out his best bottle of whiskey. "I have a confession to make, and I hope you won't be too upset about it." He poured two shots, joined Aru in the living room, and handed him one. "Syssi knows about your telepathic communication with Aria."

The temperature in the cabin dropped by at least ten degrees. "You vowed not to tell anyone." Aru's tone was frosty. "My own mate doesn't know."

Kian raised a hand, signaling for him to calm down. "Syssi didn't hear it from me or anyone else. She saw Aria in a vision, and she recognized her as your twin sister. She says that you look a lot alike. When she confronted me about it, lying to her would have been futile and would have only upset her, so I confirmed her guess."

"Who else knows?" Aru asked.

"Just Syssi and my mother," Kian assured him. "You know that Syssi is a seer. You must have assumed that sooner or later, she would see your sister."

Kian watched as Aru processed the information, his initial anger giving way to reluctant acceptance.

"I was afraid of that, but I hoped that she wouldn't get a vision about me and my sister." Aru rubbed a hand over his face. "Aria and I have guarded this secret throughout our lives, and the only reason we were discovered was that the Supreme Oracle saw us in one of her visions. Since then, we have lived in fear that other seers will discover us. The Supreme promised to somehow hide us from other seers, but apparently, she wasn't successful. If Syssi saw us, others could as well."

"Syssi knew you, and she knew that you were communicating with someone on Anumati. When she saw Aria with the queen and the Oracle, it was clear to her that she was the one you were communicating with. Others don't have the same knowledge."

Aru let out a breath. "I hope you are right. I fear for my sister."

"I bet you do." Kian cast him a sympathetic look. "I would be worried too, but not because Syssi is privy to the information. You have nothing to fear on her account."

"I hope so." Aru finished the whiskey in his glass and put it down on the table. "So, this is it? You wanted to tell me that she knows?"

Kian shook his head. "When I told Syssi about the meeting tonight, asking her advice about the best way to excuse our absence from the celebration, she had a few good suggestions. She offered to come along and transcribe what was being said. She pointed out that the information the queen would share with my mother was too important to entrust to memory. It should be written down."

"I hadn't thought of that, but I agree with your mate. I hoped to conduct the meeting in Anumatian, which would have made it easier for Aria and me, but it might not have been possible anyway because your mother is not fluent in it."

"She's not." Kian regarded Aru, noting the furrows on his forehead. "Perhaps you should tell Gabi about Aria. Keeping a secret from your mate is not healthy for the relationship. It would also make your departure less suspicious if you leave with Gabi. People would just assume that you wanted to continue celebrating in private."

He was such a hypocrite, giving advice to Aru about keeping secrets from his mate when he was doing it himself. Only in his case, he was doing it to protect Syssi more than his mother.

Aru shook his head. "I can't. I will tell Gabi that I need to do something in secret and ask her to cover for me. She will back me up."

"Of course. Syssi and I will claim that Allegra is fussy. I will also ask for the wedding ceremony to be scheduled earlier. If we start at eight o'clock in the evening instead of ten at night, by the time we need to leave the party will start dwindling, and it will look less suspicious."

Aru smiled for the first time since arriving at Kian's cabin. "That's the best idea you've had so far."

22

MARGO

Margo walked down the softly lit corridor with Frankie on one side and Mia riding her wheelchair on the other. "Toven looked like one of those evangelical preachers on television when he showed up declaring that he was sent by the Clan Mother to give Karen a blessing, and he was glowing like a neon sign. I've never seen him act like that."

"Are you serious?" Mia laughed. "I had no idea that he was going to do it."

Margo had known Mia since she was five years old, and she'd never been a good liar. "Toven didn't tell you that he was going to bless Karen?"

"He said he was going to visit her and Gilbert and offer his support. He didn't say anything about a blessing."

For some reason Mia was lying, and Frankie wasn't calling her out on that, which was suspicious as hell.

Margo stopped walking and put her hands on her hips. "Okay, you two. What are you hiding from me?"

"Nothing." Mia looked at her with fake innocence in her eyes. "Toven really didn't tell me. Perhaps the Clan Mother called him while he was on his way to see Karen and Gilbert and asked him to bless Karen."

Frankie nodded. "Yeah. That's probably what happened."

Margo shook her head. "Fine. Be like that." She resumed walking. "It's a shame I can't tell Jasmine about it. She would have gotten a kick out of Toven's performance."

Frankie snorted. "I can teach you a few workarounds, but perhaps I shouldn't right before we are going to see Jasmine. You really shouldn't tell her anything that will make her suspicious."

Margo stopped in front of Jasmine's cabin door and rang the bell. "I'd rather not know. Don't tell me."

Knowing Frankie, she wouldn't be able to help herself and would tell her anyway.

She rang the doorbell again and waited a couple more seconds before turning away. "Jasmine is never in her cabin. She spends her days in the staff lounge."

When they reached the lounge, Margo was surprised to find Jasmine sprawled on one of the comfy-looking couches and not sitting at one of the tables, playing poker with the staff.

"Hi." She waved them over. "Are you here to see me?"

"Who else?" Margo sat down next to her on the couch. "Are you resting after a long day of poker wins?"

"I wish." Jasmine pushed her thick hair behind her shoulder. "Do you know a lady named Amanda?"

Margo nodded. "Where did you meet her?"

"She came to see me. My poker playing has made me famous, and she wanted to see if I had any paranormal talents. She is a professor of neuroscience who researches paranormal abilities, and she wanted to test me."

Kian's gorgeous sister was a professor?

To Margo, it was almost as impressive as being a demigoddess, which actually meant a demi-alien. "I met Amanda at the wedding last night, but she didn't say anything about being a professor." She turned to Frankie. "Did you know that she was a researcher?"

Frankie shook her head. "I didn't."

"I did," Mia said. "She tested me too."

Margo already knew what Mia's talent was, but she hadn't known that she'd been tested by a neuroscientist. According to what Mia had told her, it had been Kian's wife who had figured out her talent.

"What kind of tests did she run on you?" Margo asked Jasmine to preempt her asking Mia the same question.

"Oh, the usual stuff you see in movies," Jasmine said with a playful roll of her eyes. "Card guessing, identifying objects without seeing them, guessing what she was thinking about, etc. It was pretty out there, but I cooperated because I was curious to see if I had any paranormal talents."

"And?" Frankie prodded. "Do you have any?"

Jasmine shrugged. "My so-called 'talents' are more about observation and intuition than anything mystical. I guessed a few cards more or less correctly, but I got most of them wrong, so I guess it was just luck."

Margo was fascinated by the fine line between science and the supernatural, and now she knew an expert in the field. Would Amanda mind if she asked her a few questions?

"Your exceptional ability to read people might be a paranormal talent," Mia pointed out. "If it was normal, everyone could do it, right?"

Jasmine smiled with a hint of pride flickering in her eyes. "I trained myself to notice all those little details. Observing human behavior is essential for an actor. After all, I need to be able to portray emotions in a thousand different ways according to the characters I'm supposed to play."

As a conversation about different acting methods ensued, Margo's mind wandered to Negal and her quest for a romance novel that would put her in the right mood.

"Daydreaming about your new boyfriend?" Jasmine pulled her out of her reveries.

"How did you know?"

"Easy. You had this dreamy expression on your face, with your lips lifting in a ghost of a smile. Things are going well with Negal, I assume?"

Margo nodded. "You could say that." She felt a blush creep up her cheeks as she remembered the kiss they had shared.

Jaz laughed. "So, are you taming the rogue?"

"Negal is not a rogue. He's gentle and patient and kind of sweet. But speaking of rogues, do you have any romance novels that I can borrow? I need something relaxing to read before going to sleep."

"I have a couple." Jasmine rose to her feet. "But I have to warn you. They are quite racy."

"Perfect." Margo smiled up at her. "That's precisely the kind I need."

Jasmine's lips twisted into a knowing grin. "So, it's that kind of relaxing."

Margo rolled her eyes. "You have a dirty mind."

"That I do." She laughed.

As Jasmine left to retrieve the books from her cabin, Mia leaned closer to Margo. "Having paranormal talent is a possible indicator of immortal genes," she whispered conspiratorially. "The other is affinity, which we all seem to feel toward Jaz. Your friend might be a Dormant. Wouldn't that be great?"

"Yeah, it would." Margo felt a pang of jealousy.

If Negal knew that Jasmine was also a potential Dormant, would he have courted her?

She was much better looking than Margo, had a better disposition, and seemed to have no hang-ups about sex. She was a superior catch.

Jasmine returned a few minutes later with two tattered paperbacks. "Excuse the condition they are in." She smiled. "It's not that I read them so frequently. I buy them secondhand."

"Thank you." Margo took the books and put them in her tote without checking out the covers.

"Did you have your job interview already?" Jasmine asked.

"Not yet. Everyone is busy with the weddings."

"Right." Jasmine nodded. "I became friends with two of the servers. They were invited to tonight's wedding as guests, but they have nothing to wear because they didn't expect to be dancing at the weddings they were supposed to wait." She told them about Marina and Larissa.

"I saw the one with the blue hair dancing with Peter," Mia said. "She's very pretty, and she had a beautiful dress on."

"It was mine," Jaz said. "But she returned it, and now she needs another one."

"Maybe I can help her," Frankie said. "I have plenty of dresses."

23

KRI

"**M**om, stop." Kri put her hand on her mother's shoulder. "The tray looks perfect as it is."

Her mother lifted a pair of frantic eyes at her. "I'm sorry. It's the stress. It's making it worse." She took a deep breath. "I thought we would have more time to put up the decorations."

Kian had called less than an hour ago, informing Kri that the wedding party needed to start two hours earlier than planned, which also affected the timing of her and Michael's bachelorette and bachelor parties.

She didn't really mind, but the sudden schedule change wreaked havoc on her mother's ability to control her OCD. With Vanessa's help, she'd made great progress in the last year or so, but when stressed, the obsessive need to arrange everything in neat groups of three resurged with a vengeance.

"So did I, but we made it on time." Kri leaned to kiss her mother's cheek. "The cabin looks awesome, and appetizers are ready, and all that's left to do is welcome our guests."

"Your guests, sweetheart." Her mother smiled. "Not mine. This is your day. You are the bride."

The tone of wistfulness in her mother's voice made Kri wish that there was a mate for her out there, but given that her mother rarely left her house, she wouldn't find him even if he was in the village.

Kri had tried to introduce her to some of Kalugal's men, but her mother was terrified of them as if they were still members of the Brotherhood, and it didn't matter how many times Kri had explained that they had escaped Navuh's camp because they were not like the others.

Her mother needed to find a gentle soul who wouldn't mind her oddities and her constant state of fear-fulness.

As the doorbell rang, her mother's hand flew to her chest. "Oh, my. That's such a shrill sound."

"It's okay, Mom." Kri patted her slim shoulder. "My guests are starting to arrive, so prepare yourself for more shrill sounds or step out onto the balcony until the last one gets here."

Kri walked over to the door and opened it.

"Amanda? I can't believe it. You're the first one."

Amanda was usually the last to arrive, whether at a social gathering or a council meeting. Kri suspected that she did that on purpose to make a grand entrance and get everyone's attention.

"Hello, darling." Amanda leaned and kissed the air near Kri's cheek. "Dalhu took Evie to the pool, and I had nothing to do, so here I am." She walked toward Kri's mother. "Mona." She leaned in to kiss the air next to Kri's mother's cheek. "I haven't seen you the entire voyage. Where have you been hiding?"

Her mother darted her eyes to the dessert table, probably searching for something that wasn't grouped in threes yet. "I attended the weddings, but I stayed in my cabin the rest of the time. I don't like crowds. Dolores, my cabin mate, brought me food from the dining hall."

Amanda shook her head. "You should mingle more."

"I know." Mona walked over to the bar and started arranging the glasses in groups of three.

Kri decided not to comment. It was not only futile but usually made the problem worse.

"I'm dying to see your dress," Amanda said. "I bumped into Stella earlier, and she said it's one of her best creations."

Everyone was so excited about the damn wedding gown that Kri didn't have the heart to admit that she hated everything about it.

"You'll have to wait until the others get here."

It wasn't that there was anything wrong with the dress, or that Stella's creation wasn't beautiful. It was just that any dress, no matter how gorgeous, looked ridiculous on Kri. With her height and broad shoulders, it wasn't a pretty picture. It was like stuffing John Cena into a white wedding dress and expecting him to look wonderful in it.

She could have insisted on getting married in a white tuxedo or even pink, but the way she saw it, letting Stella design the dress, and Mey and Jin produce it in their shop, was more for their benefit than hers. It was a prototype for their new line of wedding dresses for tall women.

Amanda pouted. "Don't I deserve at least a peek?"

Thankfully, the doorbell rang again, so Kri didn't have to respond.

As she opened the door, she found the rest of her bridesmaids in the corridor, already dressed in their gowns, which had also been designed by Stella and produced by Mey and Jin.

The big square case Eva was holding most likely contained the makeup she was going to use on Kri's face, and the bag in Callie's contained the hair styling tools she was going to use on her.

Oh, the joy.

Amanda put her hands on her hips. "How come no one told me to dress in my bridesmaid outfit?"

"Didn't you get my text?" Carol asked.

Amanda pulled out her phone. "Oh, damn. I didn't notice it." She cast an apologetic glance at Kri. "Do you want me to go get it?"

Kri shook her head. "You can do it right before the ceremony."

"Can we see the dress?" Carol asked. "Stella has been gushing over it for days."

"I was," Stella admitted. "I love that dress. When Richard and I get married, I will design one for myself in the same style."

Well, duh. Stella was of average height, and her shoulders were slim and feminine. She would look awesome in something like that.

"It's in the bedroom." Kri walked over to the door and opened it. "Go ahead. Take a look."

"We want to see it on you," Stella said. "You refused to come for fittings, and I'm terrified that it doesn't fit. I brought my sewing machine on the cruise in case I need to make last-minute alterations."

Kri grimaced. "I'm sorry, but I just didn't have time. You know how hectic things were before the cruise."

The look Stella gave her made it clear she hadn't bought the explanation even for a second. "I'm armed with pins and ready to use them. Get in that dress."

Kri chuckled. "Yes, ma'am."

24

MARGO

"Are you sure?" Margo eyed the pile of dresses Frankie had dropped on the bed. "What if Marina and Larissa don't take good care of them? Your cousins will be upset if you return them damaged."

"Don't be silly." Frankie waved a dismissive hand. "What could they do to them?"

"Stains, tears," Mia supplied. "But if they do, I'll happily cover the cost of replacements."

It was nice to be in Mia's situation and not have any more worries about money. Margo had never dreamt about being rich, but being able to pay her bills and do nice things for others from time to time could have been nice.

Hopefully, her new job at Perfect Match would pay enough to cover the basics. The problem was that her future was uncertain at the moment, and she might not be able to take the job because she had to leave, either because she had no godly genes and didn't become immortal or she had them and had to follow Negal to Tibet.

She pulled out her new phone to check if Negal had left her a message and was disappointed that there was none.

After the visit to the clinic, she'd gone to see Jasmine with Frankie and Mia, and Negal had returned to the Lido deck with Dagor. Since Dagor wasn't back yet either, they were probably still up there.

"We don't have to deliver the dresses right now," Margo said. "They are still short-staffed, so Larissa and Marina have to work tonight and won't need them until tomorrow. Let's join the guys on the Lido deck."

Frankie perked up. "I like the way you think. I haven't had a drink in forever." She turned to Mia. "You can call Toven and ask him to meet you up there."

"I'll do that." Mia pulled out her phone.

As they headed out, Margo leaned toward Frankie. "Are you allowed to have alcohol so soon after your transition?"

"Bridget didn't say anything to that effect, so I assume it's fine."

"You should ask," Mia said.

"Why? So, she can tell me no?" Frankie called the elevator. "If I don't ask, I can claim ignorance."

It wasn't smart, but Margo knew better than to argue with Frankie. She was a sweetheart but had a stubborn streak a mile long.

When they reached the Lido deck, they found Negal and Dagor sitting at a table, sipping on beers and munching on pretzels.

Both rose to their feet when they saw them approaching, and then Negal walked over to Margo. "I've missed you." He feathered a kiss on her cheek.

She arched a brow. "You did?"

"Why does that surprise you?" He pulled out a chair for her.

"You didn't text me." She sat down.

"Was I supposed to?"

Dagor chuckled. "Yeah, you were."

Negal turned to him. "How do you know?"

"Frankie made a list of rules for me. One of them is to always let her know where I am and what I am doing."

Margo looked at Frankie, who nodded. "Don't forget that they are not from this planet. How are they supposed to know what human women expect from their significant others?"

"I suspect that females on Anumati are not all that different from us. After all, we are biologically compatible, which means that we are more similar than different."

"Culture plays a big role," Dagor said. "Expectations are different." He glanced at Negal. "Right?"

Negal nodded. "Couples don't get as close emotionally on Anumati unless they are fated mates, and that's extremely rare."

"That's strange," Mia said. "There are so many fated matches in the clan. Most of them are, in fact."

It was indeed strange, but if Mia didn't know the reason for that, Margo doubted anyone else did. "What about children?" she asked. "Are parents close to their children on Anumati?"

Negal nodded. "Very much so. The birth rate is so low that every child is treated like a miracle."

That was surprising for a society with such advanced knowledge in genetics.

"Given what Anumatians can do with gene manipulation, I would assume that anyone who wanted a child on Anumati could get one." Margo looked at Negal. "Even humans know how to make babies in a lab, and then implant them in a female's womb. I'm sure Anumatian scientists know how to make test tube babies."

Negal nodded. "You are correct, but to make a test tube baby, as you call it, a couple needs to apply, get approved, and have the funds for it. The wait line is centuries long, and the procedure is above most citizens' means. On the other hand, having a child naturally does not cost anything and doesn't require approval."

"It's sad," Mia said. "I imagined that a society as advanced as the gods' would do away with money, and that everyone would get what they need while contributing what they can."

Dagor chuckled. "It doesn't work like that. Not here and not on my home planet. People need incentives to put in an effort. Regrettably, praise and recognition, or even social pressure, are not enough to encourage people to put in the work. Fear of destitution on the one hand and monetary rewards on the other are much stronger motivators, and at the end of the day, we are better for it. Laziness and lack of motivation lead to low self-esteem, which in turn might lead to depression, drug abuse, and distractive behaviors to alleviate the boredom."

Margo agreed, but Mia didn't look convinced. "The clan has a good system, but I doubt it could work for a large society. Every member gets a share in the clan's profit, and it's enough to live on comfortably without having to work, but if they do choose to work, they get paid for their efforts and have more than just the basics."

"That's amazing," Margo said. "I would love to have the security of knowing that my bills are covered, and that I could do whatever I'm passionate about without having to worry about money."

Negal grimaced. "We don't have that on Anumati. But to tell you the truth, I have no idea what I would do with myself if I didn't have to work. I don't love what I do, and I don't hate it either, but I'm not passionate about it."

"Speaking of work," Margo said. "Did Aru speak to your commander about postponing the trip or letting you stay behind?"

Negal shook his head. "Aru didn't speak to the commander, and he won't unless you start transitioning."

Margo's heart sank. She was out of time, and she needed to get over her inhibitions or lose her chance with Negal. If he left before inducing her, she would have to choose someone else, and there was no way she would be able to do that.

It was either Negal or no one.

25

MICHAEL

Surrounded by his fellow Guardians, including the chief, Michael felt a profound sense of camaraderie. These males had become his family, taking him under their proverbial wings, teaching him, and supporting him through his transition and beyond. Still, as laughter filled the air and stories of past exploits were shared, Michael's mind drifted to his old friends from college.

He wished they could be there with him, along with his parents, to celebrate his bachelor party and attend his wedding.

It had been a spontaneous decision to secure one of the nights on the cruise for their wedding, and although Michael had agreed to it, he hadn't been happy about celebrating without at least his parents attending.

Perhaps once they returned home, he and Kri could have another wedding in Vegas with his parents, his best friends Eddie and Zach, and maybe also Kri's mother if she was up to it. After all, the cruise wedding did not provide any official documentation, so in the human world, they wouldn't be considered married.

The more occasions to celebrate, the better, right?

Since stepping through the veil separating their worlds, Michael had met with his college friends from time to time, but they had drifted apart.

Zach and Eddie did not belong in his new world, where gods and immortals were real, and he had become an immortal himself, but he did not want to let go of them just because he had been changed.

He still remembered vividly introducing Kri to them over four years ago. He'd been anxious about how his friends would react to his new girlfriend and the fact that he was not returning to college.

Even though his buddies had been with him when he'd been thrust into this new world, they had no recollection of how it had happened. Yamanu had thralled them to forget the Doomers' attack, replacing their memories with a story about a drunken brawl and a sudden family emergency that Michael had to attend to, necessitating his leaving right away.

He'd met Kri the next day, and his life had been irrevocably changed in more ways than he could count.

It had taken him months to arrange a get-together with Zach and Eddie and introduce Kri to them.

Michael chuckled.

He'd fabricated a story about joining a secret government training program and meeting Kri there, but the truth wasn't that far removed from the lie. He'd joined the Guardian force as a trainee, hoping to one day become a Guardian like her.

He'd been told that it would take him decades to reach her level, and at the time, he'd naively believed that he'd do it faster, but four years later, he was still a trainee, and Kri was still light years ahead of him in her level of skill and ability.

Michael had learned to live with it. He'd realized that he didn't need to be better than she was or even as good. He just wished to be a full-fledged member of the force and get all the perks the position entailed.

Looking around at the immortal warriors who had become his best friends, he felt a twinge of nostalgia for his old, simpler life, but he wouldn't have traded his new one for anything.

"You seem miles away, kid." Bhathian clapped him on the shoulder, jolting him back to the present.

Michael shrugged. "I was thinking about the old times and about being a full-fledged Guardian. I always thought that Kri and I would get married after I got accepted, but the wedding cruise came up, and suddenly, she was talking about getting married on the ship, and I just went along with it. I couldn't say no."

Bhathian let out a low chuckle. "I'm married too, kid. The secret to a happy marriage is saying yes at least ten times for every no."

Smiling, Arwel leaned over Bhathian's shoulder. "You should have a relationship advice column on the clan's virtual bulletin board."

"That's not a bad idea." Bhathian raised his glass in a salute. "I might just do that."

Anandur snorted. "It'll have to be a very short column. It will answer every question with, 'yes, dear'."

Brundar's lips lifted in a ghost of a smile, but as usual, he didn't say anything. Instead, he walked over and clapped Michael on his back, offering his silent support.

"A toast." Onegus raised his glass and waited until everyone hushed. "To Michael, who works harder than any other trainee in the history of the force."

The statement surprised Michael. Onegus had never praised his progress, and Michael had been under the impression that he was pretty average.

"Thank you." He lifted his glass and clinked it with Onegus's.

"You are welcome, but I'm not done." Onegus kept his glass aloft. "I've been watching you, Michael. You've done very well on the missions I've sent you on, and your team leaders have had nothing but praise for you."

Hope rose in Michael's chest. Was Onegus praising him just because it was his bachelor party, or was he getting promoted?

Onegus reached into his pocket, pulled out a scroll tied with a red ribbon, and handed it to Michael. "Welcome to the force, Michael."

The sudden eruption of cheers and applause from everyone was overwhelming. Bhathian slapped him on the back, Arwel smiled and clapped his hands, and then Yamanu enveloped him in his arms. "Congratulations, little brother."

For a long moment, Michael was speechless. This was so unexpected that he suspected he was dreaming. He must have fallen asleep and dreamt about the bachelor party and the scroll clasped in his hand.

"Can someone please pinch me?"

Bhathian's booming laugh was soon joined by four more, with Brundar the only one not laughing.

"This is not a dream," Onegus said. "You've done so well on the test missions I've sent you on that there was no point in delaying your acceptance. You've earned it in record time like you've said you would from the very beginning."

"Thank you," Michael managed to choke out. "I'll make sure that you never regret the decision to grant me fully-fledged status after only four years of training." He swept his gaze over the smiling faces of his friends. "I won't let any of you down."

Onegus nodded. "We all know that you won't. That's why you are holding this scroll. Otherwise, I would never have given it to you."

26

PETER

Peter scrolled through the selection of movies on the ship's server, clicked on a comedy he'd already seen, watched a few minutes, and clicked it off. He was bored and restless. He missed Marina.

Dropping the remote on the couch beside him, he leaned back and closed his eyes.

He was doing it again. Falling for a female that was no good for him and with whom he could have no future.

'You are in love with the notion of being in love.' Kagra's words reverberated through his mind. *You need to learn to live in the moment.*

"If only I could."

He wouldn't admit it to anyone, not even to himself, but in the back of his mind, he entertained the hope that Marina was a Dormant. It wasn't likely, because what were the chances of that?

Practically none.

If she had the genes, she would have started transitioning already, given how many times he had bitten her.

Then again, several of the Dormants had taken weeks to transition. Mey and Yamanu had almost lost hope before the first signs began manifesting.

But even if Marina was just a human, which was most likely the case, she wasn't like all the other human females Peter had been with. She knew who he was, and nothing was preventing him from bringing her to the village. Several of the humans from the Kra-ell compound were already living there, so Kian couldn't use the secrecy excuse to forbid it, and there was no reason to deny Marina.

Well, except that it wasn't good for Peter.

He was well aware that it was a prescription for heartache and that watching her get old and die would slay him, but he just couldn't think of not being with her.

If he had any brains, he would end things between them before his attachment to her grew even stronger, but it wasn't his brain that was in charge. It was his heart.

With a groan, he picked up his phone and dialed her number.

She answered on the second ring. "Peter. What's up?"

"I just wanted to hear your voice. How's your day going?"

"Hectic. How is yours?"

"I'm bored, and I want to see you."

She chuckled. "It would have sounded better if you'd said that you missed me, and that's why you wanted to see me."

"But that's what I said."

"No, you said that you were bored."

He rolled his eyes. "Can I come down to the kitchen? I can help out. Wash dishes or cut vegetables. I don't care what task I'm assigned as long as I can be near you."

She sighed. "That's so sweet of you, and I would love it, but you'd just be underfoot because you don't know your way around a commercial kitchen. Besides, you'll make everyone nervous. Humans and immortals usually don't mix well."

"I can be useful, though. I can carry heavy stuff."

Marina laughed. "I know you can, but it's not going to work. The kitchen is a well-oiled machine, and you'd be like a wrench thrown into the gears."

Peter slumped against the back of the couch. "Can I at least come visit and steal you away for a few minutes?"

There was a moment of silence, and then she let out a sigh. "I've already taken a break to return the dress to Jasmine, and Mila will not be happy about me taking another one, especially since we were informed that the wedding would start two hours earlier than scheduled, but perhaps I can come up with an excuse that's more convincing than a long visit to the bathroom."

Peter perked up. "Just tell me when, and I'll be there."

"Hold on, I'm thinking. Do you still have the dresses you borrowed for me from your relatives?"

"Of course. You returned the one you borrowed from Jasmine, and there are still four weddings to go."

"Three. I'm not accompanying you to tonight's wedding. But I hope that Larissa and I can attend tomorrow's wedding, and Larissa has nothing nice to wear. Could you possibly bring her one of the dresses? That would be a great excuse for me to take a break."

Peter sighed. "They were meant for you, and none of them will fit Larissa, but we can pretend that I'm bringing a dress for her, right?"

"Yeah, I guess. Poor Larissa will be disappointed. I need to find her something. I just hope that the two servers are back to work tomorrow. If they are not, I will drag them out of their beds even if one needs to work one-handed and the other is loopy from pain medication."

"They'd better. If not, I'm coming to help prepare breakfast and lunch so you and Larissa can take the evening off. I might be inexperienced in the kitchen, but with my speed and strength, I can do the work of two people with ease, and it's not like I have anything better to do when you're not around."

"I'll tell that to Mila." Marina chuckled. "You helping in the kitchen should be threat enough to make sure we get the time off no matter what."

27

MARINA

Marina's hands moved with practiced efficiency as she chopped vegetables. Usually the monotony of the task, along with the clatter of pots and pans and the sizzle of frying food, calmed her down and centered her, but today it wasn't enough to distract her from thinking about Peter.

Reaching for another tomato, she placed it on the chopping board, but as she lifted the knife, she heard the kitchen doors swinging open. It could have been anyone, but she knew it was Peter even before she turned around.

He strode in with his typical swagger, a broad smile on his handsome face, and looking good enough to eat.

Everyone seemed to pause for a heartbeat, every pair of eyes flicking toward him and then quickly back to what they were doing before the interruption.

Peter didn't seem to notice, his focus on her and his smile getting broader the closer he got to her.

A flutter of anticipation stirred in her stomach.

Without a word, he took the knife from her hand, put it on the chopping board, and pulled her to him for a quick kiss. "I missed you too much to wait," he murmured against her lips.

Behind his back, several of her friends snickered, and the indignant huff had no doubt come from Mila.

"Take it outside," the cook barked in Russian. "You have five minutes."

Chuckling, Marina rested her forehead against Peter's chest. "Mila told me to take it outside."

Peter turned around to look at the cook and dipped his head. "*Spasibo.*"

Mila waved him off with her mixing spoon, a stern expression on her round face, but Marina caught the slight twitching of the cook's lips. She wasn't really mad.

As Peter took her hand, she smiled at Mila and mouthed '*Spasibo*' as well.

This time, Mila allowed her lips to lift in a lopsided smile.

Outside, he led her to the small alcove they had discovered during one of his previous visits to the kitchen.

Leaning against the wall, he spread his legs and pulled her between them. "I need to kiss you."

"You just did."

"That was just a taste." His hand wrapped around the back of her neck, and then his lips were on hers.

Marina closed her eyes and wrapped her arms around his neck, the tips of her fingers playing with the strands of hair on the back of his head.

He needed a trim.

For a moment, his hands settled on her waist, but they didn't stay there. His fingers stroked up her sides, skimming the swell of her breasts and eliciting a moan, which he caught with his mouth.

She tightened her hold on his neck to bring him closer so she could rub her hardened nipples against his chest, but the thick fabric of her apron was in the way.

They had made love that morning, and yet the kiss ignited a hunger in her that had her forgo caution and lift one leg to wrap it against Peter's waist, so her achy center was aligned with the delicious bulge in his pants.

"Marina." He broke the kiss and leaned his forehead against hers. "I can't get enough of you."

"Me too," she said breathlessly and then sighed. "Unfortunately, I think the five minutes are up."

"What a shame." The look he gave her was lustful, but it was also so tender and full of feeling that it made her heart flutter.

Could it be that he was falling for her?

Did his emotions run as deep as hers?

Probably not. Immortals didn't fall in love with humans, and she would never be his mate, but she wouldn't mind being with him as his lover, or a friend with benefits, or even his housekeeper whom he occasionally shagged.

Scrap the 'occasional' part. She would accept daily shagging as payment for her cleaning and cooking services.

"You didn't bring the dress," she said, to hide the manic laughter bubbling up in her throat.

"I forgot." Peter grinned. "Which means that I have an excuse to whisk you out of the kitchen again."

"Mila will chase you off with a rolling pin in hand."

"No way." He planted a chaste kiss on her cheek. "She likes me."

Of course, she did. Everyone liked Peter. What was there not to like?

Back in the kitchen, she ignored the knowing looks and the smirks as she walked over to her station and resumed chopping vegetables for the salad.

She was lost in the rhythm of her task when Amanda breezed into the kitchen to give last-minute instructions for tonight's wedding and check that everything would be ready on time.

When she was done, she walked over to Marina's station and leaned against the counter. "Are you accompanying Peter to the wedding tonight?"

Marina shook her head. "We are understaffed, so I can't get tonight off, but I will be there tomorrow." She regarded Amanda with a challenge in her eyes, waiting for the lecture about how inappropriate it was for her to date an immortal.

"It's a shame that you can't be his date tonight. I haven't seen Peter so happy in a long time."

Marina's eyes widened in surprise. Amanda was an important immortal, the sister of their leader. If she wasn't against Peter dating a human, then maybe others wouldn't be either.

She schooled her expression to hide her surprise. "My friend Larissa was supposed to accompany Jay, but she's in the same situation as I am." She watched Amanda's expression to see if her reaction would be different to yet another human and immortal pairing.

"I'm sure that Jay is thrilled," Amanda said, sounding genuine.

"Larissa surely is, but if she doesn't find something nice to wear, she might not attend." Marina sighed. "Thanks to Peter's cousins' generous contributions, I'm covered, but none of their dresses will fit Larissa." She turned to smile at her friend across the kitchen.

Following her gaze, Amanda also smiled at Larissa and gave her a small wave hello. "I will ask around for her," Amanda said. "Perhaps I can scavenge something for her to wear."

That was so kind and unexpected that Marina was lost for words for the second time in mere minutes.

"Thank you so much. Can I do something to repay your kindness? Does your cabin need sprucing up? Do you need breakfast delivered tomorrow morning?"

Amanda laughed. "Thank you for the offer, darling, but my butler would be mortified if anyone tried to take the job of sprucing up and making breakfast from him."

Amanda had her own servant on board?

"Oh. I didn't know that you had a butler."

"Onidu rarely leaves the cabin," Amanda said. "He's also my nanny."

"You are lucky to have such a capable person in your employ."

"I know." Amanda pushed away from the counter. "I'll see what I can find for Larissa and come back. If not today, then tomorrow."

"Thank you."

As the doors flung closed behind the gorgeous brunette, Marina sighed. "It must be nice to be a princess."

28

ANNANI

Annani put the brush away, rose to her feet, and walked into the living room. The afternoon sun filtered through the curtains, casting a serene light over the table that her Odus had set in preparation for Syssi's parents' visit.

The cruise offered a rare occasion for Annani to interact with her in-laws, and she was looking forward to a stimulating conversation with Anita and Adam.

They always had so many fascinating stories to tell about their exploits in the Congo. Listening to Anita talk about her work with children, Adam about his wildlife photography, and the dangerous situations both often found themselves in might take her mind off tonight's first telepathic meeting with her grandmother.

It was a shame she could not share that piece of information with them or the rest of her clan. If it was up to her, she would have told everyone about it, but Aru insisted on secrecy, and she had to honor his wishes even though she did not believe it was necessary.

Well, it was true that letting Dagor and Negal in on the secret carried some risk. If they ever got picked up by the Anumati patrol ship, the knowledge of Aru and Aria's telepathic connection could be extracted from them.

When the doorbell rang and Oridu let Anita and Adam in, Annani greeted each one with a warm smile and a gentle embrace.

She might be petite and look delicate, but she could easily crush a human's ribcage if she was not careful.

"I hope you have not eaten yet. My Odus prepared afternoon tea."

"Not since lunch." Adam patted his belly. "I'm going to gain so much weight on this cruise that I will need to go on a diet when we return to Liuma."

Anita sighed. "That won't be difficult." She cast Annani a sad smile. "It's hard to eat well when people are hungry around you."

"Is hunger still such a severe problem in the Congo?" Annani asked.

Syssi's mother nodded. "Yes, hunger remains a significant issue in DRC. Many are experiencing food insecurity, and many children are acutely malnourished. Poor harvests, violence-driven displacement, disease, unemployment, and collapsing infrastructure are to blame, and there are no fast and easy solutions to any of that."

Annani shook her head. "It is hard to believe that hunger is still an issue in today's world."

Adam snorted. "And what about barbarism? When I was a boy, I believed the world was getting better and that there were no more barbarians left."

Annani leaned back, Oridu filled her cup with tea, and then she waited for him to fill Anita and Adam's cups.

"I assume that you are referring to what happened in Acapulco."

Adam let out a sigh. "Among other instances. There are too many to count even though the media tends to focus on only one or two while completely ignoring the worst travesties."

"It's all ugly politics." Anita lifted her hand. "But let's talk about more pleasant subjects." She forced a smile. "I've loved all of your wedding speeches, Annani. How do you come up with all those beautiful words for all the ceremonies?"

Annani smiled. "Every couple has a unique story that inspires my words."

Anita leaned forward. "Do you write them in advance?"

Annani laughed. "I used to wing it, but with a different wedding every night, I need to make sure I don't repeat myself, so I write down a few bullet points and read through them before the ceremony. Some repetition is unavoidable, of course, but I try not to bore my audience."

Nodding, Anita smiled. "I must admit that I tear up each night, and you know me. I'm not usually the emotional type. And it's not just during your speech but also during the vows the couples exchange. They are so heartfelt." She cast a smile at her husband. "When we got married, exchanging personal vows wasn't a thing. I wish it was."

"Our golden anniversary is approaching." Adam reached for her hand and brought it to his lips for a kiss. "We can renew our vows, and this time not use the standard wording."

"That is a marvelous idea." Annani clapped her hands. "I would love to preside over your vow renewal ceremony." She leaned closer to Anita. "Perhaps it could coincide with your retirement? Allegra and Phoenix would love to have their grandmother near."

Anita let out a sigh. "My granddaughters are surrounded by a loving and supportive community. I'm sure they would love to have me close, and I would love that as well, but the children I help in Liuma need me, and I can't abandon them."

"I am sure you can find a replacement," Annani said.

"I wish that was true. People are willing to volunteer for a few months, sometimes a year, but it's a rare soul that is willing to make Liuma their home."

29

KRI

Kri stood just outside the dining hall doors, her fingers twisting the simple wedding band she was about to put on Michael's finger. Her bridesmaids were smiling, but she was too nervous to even pretend, and it had nothing to do with being unsure about the male she was marrying.

It was the damn wedding gown.

It was grand, a true masterpiece, but she was not used to wearing dresses, especially not one as constricting as what Stella had designed for her. The corset was tight, making it difficult to take a full breath, and with her ample cleavage, Kri was afraid that if she fully expanded her chest, the zipper would give up.

Served her right for not making time for fittings. Stella had taken her measurements, and Kri had thought it would be enough, but apparently it hadn't been.

Her large breasts were pushed up uncomfortably, making her self-conscious despite her bridesmaids' gushing over how lovely she looked in the damn dress.

Instead of succumbing to peer pressure and her mother's pleading, she should have gotten married in an elegant white pantsuit like she'd wanted to. The dress, while stunning and crafted to fit her six-foot-tall broad-shouldered frame, did not complement her Guardian's body.

Her bridesmaids, on the other hand, looked effortlessly beautiful in their dresses.

Taking a shallow breath, Kri turned inward to calm her nerves.

After all, it was just a ceremony. She and Michael had pledged their lives to each other a long time ago.

Their relationship hadn't been all smooth sailing, and they had weathered some rough waters, but once Michael had given up on his preconceived notions of masculinity and femininity, it had been as close to bliss as she could have hoped for.

Kri smiled, thinking of their first meeting.

Curious about the newcomer housed in the keep's dungeon, she'd volunteered to deliver him lunch, and the connection had been immediate.

Michael had been taken aback by her. She was so different from the girls he'd encountered in college. She'd teased him, and he'd almost choked on his food, but then he'd expressed his admiration for her in such an earnest and uncommon manner that he had won her over.

In no time, they had found themselves deeply in love, and despite a few rough spots along the way, she had zero hesitation about pledging her life to Michael.

Taking as deep of a breath as she could in the damn corset, Kri steeled herself for the walk down the aisle and the reaction of her clan members to seeing her stuffed like a big sausage into a too-tight white dress.

It was nothing compared to facing traffickers and other scum, and if she could handle that, she could handle a few snide remarks. She would walk into the hall with her head held high.

So yeah, today she was a bride, but above all she was a Guardian, and Guardians feared nothing.

When the music started, and the doors opened, Kri trained her eyes on Michael's smiling face and strode forward.

When she and her bridesmaids reached the podium, she took Michael's extended hand while her bridesmaids took positions next to their mates, who were Michael's groomsmen.

Standing on top of the dais, the Clan Mother was so petite that her eyes were on the same level as Kri's and Michael's, and as she turned to them, her gaze was full of warmth.

When the room fell silent, Annani turned back to face the guests. "My beloveds, today, we gather under the auspices of love and community to witness the union of two extraordinary souls—Kri and Michael."

She turned her gaze affectionately towards Kri. "Kri, our fierce and brave Guardian. You embody strength, courage, and loyalty. From the moment you took your first baby steps, it was clear to everyone that you would grow up to be a warrior. You have always stood tall, not just in stature but in spirit. You have never backed out of a challenge, and when you found your one and only, you conquered him the same way you conquered every goal you have set for yourself."

As a few snickers sounded from the assembled guests, Kri gave Michael's hand a gentle squeeze, and he returned it along with a wink.

Annani turned to Michael with a brilliant smile. "My dear Michael. You entered our world unexpectedly but have since become a cherished member of our community. Your openness, humor, and bravery have not only won Kri's heart but have earned you the respect and affection of all who have come to know you. You remind us that strength is shown not just through acts of valor but through determination, hard work, and the courage to embrace a vastly different world from the one you were born to."

The goddess then addressed them both. "May the love that has brought you together continue to grow and deepen with each passing day. May you face every challenge hand in hand and side by side. And may your lives be blessed with endless joy, unwavering support, and love that deepens and grows along with your joined journey."

Annani lifted her hands. "In the presence of your family and friends, I bless this union. Kri and Michael, would you like to exchange vows?"

Kri dipped her head, "Yes, Clan Mother."

30

MICHAEL

Michael felt a lump form in his throat as he saw Kri walking down the aisle, looking every inch the warrior princess that she was.

Her strength and beauty left him breathless.

The dress, which he hadn't been allowed to see, was exquisite. It complemented her tall, powerful frame, capturing the essence of Kri, which was fierce yet beautiful and feminine, formidable yet graceful and kind.

Beside him stood his groomsmen, a solid wall of muscle and fierce loyalty. They were more like family to him than friends and mentors, but he once again regretted not having his family by birth and his old friends with him at this monumental moment.

His father.

His mother.

Zach and Eddie.

Reminding himself of his plan to have another ceremony with them in Vegas, Michael took a deep breath and focused on the present. He hoped he would remember all the beautiful words that Yamanu and Bhathian had helped him craft and that they would please Kri, conveying the depth of his feelings for her.

As she reached him, Michael took Kri's hands in his, feeling the familiar rush of energy that always flowed between them. He looked into her blue, smiling eyes, which had captivated him from the first moment he'd seen her and hadn't loosened their hold on him ever since.

"I love you," he mouthed, but she was already turning to the Clan Mother.

Listening to the goddess deliver her speech, he waited for her to finish her blessing over their union and give them the go-ahead to recite their vows.

He'd won the privilege of going first in a fierce game of *War of the Godzillas* they had played the day before, which made him anxious.

What if Kri's vows were more beautifully worded than his?

It wasn't a competition, he reminded himself. And even if it was, he should happily accept Kri winning.

Turning to the love of his life, Michael smiled. "My beautiful Kri. From the moment I met you, I knew that my life would never be the same. The man I became, thanks to you, is very different from the boy I was before. You challenged me, you laughed with me, and you showed me what it means to be truly strong. You've taught me that true strength is in the heart and mind and that bravery manifests in many ways. But most of all, you taught me all I know now and will ever know about love."

As her eyes glistened with unshed tears, he rubbed his thumb over her racing pulse. "I vow to honor the incredible woman you are, to support you in your battles, and to be your partner in every adventure life throws our way. I vow to respect our differences as much as our similarities and to cherish the love that binds us. For better and for worse, you are stuck with me."

As their audience laughed, Michael took a deep breath and continued, "I pledge to stand by you, to be your confidant, your ally, and your partner in all things. I will be your shelter in the storm, your light in the darkness, and the one who holds you close through all the seasons of our lives."

He paused, looking into her glistening eyes and hoping that she could see the sincerity and love he felt for her. "Kri, my mate, my one and only, the owner of my heart. Today, in front of our friends and family, I pledge myself to you for eternity." He pulled a ring out of his pocket. "Kri, my love. With this ring, I thee wed."

As Michael finished with the traditional words, the weight of the moment settled upon him. He felt blessed beyond measure to have Kri by his side and to call her his mate.

As Kri's eyes held his, shimmering with unshed happy tears, he was awed by the power of her presence, the strength of her spirit, and the tenderness of her heart.

She took a steadying breath. "Michael. Before you entered my life, I thought that I had all that I needed to be happy, but I was wrong. You brought me joy, friendship, and companionship, and you even managed to convince me to enroll in online college. Thanks to you, I now hold a bachelor's degree in criminal justice."

As the crowd clapped and cheered, she lifted their joined hands in the air. "Michael earned a degree in business, so give him a cheer as well."

She waited for the applause and cheers to subside before continuing. "And that was in addition to training for long hours every day." She smiled at him before turning to look at their guests. "Respect, people."

The applause and cheers were deafening.

He dipped his head. "Thank you."

This was the Kri he knew and loved. The female who took charge and led the crowd even at her own wedding and with the Clan Mother standing inches away from her.

His mate wasn't afraid of anything.

Kri smiled and squeezed his hand. "Michael, my love. I vow to support you, to stand by your side, and to be your partner in all things. I vow to be your shield in times of war and your solace in times of peace. I vow to laugh with you, to dream with you, and to shoulder any burden or challenge that comes our way. Together, we are stronger, braver, and more complete than the sum of our parts. I promise to cherish and love you forever and beyond." She reached into her corset and pulled out a ring from between her breasts to the cheers and laughter of their guests.

"Michael, my love, with this ring I thee wed."

Their audience erupted with hoots, cheers, and applause, and then someone started a chant, "Kiss, kiss, kiss…"

Michael lifted a hand to shush them. "The Clan Mother hasn't said the last words yet."

The room fell silent in an instant.

Stepping forward, the goddess raised her arms, signaling the culmination of the ceremony. "Kri and Michael, I pronounce you mated and bonded for life. May your union be blessed by the Fates and as enduring as the fabric of the universe." She paused, allowing her words to settle over the congregation. "You may now seal your promises with a kiss," she announced with a twinkle in her eye.

As Michael wrapped his arms around his bride's narrow waist, she wound hers around his neck, and the kiss they shared was an affirmation of their vows, tender yet full of strength—a perfect balance of passion and promise.

NEGAL

J ust like the one the night before, the wedding ceremony had been touching, and the vows Kri and Michael had exchanged echoed in Negal's mind long after the words had faded into the ether and the festivities had commenced.

The hall was alive with laughter and the soft clink of glasses, and as the music started, couples took to the dance floor.

"Would you like to dance?" he asked Margo.

"I would love to." She swiped a finger under one eye and then the other.

He smiled. "Got emotional?"

She nodded. "For a cynical skeptic, I love weddings too much." She cast a glance in Kian's direction. "Apparently, I share this weakness with the big boss, so maybe it's something that grouches like us have in common."

"You're not a grouch." Negal rose to his feet and offered her a hand up. "Maybe you just need more reminders that not everything is as bad as you think it is."

Chuckling, Margo took his hand. "Oh, it's much worse. The older I get, the more I discover how naive I was, believing in a better future and the integrity of the system."

"I'm not well versed in human affairs, but I experienced the same on Anumati. Sometimes, I miss the days of my youth, when I worshipped the Eternal King and believed wholeheartedly that he had my best interests at heart along with all the citizens of Anumati, whether residing on the home world or the colonies."

"I'm glad that you understand my way of thinking." Margo smiled up at him. "Not many do."

As he led her to the dance floor, Negal scanned the room, noting all the males whose eyes followed her, and he had the absurd urge to wrap her in his arms and hide her from view.

Margo looked exquisite in a dress made from a shimmery gold fabric. The bodice hugged her curves gently while the skirt flowed like liquid gold, cascading to the floor in a series of gentle waves. Her long blond hair was gathered atop her head, and a few strands cascaded like a golden waterfall, framing her face and highlighting the clear blue of her eyes.

His thoughts drifting to Kri and Michael's vows, to the joy and love he glimpsed in their exchange, Negal couldn't help but yearn for an everlasting bond like theirs.

As the slow dance began, Margo looked into his eyes and frowned. "Did something upset you?"

"Why do you ask?"

"Your eyes are glowing."

He wasn't sure whether they were doing that in response to the male gazes that had trailed Margo or what her nearness was doing to him, but it was unacceptable in either case.

"My apologies." He blinked a couple of times until he was sure they were no longer glowing.

"You have nothing to apologize for. I was just curious about the reason." A smile lifted her lips. "Were you having naughty thoughts about me?"

He chuckled. "I'm always having naughty thoughts about you, but I'm usually in better control of my responses."

As her cheeks pinked, she got closer and rested her forehead against his chest. "I'm having naughty thoughts about you as well," she admitted in a whisper. "But they are probably much tamer than yours."

His shaft swelled in an instant. "Now I'm dying to hear all about those naughty thoughts."

She shook her head. "I'm not going to tell you."

Negal hoped she would show him, and that she wouldn't keep him waiting for too long. Delayed gratification had its merits, but he preferred to end the delay sooner rather than later.

As they swayed in place to the rhythm of the music, not really dancing but rather enjoying each other's closeness, the world around them seemed to fade. The music and the couples dancing next to them all receded until it was just the two of them, moving to the beat.

As the song ended and they stepped apart, Negal was reluctant to let go. "Another dance?"

Margo stepped closer to him. "Of course."

As Dagor and Frankie glided onto the dance floor to join them, the dynamic shifted, their bubble expanding to include their friends.

Watching how happy and in love they looked, Negal was glad for Dagor and Frankie, but he was also a little envious.

The obstacles that they had faced together were behind them. Frankie had successfully transitioned, and her future with Dagor was set on the right path. They would still face challenges, but their relationship was cemented, their bond just as everlasting as Kri and Michael's.

Still, Dagor would never be able to bring Frankie home to his parents on Anumati because she was a hybrid, part human, part goddess, and mating with created species was not allowed on the home planet. The same was true for Negal, but he no longer cared about that.

His gaze flickered from Dagor and Frankie back to Margo, who was watching the other couple with a smile.

Was she thinking about all the obstacles that still stood in his and her way before they could bask in each other's company with the same ease?

The crux of it all was her transition, but for that to have a chance of happening, they needed to overcome Margo's intimacy problem.

Not that he was overly concerned about that. The way she was looking at him, her eyes full of desire and perhaps even love, it wouldn't be long now, but the biggest question was whether she possessed the godly genes at all. He believed that she did, that the Fates wouldn't be cruel to him by sending him a mere human to taunt him, but until it happened, the uncertainty was gnawing at him.

The thought of a future without her was unbearable. He loved her, more than he had ever thought possible, and the realization that her transition might never occur and that their time together could be limited was weighing heavily on his heart.

3 2

MARGO

Margo smiled and moved to the beat, but her mind was a whirlwind of thoughts and anxiety.

She had made up her mind that tonight would be her first time with Negal, but she had no idea how to make it happen. She was sharing a cabin with Frankie and Dagor and Negal was sharing a cabin with Aru and Gabi. She was nervous enough as it was without the added complexity of the lack of privacy.

Margo tried to keep her expression serene, to lose herself in the music, the dancing, and in Negal's eyes, which looked at her with such depth and warmth. But given the crease between his brows, Negal was sensing her disquiet.

"What's the matter?" he asked. "Are you tired? Do you want to sit down?"

"No, I'm fine." She smiled up at him. "Are you enjoying yourself?"

The crease between his eyebrows deepened. "I have you in my arms, so of course, I'm having a good time, but I know that something is troubling you." He leaned closer and brushed his lips over her ear, eliciting a shiver. "You can tell me anything, sweetheart."

The sudden flash of desire loosened her tongue. "I was just thinking about our lodging situation," she whispered. "It's not very conducive to romance. When we are ready to take the next step, and I'm not saying that it is now, but when we are, I would have liked for us to have a cabin to ourselves," she finally confessed.

His expression shifted from concern to understanding, and then his eyes started glowing again, but this time, she had no doubt about the nature of the catalyst.

Leaning so his mouth was at her ear, he whispered, "I believe that there are plenty of staff cabins available if you are willing to lower your standards a little."

The idea of having a space just for them ignited a spark of hope, but the logistics of arranging that seemed daunting.

Her cheeks heating up, Margo pressed closer to him and whispered back, "I would be more than happy in a bare necessities cabin if that's what's available, but who can we ask about it?"

It felt so awkward to talk about it. Those things should be spontaneous, not planned like a military operation.

"I'll find out." His hand ran small soothing circles on her back. "Leave it all up to me."

She'd known he would say that and was relieved that he would spare her the embarrassment of inquiring about a spare cabin herself, but on the other hand, she hated relying on others for things she could easily do but preferred not to because of nonsensical considerations like outdated attitudes toward sex.

When the song ended, Margo stepped out of Negal's arms. "Would you excuse me for a few moments? I need to visit the ladies' room."

"I'll come with you," Frankie said. "I need to freshen up as well."

Had Frankie heard their conversation and was about to suggest a solution?

Perhaps Margo should have started there and asked her bestie for advice.

When they reached the bathroom, though, Frankie immediately ducked into one of the stalls, which implied that her visit to the bathroom had nothing to do with the lodging dilemma.

With a sigh, Margo entered the stall next to her friend and relieved her bladder.

As they both stepped up to the sinks to wash their hands, Frankie cast her a sidelong glance in the mirror. "What's going on with you? You look stressed."

"It's a stressful situation." Margo tucked a few loose strands into her chignon. "It's such a weird feeling to know that everyone is expecting me to get in bed with Negal."

Frankie chuckled. "Everyone probably assumes that you are already sharing his bed. Immortals are, by and large, a lustful and uninhibited bunch. None of them would think that you are holding off on the fun." She smiled at her in the mirror. "The truth is that I don't know why you are doing that either."

"Lack of privacy, for one," Margo shot back.

"The moment you close the door to your bedroom, you have all the privacy you want. You can moan and groan to your heart's content, and we will not hear you. If you scream, though, we might, so don't. I mean, do, just no screaming. Not that I care if you do, but you seem to, so yeah." Frankie put a finger over her lips. "Turn down the volume."

Margo shook her head. "I envy the ease with which you approach sex. I wish I could be as open and outspoken about it."

Frankie narrowed her eyes at her. "You've never seemed to have a problem talking about it before. Is it just because it's Negal? Does he intimidate you because he's a god?"

She could have lied and said yes, but maybe it was time that her friends knew the truth. "Negal doesn't intimidate me. I have a problem with getting intimate with a man I've just met. Your rule about having sex for the first time with a guy used to be at least three dates, mine was more like thirty."

Frankie's eyes widened. "No wonder you had a problem keeping boyfriends. Who was willing to wait that long?"

"I exaggerated a little for emphasis." She hadn't.

Shaking her head, Frankie glared at Margo and then pulled a tube of lipstick out of her clutch. "You had me there for a moment." She refreshed the color on her lips.

"I might have exaggerated, but you get the gist of it. I'm also a very private person in that regard." She reached for Frankie's lipstick. "Do you happen to know who is in charge of assigning cabins?"

"Ingrid. Why? Do you want to move out? I don't think there are any cabins left."

"Negal said that there are plenty of available cabins in the staff quarters." Margo dabbed a few touches of color on her lips and then smacked them together.

"You must be really desperate to settle for a staff cabin. They have single beds, but I guess you can push two together to make a king-sized one. Still, it's like making love for the first time in a closet or the backseat of a car. Not the kind of accommodations that are conducive to pleasant memories."

"Yeah, I guess you are right." Margo handed Frankie the tube. "Do you have a better solution?"

NEGAL

As Margo and Frankie headed out to the ladies' room, Negal tried to come up with a plan. He hadn't expected Margo to announce that she was ready so soon, especially not in the middle of the dance floor at Kri and Michael's wedding, but now he had to solve their lodging problem so he could make this night special for her.

The thought of having Dagor and Frankie in the next room in her cabin suite or Aru and Gabi in his was far from ideal for their first night together. He didn't particularly mind, but Margo obviously did.

He needed a plan. But who to ask?

Negal's gaze drifted across the room, landing on Gabi, who was laughing at something Aru had said. She knew many of the immortals and had family in the village. Perhaps she could tell him who the person in charge of lodging was.

It was also possible that the task had been assigned to one of the humans, but he had to start somewhere.

"I'm heading to the bar," Dagor said. "Want to join?"

"Perhaps later. I need to talk to Gabi."

Negal walked over to where Gabi was sitting with Aru and a female he knew but whose name he had forgotten.

"Good evening." He dipped his head to the female and turned to Gabi. "Can I steal you away for a few moments?"

She lifted a brow. "Lady troubles?"

"No troubles. I just need to ask you something, in private if possible."

His quest for new lodging would make his intentions obvious, and although he didn't mind who knew, Margo would be embarrassed, so he needed to be discreet.

"Of course." She cast Aru a smile. "Can I get you something from the bar after I'm done talking to Negal?"

"No, thanks, I'm good." He trained his dark eyes on Negal. "Is everything okay?"

"Everything is great. I just need Gabi's help with something."

Aru nodded.

As they walked out of the dining room, Gabi turned to him. "What's up?"

He glanced around, lowering his voice. "Margo and I need a cabin of our own, preferably as soon as tonight. Do you know who takes care of assigning cabins?"

Gabi's eyes widened, and then a smile spread over her face. "Congratulations. I'm glad that my advice worked." She tapped her lips with a long-nailed finger. "I don't know who is in charge of assigning lodging, but I might know someone who knows. Wait here." She flounced away without waiting for his response.

Moments later, she returned with the female who had been sitting next to her and Aru.

"Negal, this is Darlene. My brother's mate."

Now he remembered who she was. Gabi's family had visited often during her recovery, and although he and Dagor had tried to make themselves scarce during the family's visits, he'd been introduced to Darlene.

"Hi, Negal," Eric's mate smiled. "Gabi tells me that you need help with something."

"I need a private cabin. Sharing one with Aru and Gabi doesn't work for me right now."

Hopefully, she wouldn't need further explanations.

Frowning, Darlene glanced at Gabi. "Did the boys have a fight?"

Gabi laughed. "Not at all. Negal's changing needs are romantic in nature."

Darlene's eyes widened with understanding. "I see. Well, in that case, Ingrid is the person to talk to. I can give her your phone number, and she will contact you tomorrow."

"I need the cabin tonight. Time is of the essence."

"I see." Darlene was trying really hard not to smile, but her lips twitched, betraying her amusement. "I'll go find Ingrid."

"Thank you. Should I wait here?"

Darlene hesitated but then nodded. "Ingrid is a sweetheart. She'll be happy to help."

When Darlene left, Gabi remained standing by his side. "Where is Margo?"

"In the ladies' room with Frankie."

Gabi shifted to lean against the wall. "What prompted the sudden urgency?"

Negal wondered the same thing. Their kissing had been full of passion, so maybe that was what had cut through Margo's resistance.

But what was more likely was that she'd decided that she couldn't wait after hearing that Aru had refused to contact their commander about postponing their departure or letting Negal stay behind.

"Pragmatism, I guess," he finally said. "The cruise is almost over."

Darlene returned, accompanied by an elegant blond who regarded him with a twinkle in her eyes.

"Negal, this is Ingrid, the clan's interior designer and the person in charge of allocating lodging," Darlene introduced her. "Ingrid, this is Negal, who doesn't need introductions."

Ingrid shook his offered hand. "Darlene told me that you need a private cabin and that it's somewhat urgent, but I really can't help you tonight. The upper decks are at full capacity, and all I can offer are staff cabins that are pretty utilitarian and not really conducive to romance if you know what I mean." She chuckled. "It will be like taking a virgin to a motel. A shared cabin is preferable to that. But what I can try to do tomorrow is to move some people around to free a guest cabin for you and Margo."

He didn't want to move people from their cabins. "If you can get us a staff cabin, I can try to spruce it up."

She gave him an apologetic look. "I'm sorry, but that too will have to wait for tomorrow. With the extra passengers we've collected, I'm not sure what's available, and if it's in habitable condition."

To say that Negal was disappointed was an understatement. "I understand. Thank you for your help, and I apologize for dragging you away from the party."

Ingrid waved a dismissive hand. "Don't mention it. I'm always glad to help a couple in love."

Were they a couple in love?

Yeah, they were. Margo hadn't told him that she loved him, and he hadn't told her how he felt about her either, but he knew it to be true.

Relief flooded through Negal, though he felt a twinge of disappointment at the delay. "Yes, that will be perfect. Thank you, Ingrid, and thank you, Darlene and Gabi. Margo will be thrilled."

As Ingrid and Darlene left, Negal turned to Gabi. "Thank you."

She waved him off. "I wish I could do more." As she turned to leave, the dining room doors pushed open, and Dagor walked out.

"Did you see Margo and Frankie?"

Negal frowned. "They are not back from the ladies' room yet?"

Dagor shook his head. "I thought that they were out here with you."

"I'll go check on them," Gabi offered. "They are probably having a girl talk." She winked before walking toward the bathrooms.

"What's going on?" Dagor asked. "Were you also looking for our missing mates?"

First Ingrid with her comment about them being a couple in love and now Dagor, it seemed like everyone assumed that Margo and he were a done deal.

If only he could share their confidence.

"I needed to find a private cabin for me and Margo, and I enlisted Gabi's help."

Dagor regarded him with a knowing look. "Given your expression, you were unsuccessful."

"The person in charge of lodging can't do anything tonight, and the prospects of her finding anything decent for us tomorrow are not good either."

Dagor's lips lifted in a grin. "As always, your thinking is too linear. The solution is quite simple." He clapped Negal on the back. "You just need to think a little creatively. Tonight, you will pretend that you're going to sleep on the living room couch because Frankie and I can't watch over Margo for another night, and you are still worried about her having a delayed reaction to the drugs she was injected with. And that's not even a lie. We will make ourselves scarce as soon as we enter the suite, so you will have the living room to yourself and can pretend that we are not even there. Then, if things go right," he paused, giving Negal a knowing look, "you can join Margo in the bedroom later. That way, she will not be embarrassed about inviting you to stay the night. On our part, Frankie and I will not emerge from our bedroom until you text me that it's okay."

Negal considered the idea. It wasn't perfect, but it was simple and didn't require any preparation or moving to another cabin.

"That might just work." He clapped Dagor on the back. "Thanks."

"Anytime."

34

MARINA

Marina maneuvered through the crowded wedding hall, balancing a laden tray, her arms shaking with the effort.

The damn immortals could have invested in carts so moving dishes from the kitchen to the dining room wouldn't have been such an onerous task.

Were they even aware of how heavy these things were?

For them, the trays probably weighed nothing, but they hadn't stopped to think how heavy they were for human females.

Marina let out a breath.

She was just irritated because she'd been working almost nonstop for two days and didn't get to spend enough time with Peter. The cruise was almost over, and she was running out of time to make him fall in love with her.

Heck, who was she kidding. She was in love with him already, and he was merely infatuated. When the cruise ended and they had to part, he might be sad for a day or two, but she would be devastated.

"Serves you right for scheming," she murmured under her breath.

The scent of roasted meats and exotic spices filled the air, clashing with the sound of love songs floating through the room. Marina didn't know why, but in her mind, romantic music went with wine and dessert, not meat and potatoes.

Not that she had anything against either. She loved both in any form or shape.

"You look beautiful tonight," a deep male voice said behind her.

She nearly dropped the tray as she spun around to find Peter watching her with an amused grin.

"You startled me. Not a smart move when I'm carrying a heavy load."

"Dance with me." With a swift motion, he plucked the tray from her hands and set it down on a nearby table. Then he grasped her hand and pulled her toward the dance floor.

Marina tried to resist. "Peter, stop it. I can't dance with you. I'm working, and look at me!" She gestured at her apron, but that wasn't the worst part of her appearance.

Her hair was pulled back in a messy bun, a few loose tendrils sticking to her flushed face from the heat of the kitchen. She had hastily applied some eyeliner that morning, but it had no doubt smeared over the course of her long workday.

Couples swirled around them as Peter pulled her close, his large hand settling at the small of her back. "You deserve a break."

"I look messy, and you are set on embarrassing me in front of your family, and especially your mother."

Peter laughed. "First of all, you look as beautiful as always, and secondly, I love my mother, but she has no say in my love life."

The word 'love' hung between them, charged and bold and painfully irrelevant.

Marina couldn't resist teasing him about it, even though it would no doubt backfire. "Love, huh? That's a strong word."

Peter didn't shy away. Instead, he pulled her closer. "Yes, love. I'm not taking it back because it's the truth. I've fallen for you, and I don't want to let you go."

The breath stalled in Marina's lungs. She swallowed hard, peering up at him through the fan of her lashes. "Then don't," she blurted.

"I don't intend to."

As Peter's words lingered in the air, the music around them seemed to fade, and the chatter and laughter of the other guests became a distant murmur.

Regrettably, his expression looked teasing rather than serious, and Marina knew he didn't mean it the way she wished he would.

Afraid that her disappointment showed on her face, she shifted the conversation away from that dangerous territory. "Amanda was really sweet today," she said. "When I told her about Larissa not having anything to wear tomorrow, she promised to find something for her. I was so touched that the clan's princess volunteered to assist a lowly human."

Peter's brows furrowed. "Every member of our clan helps humans. We made it our mission to save victims of trafficking and rehabilitate them, and we fund most of the effort from our own coffers. Not to mention that we liberated you and your people from the Kra-ell."

Evidently, she'd hit a nerve. "I'm sorry. I didn't mean it that way. It's just that Amanda is such a princess, and she comes into the kitchen issuing orders without asking anyone if we can actually do what she wants, so I assumed she was stuck up. I was surprised at how nice she was and how accepting of our relationship."

The furrow between his brows smoothed out a little but didn't disappear. "What did she say?"

"She said that it was a shame I couldn't be your date for tonight because she hadn't seen you so happy in a long time."

Marina waited with bated breath for him to confirm what Amanda had said, and after what seemed like forever, he nodded. "That's true. Being with you makes me happy."

"Same here." She stretched up on her toes and kissed him lightly on the lips. "But I need to go."

As the song ended, Peter released her, his demeanor pleasant but distant.

With unease churning in her gut, Marina returned to work, her mind a whirlwind of what-ifs and maybes.

Peter had confessed that he was falling for her, and he'd even said that he didn't want to part with her, but when she'd blurted that she wanted him to take her with him, his reaction was far from enthusiastic.

Had he guessed her intentions? Did he think that he was just a means to an end for her?

It might have started that way, but it no longer was.

It was as real as it got.

35

KIAN

Kian glanced at his watch and then surveyed the party, the dim lights casting long shadows across the faces of the dwindling number of guests. It was only a few minutes past midnight, and the dance floor was not as packed as it had been an hour ago, but it was still quite lively, and laughter bubbled from a few clusters of seated guests. If he could wait another half an hour, his and Syssi's departure wouldn't arouse suspicion, but the clock was marching relentlessly toward half-past twelve, which was the latest they could afford to stay.

He caught Syssi's eye across the table and gestured with his head toward the exit.

Nodding, she pulled her phone from her clutch and affected a concerned frown. "Allegra is fussy," she said out loud and looked at Kian. "We need to go."

Amanda quirked a perfectly arched brow. "Isn't Parker babysitting her with Okidu?"

"She's asking for Mommy and Daddy." Syssi smiled. "She won't go back to sleep unless we show up." She stood, smoothing the folds of her purple gown.

Kian rose to his feet and took Syssi's hand. "Good night, everyone. Continue to enjoy the party."

A small chorus of good nights followed them as they made their way out of the dining hall and into the blessedly quiet corridor.

Kian let out a breath once they were alone. "Well played, my love." He pressed a quick kiss to Syssi's temple.

As they entered their cabin, Parker looked up at them with surprise in his eyes. "Why did you come back so early?" he asked, a hint of disappointment in his voice, perhaps at the evening ending sooner than expected and his babysitting fee shrinking.

"Syssi had a feeling Allegra was going to wake up and ask for us," Kian said, hoping the explanation sounded plausible given Syssi's psychic abilities.

He also pulled a crisp hundred-dollar bill from his wallet and handed it over with a conspiratorial wink.

Parker's eyes lit up at the sight of the bill, his disappointment quickly forgotten. "No problem, Mr. Kian. Allegra was great," he said with a broad smile. "Good night!" He waved cheerfully as he exited.

Once the boy was gone, they hurried to trade their elegant evening wear for comfortable clothing, and

Syssi gently transferred their sleeping daughter from the portable crib into her stroller, covering her in a soft blue blanket.

Allegra didn't so much as stir throughout the transfer.

Kian swept his gaze over his two favorite girls, his heart swelling with love. He would walk through fire a thousand times over for them.

A glance at his watch had him tensing again. They had ten minutes to get to his mother's cabin and get ready for the session.

"We should get moving," he said in a hushed tone. "Aru will meet us there."

"I'm ready." Syssi put a yellow paper pad into a compartment of the stroller and pushed it toward the door.

"Where did you get that from?" Kian opened the door for her.

"Turner, of course. I asked him if he had a spare one, and he did. He didn't even ask what I needed it for."

"Naturally." Kian took command of the stroller.

As they made their way down the corridor to Annani's cabin, the short walk was done in silence, each lost in their own thoughts about what was to come.

Kian was nervous.

His mother had been waiting for this first meeting with her grandmother with such great excitement that he was worried she would be disappointed.

What if the queen of Anumati turned out to be a condescending monarch who would belittle her granddaughter?

Annani was the Clan Mother, the most superior being on Earth, and she wouldn't take well to being regarded with anything other than the utmost respect.

Syssi stopped in front of Annani's door. "Why are you so stressed?" she asked. "I know it's a monumental event, but you look like you are about to enter the lions' den, or the lionesses' as the case may be."

"I don't want my mother to be disappointed. She's been looking forward to this meeting with her grandmother, expecting to learn about the planet of the gods, their culture, their politics, but that is not what's going to happen during this initial meeting, and if the queen doesn't get what she wants, there might not be another one."

Syssi frowned. "What do you mean?"

"The queen needs to assess my mother, and she will be asking more questions than answering them. If she's impressed with my mother, she will schedule another meeting. If she's not, she might decide that it's not worth the risk she's taking."

Smiling, Syssi lifted her hand and cupped his cheek. "You have nothing to worry about. Your mother is the most impressive person I've ever met, heard of, or read about. There is no way the shrewd queen of Anumati wouldn't recognize her greatness."

He let out a breath. "I hope you are right. To me, my mother is second only to my wife, but the queen of the gods might not share my opinion."

Syssi laughed. "I'm sure she won't share your opinion about me, but I'm just as sure that she will agree that your mother is the most important person on Earth."

36

ARU

Aru clenched his jaw as he watched Kian and Syssi make their excuses and exit the wedding reception. As a wave of anger washed over him, a muscle ticked in his cheek. He couldn't forgive Kian for betraying his trust and telling Syssi about the telepathic connection Aru shared with his twin sister.

Being a seer, Syssi had seen Aria in a vision and guessed the truth, but Kian shouldn't have confirmed it for her. Visions were often unreliable, and without confirmation, Syssi might have dismissed it.

The knowledge of Aria's telepathic connection with Aru was supposed to be safeguarded at all costs, hidden away from the Eternal King and his numerous spies. Aru had stressed the importance of secrecy to Kian, and yet, his trust had been shattered. Part of him understood that the bond between mates made it difficult to keep things from each other, but this was a matter of life and death.

His sister's life depended on her ability to stay hidden from the ruthless dictator occupying the Anumati throne and, even more so, her part in assisting the queen, who was supporting the resistance.

The queen herself was in danger.

Queen Ani was too beloved by the citizens and too connected to the ruling families to dispose of outright. But the Eternal King was a master at orchestrating unfortunate "accidents" when it suited his purposes.

The king also had to remain oblivious to the fact that his son had sired a daughter on Earth before his untimely demise. If he ever learned of Annani's existence, the sole remaining legitimate heir to his throne, Aru shuddered to think what he would do.

Destroying Earth to eliminate Annani was a very real possibility.

The heir represented their best chance for a peaceful revolution. Her ascendancy to power could herald a new era for Anumati. Unlike her grandfather, Annani was no tyrant and had no greed for power. But like her grandfather, she was powerful and impressive. If the people of Anumati accepted her as their queen, she would rule them with a firm but kind hand and always look after their best interests.

Or so Aru hoped.

Power was corruptive, and once upon a time, the Eternal King hadn't been the monster he was today. He'd united Anumati's ruling families and brought prosperity to all, but he'd become too attached to his throne, so much so that he eliminated his own flesh and blood, his only son by his official mate, just so there would be no suitable contender to replace him.

A warm hand settling over his clenched fist drew Aru's attention back to the present. He blinked to find Gabi watching him with concern.

"What's wrong, my love?" She leaned closer to him. "You look troubled."

Aru forced his lips to curve in a reassuring smile as he turned his hand to lace their fingers together. "I have something I need to do that will take about an hour, and I will have to do it every night at the same time from now on. I wish I could tell you what it is, but I can't."

Gabi worried her lower lip briefly between her teeth as she studied him. "Does it have to do with Anumati?"

He nodded. "You don't have to leave with me. You can stay and enjoy the party."

Aru's chest twinged with a pang of remorse. Keeping things from his mate didn't sit well with him, instilling a dull ache of guilt. But it was a necessity. His sister's life was more important than even his bond with his mate.

Gabi smiled. "I know it must be important or you wouldn't keep it from me. I don't need to know the particulars."

The truth of her words was like a soothing balm gliding over the frayed edges of his nerves. He surged forward to capture her lips in a fierce kiss.

"Thank you," he rasped when they finally broke apart, his forehead resting against hers. "I don't know what I did to deserve such a perfect, understanding mate, but I'm grateful to the Fates for you every day."

Gabi's face glowed with pleasure at his words, smoky lashes sweeping low to veil her shining eyes. "I'm the lucky one, my love. I'll leave with you," she said with a teasing lilt. "I'll just head back to our cabin and relax until you return. I'll be waiting for you in something skimpy and lacy." She waggled her brows.

Aru groaned low in his throat, capturing her mouth once more in a hungry kiss. When the need for air became too pressing to ignore, he finally tore his lips away with a shuddering inhale.

"You're deliciously wicked, my love," he growled hoarsely, drinking in the sight of her tousled curls and passion-glazed eyes. "Now, I will have to conduct my business with a raging hard-on."

She laughed, smoothing her hands over the plackets of his tux jacket. "Try to finish your business as soon as possible. I'm not a patient woman."

37

ANNANI

nnani smoothed her hand over the soft silk of her flowing gown as she settled onto the plush couch. Though her heart was racing with excitement, she projected an aura of calm, clutching a steaming teacup in her hands.

This moment had been weeks in the making, and she could scarcely allow her turbulent emotions to overwhelm her now that it had finally arrived.

As the doorbell rang, she watched Oridu usher Kian and Syssi in with Allegra nestled in her stroller.

"Hello, Mother." Kian leaned to kiss her cheek. "Are you excited?"

"Of course." She peered down at Allegra's peacefully slumbering face, resisting the urge to brush her fingers over the downy curve of her cheek.

To wake her now would only lead to fussing that could disrupt the critical meeting ahead. Annani contented herself with drinking in the sight of her granddaughter. To compensate, tomorrow she would hold her to her chest and kiss her cheeks until the little girl pushed her away.

"She is so perfect," Annani whispered.

Kian's chest puffed up with fatherly pride. "That she is."

"You could have left her with Okidu," Annani said. "There was no need to interrupt her sleep."

Syssi sat next to her on the couch. "Allegra didn't even stir when I transferred her to the stroller. Besides, our excuse for leaving the party early was a fussy baby, so if anyone asks, Allegra demanded to see her Nana."

Annani laughed, some of the tension leaving her shoulders. "No one would doubt that story. Allegra's demands have to be obeyed, or else."

"You make her sound like a spoiled brat." Kian sat down on Annani's other side.

"Fates forbid." Annani put a hand on her chest. "She is simply assertive, which is important for a future leader."

That seemed to mollify her son, and as he gazed at the sleeping baby, his lips curved in a soft smile. "For as long as I can, I will spare her the need to take on the mantle of leadership."

Annani patted Kian's knee. "I have a feeling that when little Allegra is all grown up, she will be thrilled to ease your burden and take the mantle of leadership upon her shoulders. Leaders are born, Kian. They are not made."

"Perhaps." He sighed.

"Can I pour tea for you, Mistress Syssi?" Oridu bowed nearly in half.

"That would be lovely, thank you."

When he was done pouring tea into Syssi's cup, Oridu turned to Kian, still in the bowed position. "Master Kian?"

"Yes, please."

When Oridu was done pouring, the doorbell rang again, and Ogidu rushed to open the door.

Aru strode into the room, his brow furrowed in concentration as he bowed to Annani. "Good morning, Your Highness. Aria says they will be ready to begin in a few minutes."

"Thank you, Aru." She motioned for him to take a seat on the armchair. "Would you like some tea?"

As he nodded, Oridu hastened to fill his cup and hand it to him.

As she waited for Aru to begin, Annani's heart pounded in her chest. Soon, she would converse with her grandmother for the first time. The matriarch of her lineage, the queen of Anumati, held answers to so many questions that Annani could not think of them all.

She should have written them down, but the truth was that she did not expect to learn much tonight. The queen would want to get the measure of her, which meant that the one answering questions would be Annani.

She did not need to prepare for that.

She had many regrets, but if given a chance for a do-over, she would have most likely done things the same way, even knowing the consequences.

Well, that was not true. She would have never allowed Khiann to leave with the caravan. She would have even involved her father to forbid his departure.

Khiann's murder had started the chain of events that led to the gods' demise, and all she had needed to do to stop it was be more assertive and less accommodating.

But then, hindsight was always 20-20.

At the time, she had felt that she was doing the right thing by her husband, letting him do the things he loved and not stifling him by confining him to the palace.

QUEEN ANI

As the temple doors closed behind Ani's attendants, she embraced Sofringhati. "Finally, the day has arrived."

Sofri patted her back. "You are cold, my friend." Sofri turned to her scribe. "Could you please raise the heat in the braziers, Aria? It is a little chilly in here."

Aria bowed. "Of course."

"And also move the cushions closer to the heat," Sofri added.

"Yes, Supreme Oracle." Aria bowed again and rushed to comply with Sofringhati's commands.

Everywhere else on Anumati, the temperature in the room would have been adjusted automatically, the sensors adjusting the heating or cooling based on its occupants' biomarkers, but walking into the Supreme Oracle's temple was like stepping hundreds of thousands of years back in time.

The chamber was completely devoid of technology, with the illumination coming from burning sconces attached to the towering columns and the heating from ancient braziers that burned oil and had to be adjusted manually.

Nevertheless, to Ani the temple felt more like home than her own suite of rooms in the palace. Here, amidst the thick, isolating walls and towering columns and carvings of ancient prophecies, Ani could drop the mask of the untouchable monarch for a couple of hours and enjoy the company of her only friend.

"Please, sit down, Ani." Sofri pointed to the cushions that Aria had dragged closer to the braziers.

Ani made herself comfortable on the large square pillow and tucked her legs under her. "Whenever I am here, I am reminded of our days in the dormitories. We used to sit like this and chat for hours until the head-mistress sent us to bed."

Taking a seat on the other cushion, Sofri sighed. "I miss those days. Life was simpler when our biggest worry was passing exams. We were so naive."

"I miss being that girl." Ani sighed. "That being said, I knew even then that I would not be free to choose who I would mate, and that my marriage would be a political alliance. I just did not imagine that I would be chosen by the king." She chuckled. "Let alone one day lead a rebellion against him."

"You loved him once."

Ani shook her head. "I was blinded by his charm, but it did not take me long to realize that what he projected was very different from who he really was. I still admired him for many years, though. He was good for Anumati until he stopped being so."

Sofri canted her head. "He was never good to the Kra-ell. Ahn opened your eyes to the injustice done to them."

Tears misted Ani's eyes.

Usually, she was very good at masking her emotions, but no one other than Sofri spoke Ahn's name anymore, and hearing it said out loud was like a javelin to her heart.

Ani's thoughts drifted to Annani, her granddaughter, the living legacy of her lost son, his direct descendant who was hidden away on Earth. The knowledge that Ahn's legacy lived on, that his bloodline had not been extinguished, was like an injection of vitality for Ani, an unexpected beacon of light in the darkness.

Would Annani prove to be all that Ani hoped for?

Would she be like Ahn?

Little Ani, Ahn had named his daughter, and according to Aru, Annani bore an uncanny resemblance to Ani. Hopefully, it would not be just skin deep.

So many questions bubbled within her, so many words of guidance she longed to impart.

Ani turned her attention to Aria, the young scribe who was about to become the conduit for a conversation that spanned light years and yet was as instantaneous as a quantum communicator.

"I am ready, Aria."

The scribe nodded. "I will check with Aru if they are ready as well."

As she waited, Ani allowed her mind to wander through the past, through all the decisions and sacrifices she had made. Her relationship with the Supreme Oracle, Sofringhati, had always been her anchor, providing a safe harbor in the treacherous waters of Anumati's society. But even Sofri, with all her foresight, had been unable to predict the loss of Ani's son, not until after the fact.

There was a limit to what an oracle could see, and Ani suspected that the Fates allowed Sofringhati to see only what suited their plans and promoted their agenda.

For now, Annani was alive and well on Earth, but Sofri could not see what the future had in store for her, and that filled Ani's heart with fear.

Now that she had found Ahn's daughter, the thought of losing her as she had lost Ahn was unbearable, and if she dragged Annani into the rebellion she would be putting her at great risk.

What chance did a goddess with no knowledge of Anumati's intricate politics and power plays have against the Eternal King?

Perhaps it was best to leave her be and not involve her in the resistance. Ani could train her over many years, making sure that Annani knew all there was to know about Anumati's history, social structure, economy, and politics, and bring her home to present to their people only once the Eternal King was eliminated, but not before.

Ani could not bear the thought of losing Annani, and that was even before they had exchanged a single word.

ANNANI

Annani watched Aru's face, noting the subtle shift in his expression as he connected with his sister and bridged the vast distance between Anumati and Earth through their extraordinary link.

Finally, Aru announced, "The queen is ready."

Annani set her tea aside. "I am ready as well."

"Greetings from Queen Ani of Anumati," Aru said in the gods' language, which resembled the tongue of her youth but not precisely.

Still, she understood enough to get the message the greeting conveyed, setting a tone for their conversation.

The greeting was not from Ani, the grandmother who was overjoyed to discover that her beloved son had fathered a daughter before he died. The greeting was from the queen of Anumati.

It made Annani acutely aware of the fine line she needed to walk. She needed to show the proper deference expected when addressing a monarch, yet this was also her grandmother, her father's mother, and some warmth needed to be injected into the conversation to establish rapport.

"Please convey my deepest respects and heartfelt greetings to Her Majesty," Annani replied in English.

Her knowledge of the gods' language was not sufficient to conduct a high-level conversation.

Next to her, Syssi was writing with a pen on a yellow notepad, and Annani wondered whether she had understood Aru's words or guessed the meaning.

For the sake of record keeping, it would be better to conduct the conversation in English.

"I am overjoyed to finally meet you, my dear granddaughter," Aru translated, probably arriving at the same conclusion as Annani.

Nevertheless, the words sounded strange coming out in his masculine voice and yet sweet in Annani's ears. Her grandmother acknowledged their blood ties and addressed her as she wished to be addressed. "I wish I could gaze upon your face and see for myself the resemblance Aru reported, but regrettably, I do not possess telepathic abilities and I cannot peer into Aria's mind to see what Aru is sending to her through their connection. I can only hear what she repeats."

Annani glanced at Syssi, who had seen the queen and Aria in her prophetic vision. With Syssi's permission, Annani could peek into her mind and see her grandmother, but perhaps it was not a good idea to mention her hybrid children and their hybrid mates just yet.

The queen had been informed of the immortals' existence, but she might choose to ignore everyone other than Annani and perhaps Toven.

Even Ahn, who had been a progressive god, had ignored Areana, his own daughter, because she was a weak goddess born to a concubine. He hadn't fathered any hybrid children, but if he had, Annani had no doubt that he would have ignored their existence even more pointedly than Areana's.

She had no illusions that her father had been without fault, but he had been a rebel who fought for the rights of those who were considered second class on Anumati. Life was full of contradictions. She could imagine the queen as an elitist, even though she had believed in her son's cause enough to shoulder it after his exile.

On the other hand, Annani had nothing to be ashamed of, and if her grandmother sneered at her hybrid children, then Annani did not want to have anything to do with her.

"I am grateful to Aru and Aria for providing us this opportunity to communicate on a private channel that the Eternal King cannot spy on. For the sake of transparency, though, I would like to mention that my son and his wife are here with me, and my daughter-in-law is transcribing our conversation. My son's name is Kian, and his mate's name is Syssi. Syssi is a seer, and she had a vision of you, the Oracle, and Aria. If she permits it, I can peek into her mind and see what each of you looks like."

There was a long moment of silence as Aru transmitted what she had said to Aria, who in turn repeated it to the queen. Annani waited with bated breath for her grandmother's response.

"Greetings to my great-grandson and his mate."

Annani let out a breath. The queen had acknowledged Kian as her great-grandson, knowing that he was a hybrid.

"Please convey our greetings and deepest respects to Her Majesty," Kian told Aru.

A short moment passed before Aru spoke again. "I know that you have many questions, my dearest grand-daughter, and I will answer them in time, but today, I want to learn about you. Aru told Aria what he knew, but I want you to tell me more about your life."

Annani had expected that. Her grandmother needed to assess her and verify that she was worthy of the role the queen hoped she would one day assume. If she was not impressed, she would not invest the time and effort to groom her for the role of Anumati's future monarch.

Annani was not yet sure that she wanted the job, but she wanted to be deemed worthy.

"I have lived for over five thousand Earth years, and I have had many adventures and trials, accomplishments and setbacks, but I have never given up no matter how hopeless things seemed at the time. Where would you like me to start, Your Majesty?"

"Tell me about your father and your relationship with him. He named you after me. Did he groom you to one day become queen?"

"Yes, he did." Annani smiled. "My father, your son, taught me all I know about duty, responsibility, fairness, and respect for all, including the lowliest of humans. I have spent countless hours in the throne room, listening to proceedings that bored me to the point of despair. But he taught me what it meant to be a leader and that sometimes there are no good choices, and a leader cannot hide from her responsibility or let another shoulder it. She has to choose the least harmful one and continue forward."

Annani paused, allowing Aru time to repeat her words to Aria.

A few moments later, he said, "Tell me about your mother."

Annani smiled. The queen wanted to ensure that her parents had been officially married when they had her. Otherwise, she could not be Ahn's official heir.

"My mother was not even seventeen when she set her sights on my father and decided that he would be hers. She was not of legal age, but since it was known that he was about to choose a wife, she knew that she could not wait until she reached the age of consent and set out to seduce him before it was too late. Long story short, he succumbed to her temptation, finding out too late her real age. To avoid the legal complications of his transgression, my father proposed, and they were married. It was not long before he realized that she was his fated one and only, and that the Fates had gifted him with the greatest joy a god could hope for."

There was a long moment of silence before Aru relayed the queen's answer. "I am glad that my son found happiness with your mother, but I am not glad that their relationship had started with deceit."

Annani chuckled. "Then Your Majesty should brace herself because my tale is full of conspiracies and manipulations, although given what I have heard of Anumati, that should not come as a surprise."

Aru's lips quirked up in a smile. "That is true, my astute granddaughter. Please continue with your tale."

40

QUEEN ANI

As Aria continued relaying Annani's tale about her ill-fated engagement to Mortdh and her cunning way of subverting it, Ani's ire rose.

What had possessed Ahn to arrange such a match for his beloved daughter?

Ani had known Mortdh quite well. He had been like his grandfather, marked by the same unquenchable ambition and hunger for power but lacking the charm and sophistication of the king. Even as a child, his eyes had been full of shadows far too dark for his young age.

He had been nothing like Ekin, Ahn's half-brother by one of the king's numerous concubines. Mortdh's father had been loyal and fully dedicated to Ahn and his cause. His passion was science and engineering, and he had no ambitions other than inventing things and supporting Ahn's rebellion. It was regrettable that Mortdh had inherited none of Ekin's nobler qualities while sharing his father's sharp intelligence.

It was a bitter pill to swallow to realize that Ahn had made such a monumental error in judgment, but Ani understood his reasoning. Her son had been an idealist, and he had been willing to sacrifice even his own daughter's happiness on the altar of his people's greater good. But Ani was disappointed that he had naively believed mollifying Mortdh would ensure peace.

Sacrificing Annani would not have prevented war. At best, it would have postponed it, and at worst, it would have cost Annani's life.

"Ahn was smart, but he was also a dreamer, an optimist, and an idealist," Ani said. "He believed that given the chance and the benefit of the doubt, people would rise to the occasion. In rare instances, he could have been right, but all too often his naive belief that people were inherently good was dangerous. It was both his greatest strength and his most significant weakness."

Admitting this truth of Ahn's flaws had not been easy. His soft spot for family had blinded him to the potential dangers of binding his daughter to someone like Mortdh.

Annani's reply came a moment later. "I am just glad that my father listened to my plea when I asked him to allow Khiann to court me."

Ani listened intently as Annani recounted her daring pursuit of Khiann, the son of a merchant god whom her father would have never considered as a mate for her. She had disguised herself as a commoner to bypass the rigid structures of their society and sought out the god who had captured her heart.

Ani's heart swelled with pride.

Even at a young age, her granddaughter had displayed uncommon boldness and determination, unwilling to let her future be dictated by others.

Like her, Annani refused to be a pawn in the political games that dominated their world. She had taken matters into her own hands, changing the course of history.

Annani was precisely what Anumati needed. A bold and courageous leader with a clear vision of the right path.

The queen chuckled as Aria continued recounting Annani's exploits, detailing how she had instructed Khiann to approach Ahn, and her heart soared when she heard how Ahn had handled the situation. He had cunningly employed Khiann as a tutor to test the waters of their potential as fated mates, allowing the relationship to develop under the guise of mentorship while protecting the secrecy of the potential bond.

And then came the resolution—the revelation of Annani and Khiann's status as fated mates and Ahn's subsequent affirmation of the paramount importance of the Fates' will and dissolution of Annani's engagement to Mortdh.

The decision to offer Mortdh Annani's half-sister, Areana, as an alternative was a masterstroke, maintaining diplomatic relations while safeguarding his only legitimate heir.

Some might have viewed the move as heartless, but it was just one more example of a leader choosing the lesser of two evils.

The queen cast a sidelong glance at her best friend, who was listening to Aria with rapt attention and a smile on her face.

"Your granddaughter is a take-charge goddess, Ani. She is exactly what Anumati needs."

Ani reached for her friend's hand and gave it a light squeeze.

Her heart was full as she considered the future with Annani as queen. It would be the dawn of a new era for Anumati, one led by a goddess who understood what it meant to be a leader, and valued love, the importance of being in the driver's seat of one's own destiny, and the power of being proactive instead of reactive.

Annani continued to recount her brief marriage and the subsequent tragedy that befell her and the other gods, or at least the version that she had been told and had accepted as true. "Mortdh murdered my Khiann in cold blood. He had planned the ambush days in advance and killed my love with his own hands. The assembly of gods heard the witnesses' account of the brutal murder and sentenced Mortdh to entombment, but to do that, they had to catch him and bring him to justice first. But since he commanded a large force of immortal warriors, the assembly deliberated for days about the best way to do that. Mortdh, on the other hand, did not wait. To escape his punishment, he used a weapon of mass destruction on the assembly hall, killing all the gods inside. I managed to escape because I was afraid of him coming after me, so I ran away to the far north. My sister Areana was on her way to Mortdh's stronghold, so that was how she survived. Toven, Mortdh's brother, was away on one of his expeditions at the time, and that was how he was spared as well. We were the only three gods remaining on Earth until the arrival of Aru and his team."

Listening to the story unfold, Ani's heart went out to her granddaughter, a kindred spirit who had suffered a terrible loss and had known grief as great as hers.

When Aria fell silent, Ani let out a sigh. "Mortdh might have murdered your mate, but he probably was not responsible for the cataclysm that befell the rest of your people and destroyed a large portion of the region. Mortdh loved himself too much to go on a suicide mission, and he was too smart not to realize that he would not survive the blast in a small craft that had limited speed and maneuverability. He was most likely a pawn, used as a scapegoat for the real perpetrators."

Annani's shocked response carried over through Aria's voice. "If it was not Mortdh, then who was the real perpetrator?"

41

ANNANI

Annani had often entertained the same doubts about Mortdh's intentions that fateful day, but if not him, then who could have destroyed the assembly hall along with all the gods inside of it?

The truth was that no one knew for a fact that it had been a bomb. The particulars of the devastation suggested a nuclear weapon, but it could have been some other alien technology that had similar cataclysmic results.

The narrative she had clung to, the one that had painted Mortdh as the ultimate villain in their tragic tale, had been unraveling ever since Jade's account of Anumati's history and then Igor's, but there had been too many pieces of the puzzle missing to solve the mystery.

"If it was not Mortdh, then who was the real perpetrator?" Annani asked.

"I have no definite proof," Aru translated the queen's words. "But there is plenty of circumstantial evidence. Shortly before the catastrophe, an Anumatian patrol ship passed near Earth, and a team of scouts was deployed. By then, communications with Earth had been severed. The king blamed the destruction of the communication satellites on Ahn, the rebel who didn't want to face the accusations of war crimes that his father had trumped up against him. The truth was that the king had ordered the satellites destroyed.

"Sometime later, the Eternal King announced in a public address that the heir, along with his half-brother and sister and all the other gods who had been exiled to Earth, had perished.

"Since there was supposedly no communication with Earth, the king claimed that a seer told him of the demise of all of the gods on Earth, but it was not my friend, and when she checked with the other oracles, none of them admitted to delivering the news to the king. Still, that does not mean that the king had not had a seer in his employ who had just not reported the truth to my friend. Ahn's father pretended to be devastated by the loss and announced a day of mourning to show that he was a good father who loved his children even though they had betrayed him.

"I asked the Supreme Oracle to try to see what had really happened to them, but for some reason, Earth was hidden from her view. All she could do was confirm what the king said. The Supreme Oracle and I suspect that the Fates were shielding you and the two other surviving gods from the Eternal King's seers. If the Supreme Oracle couldn't see Earth, none of the lesser ones could either. Therefore, the only way the king could have known about the fate of the Earth-bound gods' was because he had a hand in their demise."

It was not news to Annani that her grandfather was a terrible god. She had heard the tale from Jade's perspective, but it was not the same as hearing from her grandmother how the Eternal King had spun his deceitful narrative to consolidate his power and elimi-nate any threats to his rule, even those from his own flesh and blood. It made her heart heavy. The public mourning and the feigned benevolence were all a calculated act to cloak his tyrannical reign in a veneer of paternal sorrow and righteousness.

The greatest revelation so far was that Earth was obscured from the Supreme Oracle's vision, and there-fore shielded from the prying eyes of the king's seers.

"It's a relief knowing that we are obscured," Kian said.

Aru opened his eyes and looked at him. "Do you want me to translate that for the queen?"

Kian shook his head. "I'm just an observer. Only trans-late my mother's words."

Nodding, Aru turned to Annani. "Anything Your High-ness would like to say to Her Majesty?"

"I am grateful to the merciful Fates for shielding me, my sister, and my cousin from the machinations of the Eternal King."

"So am I," Aru translated the queen's words after a moment.

The realization that her grandfather had ordered the bombing to ensure his dominion filled her with revulsion. Mortdh had become a scapegoat in the Eternal King's scheme, but she felt no pity for him. He might not have been responsible for the bombing, but his cold-blooded murder of Khiann was indisputable.

She had heard the witnesses' account with her own two ears, and their words still reverberated in her mind five thousand years later, bringing bile to her throat and an unbearable ache to her chest.

"Mortdh was a tyrant and a murderer, but it seems that he was not the architect of our people's destruction," Annani said. "He was caught in a web much larger than his own making, perhaps even unknowingly used by my grandfather."

A few moments passed before Aru conveyed the queen's response. "Our time today draws to an end. We will have to continue our talk on the morrow, my dear Annani."

"Thank you, Grandmother. I shall await our next conversation."

The understanding that she had escaped not just Mortdh's ambitions but the far reach of the Eternal King, made Annani feel blessed and a little humbler than she had been before the start of the conversation with her grandmother. She was alive, not by chance, not by her own decisiveness and clear vision, but by the Fates' design.

42

KIAN

Kian grappled with the information the queen had relayed, and so did his mother and Syssi. The only one who didn't look surprised was Aru, and Kian had a feeling that the god had known about the patrol ship and the potential assassins that had been sent to end Ahn and the other gods.

Shaking her head, his mother got up and started pacing. "If Mortdh didn't kill the gods, maybe he didn't kill Khiann either?" She looked at Kian with hope and desperation shining in her eyes. "His body was never found because his murder coincided with the earthquake. What if he is buried in the desert, alive in stasis?"

Kian's heart clenched. He understood his mother's desire to cling to any shred of hope, to believe that her beloved mate might still be alive somewhere, waiting to be found, but clinging to false hope would just reopen old wounds that had scabbed over.

Rising to his feet, he walked over to her and put a hand on her shoulder.

"I know you want to believe that, but you heard the witnesses describe the murder yourself. They saw Mortdh kill Khiann with their own eyes."

His mother's shoulders slumped, the brief spark of hope dimming in her eyes. She sighed. "I know, Kian. I just allowed myself to hope for a moment."

The familiar mask of composure settling over her features again, she offered him a smile. "We should call it a night." She cast a quick glance at her sleeping granddaughter, and the fake smile turned genuine. "Allegra will be more comfortable in her crib."

Leaning down, Kian kissed his mother's cheek. "Are you going to be okay?"

She nodded. "This is a lot to process, but we had our doubts for a long time, so it should not have come as such a big shock. We have always wondered what actually happened that day and what prompted Mortdh to act out of character. Now, we know that he did not intend to commit suicide. Perhaps he was coerced by a compeller even more powerful than he was, or maybe he just happened to be at the right place at the right moment for the assassins to frame him for what they did."

Syssi nodded. "I still wonder how the real perpetrators managed to coordinate it so perfectly that it appeared as if it was Mortdh's fault."

"We can talk more about this over brunch tomorrow," Kian suggested. "After we've all had a chance to process everything we've learned."

"That is a good idea." Annani took a deep breath. "Thank you for being here with me tonight." She smiled at Syssi. "It would have been much more difficult without you." She turned to Aru. "I am grateful to you and your sister for your help tonight. Thank you for enabling this conversation and all the future ones that will follow."

"We are glad to help." The god didn't sound convincing, which was understandable.

He and his sister were taking a great risk, and it wasn't as if either of them had a choice in the matter. They had been recruited, and saying no to the queen of Anumati had not been an option.

After they had said their goodbyes and walked out of the cabin, Kian waited for Ogidu to close the door behind them before turning to Aru. "You knew about the assassins."

"I did," he admitted. "But since it's all conjecture and speculation, I didn't want to bring it up. Maybe Mortdh was responsible after all, or maybe the assassins shot him down and caused the weapon to explode. We will never know the truth because the only one who knows it is the king."

"And the assassins," Syssi said.

Aru shook his head. "I doubt that they are still around. The Eternal King does not leave any breadcrumbs that could lead back to him."

Kian felt a flicker of irritation at Aru's admission. He understood the god's reluctance to share unconfirmed theories, but part of him wished they had been better prepared for the emotional fallout of this revelation.

"I get why you didn't want to bring it up," Kian said, running a hand through his hair. "But maybe a little warning would have been warranted. I hated seeing the hope flare in my mother's eyes only to have to quash it."

A hint of regret flickered through Aru's eyes, but then they hardened. "I apologize, but it really wasn't my place to share this information."

Was he still angry about Syssi finding out about Aria?

Probably.

Kian regarded the god with a frown. "I assume that your teammates don't know about this either."

"Of course not." Aru glanced at the cameras mounted on the walls. "I'd rather not talk about it out here."

"Don't worry about it." Kian waved a hand at the camera. "I asked for the cameras to be turned off on this deck between midnight and three o'clock in the morning every night from now until the end of the cruise." He chuckled. "I can only imagine what the Guardians in security think of my request."

Syssi groaned. "Now I understand the smirks I noticed during the wedding. They are probably imagining us chasing each other in the nude down the corridor."

Aru's eyes widened, but he was smart enough not to respond.

"No one was smirking at you." Kian kissed the top of Syssi's head before turning to the god. "Nevertheless, we shouldn't conduct such conversations out in the hallway. Would you like to come to our cabin for a glass of whiskey?"

The god smiled. "Thank you for the invitation, but I will have to take a raincheck. It's after two o'clock in the morning, and my mate is waiting for me in our cabin."

"I understand." Kian offered Aru his hand. "Thank you for your help tonight."

Aru shook it. "It was definitely an interesting hour. I'm looking forward to the next session tomorrow."

43

NEGAL

As the party dwindled, with more than half the guests having left, Negal started his slow seduction of Margo by massaging her toes.

After admitting to being ready, she'd been so nervous that he'd started to doubt her assertion, and his doubts had only increased when he'd told her that he couldn't secure a private cabin for tonight and had seen her visibly relax.

That was why he hadn't told her about the plan Dagor had suggested, deciding it would be better to just let it unfold naturally. He would offer to once again sleep on the couch in the living room and leave the initiative of inviting him to her bedroom up to Margo.

Despite the urgency of the situation, their first time together shouldn't happen under pressure.

Sitting in a chair with her feet on his knees, he kneaded and rubbed, eliciting soft moans of pleasure that stirred a predictable reaction from him. Thankfully, the lighting was dim, and his tux jacket covered the evidence.

"Are foot massages your secret talent?" Margo teased.

Working his fingers gently on her arches, he smirked. "It's just one among many."

Her eyes sparkled with interest. "What are your other talents?"

Negal hoped to demonstrate his other talents tonight, but he didn't say that. Keeping Margo relaxed was his number one priority right now, and since she was well aware of how much he wanted her, there was no chance of her misunderstanding his lack of initiative for disinterest.

When she felt truly ready, she would take the next step.

"That looks so good." Frankie plopped on a chair next to Margo and toed off her ridiculously high heels. "I could use some of that." She cast a smile at Dagor. "Any volunteers?"

Pretending innocence, he arched a brow and looked around. "Maybe I can find someone for you."

She grabbed a napkin off the table and threw it at him. "Sit."

"Yes, ma'am." He pulled out a chair on Frankie's other side and lifted her feet onto his lap.

Margo smiled. "I thought that turning immortal would mean no more toe pain from high heels."

"I still feel pain just as I did before." Frankie's expression turned blissful as Dagor went to work on her feet. "But thankfully, not for long because I recover so quickly. This, though, feels divine." She sighed. "Still, I'm a little peeved about not gaining more inches during my transition. It would have been nice not to need high heels."

"Amanda wears heels," Margo said. "And she's very tall."

"So is the bride." Frankie shifted her gaze to Kri, who was still on the dance floor with her groom after long hours of dancing. "Kri is smart. She's wearing flats."

Listening to their conversation, Negal absentmindedly kept rubbing Margo's toes while thinking of the best way to steer the four of them toward the cabin so he could put Dagor's plan in motion.

His teammate cast him a knowing look and then gently lifted Frankie's feet off his lap. "Are you ready to call it a night?" He lowered her feet to the floor and leaned down to collect her shoes. "I can carry you if you don't want to put your shoes back on."

Frankie gave the platforms a baleful look. "I don't want to put them on, but I don't want you to carry me out of here either."

Dagor affected a disappointed pout. "But I love carrying you around. You fit so well in my arms."

Frankie sighed with a small smile playing on her lips. "I'll walk to the elevator, and then you can carry me."

He grinned as if she had given him the best of gifts.

"I should call it a night, too." Margo lifted her feet off Negal's lap and slid them into her discarded shoes. "I don't think I'm up for any more dancing."

Hallelujah.

Negal got up and offered her his hand. "Neither am I."

After congratulating the newlyweds and saying their goodbyes, the four of them left the dining hall and headed toward the elevators. Negal kept some distance from the other couple and leaned to whisper in Margo's ear. "Those two are not going to leave the door to their bedroom open tonight. I need to sleep on the living room couch again to keep an eye on you."

Margo smiled at him. "I'm fine, really, and I don't need to be watched over, but I would love to wind down on the couch with you with a cup of tea and a good movie."

Had Margo been entertaining the same ideas as he was?

Negal's grin threatened to split his face in half. "It would be my pleasure to snuggle with you on the couch."

When she glanced up at him, her cheeks looked a little rosy, and he had a feeling it wasn't from the two drinks she'd had throughout the evening. "You should probably change out of the tux first. You look very handsome in it, but it's not the right outfit for snuggling."

"You are right," he agreed.

As soon as they entered the elevator, Dagor scooped Frankie into his arms and the two started kissing as if they were alone in there.

Margo and Negal exchanged smiles.

When the elevator stopped on their deck, Dagor walked out with Frankie in his arms, and Margo followed.

Negal stayed inside, holding the door from closing. "I'll change clothes and be there shortly."

Margo smiled. "I'll brew us some tea."

44

MARGO

As Margo walked into the cabin, her heart felt as if it was beating too fast in her chest, and her hands felt clammy. If she hadn't known better, she would have feared a health problem, but she'd had her annual checkup recently, and everything was great.

Her symptoms were the fault of a six-foot-three alien with blond, wavy hair and piercing blue eyes, and the soul of an angel.

Negal wouldn't agree with her on the last one, but she had seen enough of his beautiful soul to make that assertion. He was a very good person, and she wasn't saying that just because she was falling in love with him.

"Good night, Margo." Frankie waved from Dagor's arms.

"See you in the morning," Dagor said as he carried Frankie into their bedroom.

"Good night," Margo said with a smile.

As the door closed behind them, Margo sighed.

It was nice to see Frankie so happy. She and Dagor were so obviously in love, so effortlessly.

If only she could be a little bit like Frankie and not a nervous wreck whose hands shook as she thought about inviting the male she was falling in love with to her bed.

She wasn't a blushing virgin, for goodness' sake. She was a grown woman.

Inside her bedroom, Margo slipped out of her evening gown and hung it carefully in the closet. The hours of dancing had left her feeling sticky and overheated, and she needed a shower, but what if Negal arrived before she was done?

Frankie and Dagor were probably already tearing each other's clothes off so they wouldn't let him in.

She needed to let him know.

Pulling out her phone, she texted him. *I'm taking a quick shower, so if I don't answer the door, please wait for a few minutes and try again.*

His return text arrived a moment later. *I was just about to step into the shower as well, so take your time. I will be there in twenty minutes.*

Margo sent Negal an emoji of a thumbs up and put the phone on the charger.

A smile ghosted across her lips as she imagined him taking a cold shower to cool down. It hadn't escaped her notice that he'd been rock hard when he'd massaged her feet, and she'd tormented him with the sounds she'd made.

Perhaps it hadn't been nice of her, but she needed him in the mood for what she was planning. Not that Negal needed much encouragement to get aroused. He'd even admitted on several occasions that he had trouble controlling his responses to her.

As she stepped into the shower and the warm water cascaded over her skin, Margo imagined it washing away her insecurities.

She was a confident and assertive woman in all ways but one, and it was time she conquered that last frontier and allowed herself to flourish sexually. But a lifetime of reserve and self-doubt was hard to shake off, even in the face of her overwhelming attraction to Negal.

Once she was done washing and scrubbing every inch of her skin, she stepped out of the shower, dried herself off, and slipped into the new nightgown and robe he'd bought for her.

The silky fabric felt so luxurious against her skin that it was almost decadent. If not for Negal's insistence, she never would have splurged on something like that for herself, and even though he'd insisted on paying for everything, she made a mental note to calculate just how much she owed him.

Margo was determined to pay him back once she got her first paycheck from her job at Perfect Match.

With a few minutes left to spare, she settled onto the couch and reached for the historical novel she'd borrowed from Jasmine. She flipped through the pages, searching for the naughty bits, hoping to find some inspiration or courage from the fictional characters. But as she skimmed the flowery language and period-specific dialogue, Margo found herself more bemused than aroused. Without the context of the full story, the intimate scenes felt disconnected and overly dramatic.

The book painted Lord Alistair as a man of fierce passions and brooding intensity, a warrior whose mere presence could ignite a woman's heart with untold desires.

"Annabella's breath hitched as she beheld the sight of the rugged Scottish lord. With his broad shoulders straining against his tartan and his eyes as stormy as the Highland skies, Lord Alistair was a vision of masculinity."

Imagining the scene, Margo snorted softly at how ridiculous it sounded.

"In the dimly lit stables, their eyes met across the straw-covered floor. Annabella felt a wild stirring within her, an untamed yearning that drew her closer to the brawny lord."

Margo couldn't stifle a laugh. "Untamed yearning, really? What does that even mean?"

"Lord Alistair was overcome by the beauty of the wash girl disguising herself as a lady, and he took a step forward, closing the distance between them. 'Annabella,' he growled in a voice that was laden with desire, 'I ken not what magic ye possess to draw me so.'"

Margo rolled her eyes and read aloud in a deep voice and a Scottish twang. "'I ken not what magic ye possess?'"

"As their lips met in a passionate embrace, Annabella melted against the strength of Lord Alistair's embrace, her doubts and fears dissipating like mist in the morning sun."

Shaking her head, Margo closed the book.

The flowery, over-the-top prose was ridiculous, and the two-dimensional characters were not relatable, but there was something endearing about the simplicity and predictability of the story.

Margo could understand Jasmine's preference for period romances, but it wasn't her cup of tea. To truly lose herself in the narrative, Margo needed a story with more substance, and more relatable characters and situations, which was kind of funny since she loved reading about shifters and fae, and all sorts of other-worldly beings.

Glancing at the door, Margo thought about the real story unfolding between her and a god, which was much more fantastical than the story of a Scottish lord falling for the beautiful but lowly wash girl and also all the shifter romances she favored.

45

NEGAL

Negal walked out of the shower much calmer and more collected than when he'd entered it. Pleasuring himself to the image of Margo might have been a violation of sorts, but he'd excused it by the need to take the edge off, which was necessary to keeping his cool and not ravaging the woman the moment he entered her cabin.

It was good that she'd texted him and provided him with an excellent excuse not to rush.

After toweling off, he slipped into a pair of comfortable training pants and a soft t-shirt but then reconsidered his choice of attire and changed into a pair of jeans that would hopefully provide some level of concealment.

Given that she referred to an erection as a one-eyed trouser snake, he didn't want her to get a fright once she saw the large outline of the snake in his pants.

Besides, the jeans had more pockets, and he needed them for all the stuff he was carrying around.

Thinking of stuff, should he bring a bottle of wine?

Nah. First of all, it would take him too long to search for one, and secondly, Margo had already had too much alcohol for one day. When she turned immortal, she could have as much as she wanted, but as a human, it wasn't healthy for her to overindulge.

Well, that was what he had read online, so it might not be true. Anyone could write anything they wanted on the web, and Negal wasn't well versed enough in medical research to evaluate the merit of the studies those assertions were citing.

As he rang the doorbell, the door swung open a moment later, and Negal's breath caught in his throat.

Margo looked like a wet dream in the silky nightgown and robe set he had bought for her. The fabric skimmed over her curves, and the outline of her breasts was so well-defined that it took a lot of willpower to tear his eyes away from the enticing swells and up to Margo's smiling eyes.

"Hi." She lifted on her bare toes and kissed his cheek. "You smell amazing."

"Thank you." The words came out of his mouth, sounding like a hiss because his fangs had punched out.

He swallowed and commanded them to retract. "You look ravishing." As she blushed, he regretted his choice of words. "I mean beautiful. And you smell wonderful as well."

He sounded like a boy on his first date.

"Thank you." Margo took a step back and motioned for him to come in.

"Would you like some tea?" she asked. "I just finished brewing it."

"I would love some." He didn't even like tea, but right now, he would eat gravel and chew on nails if she served them to him.

Desperate much?

Sitting on one of the barstools, he watched her flutter around the small kitchen area, her robe flying behind her like a pair of colorful butterfly wings.

When she poured each of them a cup and handed one to Negal, their fingers brushed, sending a jolt of electricity through his body. He had to fight the urge to pull her into his arms right then and there.

"Let's see what they've got." He reached for the remote as they sat together on the couch. "Do you have any preferences?" He dropped his flip-flops and stretched out his legs.

"Something romantic." Margo's gaze went to his bare feet and stayed there.

Was she looking at his feet because she found them appealing for some reason, or was she embarrassed about asking for a romantic movie?

It was probably the latter. It seemed that Margo had the same plans for tonight as he had, and he wondered if Frankie had told her about his and Dagor's conversation.

Keeping his expression schooled, he leaned back against the sofa's plush cushions and started scrolling through the ship's entertainment options.

The pictures and titles flashing across were all a blur. He didn't care which movie they watched and just waited for Margo to tell him on which one to stop, or go back if he was scrolling too quickly, but she sat quietly beside him, sipping on her tea, her eyes just as unfocused as his.

All he could think about was the woman beside him, the way her thigh pressed against his, the smell of her skin, and the soft sound of her breathing.

After he had gone through the entire selection, he turned to Margo. "Nothing?"

"I'm sorry." She smiled apologetically. "I wasn't paying attention. Can you scroll through the movies again?"

"Sure."

This time he went slower and tried to actually focus on the titles, but nothing appealed to him as the right movie to set the mood, and given Margo's expression, she hadn't found any of the offerings titillating either.

Worse. The lackluster options seemed to have dampened Margo's mood, while Negal had no such problem. Just being near her, inhaling her scent, and feeling the heat of her skin was enough to undo all the good work he had done in the shower.

When he went over the selection for the third time, and it became obvious that they were out of options, he put the remote down. "I have a feeling that we will need to come up with a romantic story ourselves. Why don't you tell me about that idea you had for a Perfect Match virtual adventure? The one where I'm a dragon shifter?"

Margo laughed. "You must be really desperate to bring that up."

She had no idea.

"I am," he admitted. "But it can be fun."

She worried her lower lip between her teeth. "I'm not a great storyteller, but I was just reading a romance novel that I could use as the starting point for our story."

"Go on…"

Margo's cheeks became slightly rosy. "I needed something to read to help me fall asleep, and this is the only paperback book I found. I borrowed it from Jasmine."

Given that preamble, the book must have been either really racy or really stupid. Otherwise, Margo wouldn't have gone to all that trouble telling him that it wasn't hers.

"What is it about?" he asked.

Her blush deepened. "It's a historical romance set in the Scottish Highlands." She cleared her throat and put a haughty expression on her face. "In the wild Highlands of Scotland, there was a rugged lord with a roguish reputation and a wash girl, pure and untouched. When their eyes met across the crowded courtyard, it was as if the world ceased to exist. 'Oh, Alistair,' she whispered, her bosom heaving like the stormy sea, 'ye are the very air I breathe.'"

Negal laughed. "Let's put a spin on it. Imagine that the lord is a werewolf who is the protector of ancient lands, and you are a traveler from afar, unaware of the legends and of the magic that lurks in the misty moors."

"That's a very good start." Margo leaned in, caught up in the story. "You have a knack for storytelling. Continue, please."

He shook his head. "It's your turn."

"Okay." She straightened. "In a land of myths and legends, where the mountains touch the sky, and the lochs reflect the stars, lives a werewolf, known to the locals only as the Guardian of the Glen. By day he is Negal, a nobleman, respected and admired. But under the full moon, he roams the Highlands in his true form." She waved a hand at him to indicate it was his turn.

"One day, an American lady named Margo arrives in the Highlands. She's an adventurous soul, seeking the stories hidden in the wild lands. Little does she know that her arrival has been foretold by an ancient prophecy."

Margo smiled. "The prophecy speaks of a stranger who will enter the Guardian's domain and change his fate forever. Negal is intrigued by the mysterious woman and decides to watch over her, ensuring her safety in the treacherous terrain."

Negal continued, "But as he watches her, Negal finds himself drawn to Margo's fearless spirit. Unaware of his secret identity, Margo only sees the kindness and strength in the man."

She leaned in, her eyes sparkling with excitement. "One evening Margo wanders too close to the forest's edge and finds herself surrounded by a pack of vicious wolves. Negal reveals his true form, transforming into the werewolf to protect her from the pack."

"Despite the shock and fear," Negal continued the story, "Margo sees in the werewolf's eyes the same kindness and strength she admires in Negal, and she realizes that the Guardian of the Glen is none other than the man she has been falling in love with."

Engrossed in the story, she continued, "Margo decides to stay and learn the secrets of the Highlands. Together, they uncover the truth behind the prophecy, finding love and redemption in the wild Scottish lands."

Negal shook his head. "This story is missing something. Where are the passionate kisses? The longing looks?"

"You are right." Margo looked at him from under her lashes. "Can you add them?" Her voice sounded husky.

Negal growled softly, the sound rumbling deep in his chest. "Negal's lips found Margo's, claiming her with a passionate kiss that conveyed the depth of his feelings for her. His hands roamed over her curves, mapping every inch of her skin and stoking the flames of their desire."

Margo's hand landed on his thigh, her fingers tracing small circles over his jeans. "The American surrendered to the overwhelming passion consuming her," she breathed, her lips mere inches from Negal's. "She knew that the Scottish lord was her soulmate, and she was ready to give herself to him, body and soul."

As Negal closed the distance between them, capturing Margo's lips in a searing kiss, she responded with equal fervor, her arms winding around his neck and her body arching into his.

46

MARGO

As Negal's hands clasped Margo's waist, and he lifted her onto his lap without breaking the kiss, she wound her arms around his neck and surrendered to the passion.

He devoured her, the fierceness of the kiss and his tight hold on her so overwhelming that it became too much. Leaning away, she gasped for breath.

Negal's hold on her slackened. "Too much?"

She shook her head. "No, it wasn't too much."

Before she could let herself second-guess her decision, she pulled out of his arms, rose to her feet, and offered him a hand up.

Negal looked up at her, hesitating only for a moment before taking her hand and letting her pull him to his feet.

As she led him to her bedroom, he seemed to be in a daze, and as she closed the door behind them, he remained frozen in place.

The lights were off, but the curtains were parted, and the moon illuminated the hard angles of Negal's perfect face.

"Are you sure about this?" he whispered, his hand still clasped in hers and his blue eyes glowing with inner light.

"I'm sure." Margo pulled her hand out of his and shrugged off her robe, letting it slide to the floor.

His breathing hitched, and as she pushed the straps of her nightgown down her arms and let it slide to the floor as well, he hissed but still didn't move.

Frozen in place, he just stared at her with those luminous eyes of his, and for a moment, Margo felt self-conscious about her nearly nude body.

With only a small triangle of fabric covering any part of her, she was completely exposed, physically and emotionally, and if he rejected her offering, she knew she would never recover from it. She would never again trust herself with a male, human or immortal, because she had somehow terribly misunderstood and miscalculated his plans for her.

"You are so beautiful, Margo." Negal's whisper obliterated her insecurity, and she would have sagged to the floor from relief if not for his hands landing on her waist and then coasting up her ribcage.

Her breathing stilled as she waited for him to move them higher. Her breasts felt as if they had swollen to double their size, and if he didn't touch them soon, they were going to explode.

When his hands coasted down instead of up, she nearly cried with frustration, but then he leaned down and swirled his tongue over her nipple, and she cried out for the opposite reason.

Supporting her with a hand on the small of her back, he took the hardened peak into his mouth, and as he sucked it in, Margo threw her head back and arched into him to give him better access, but when his fangs grazed over her sensitive flesh, she whimpered, partly from fear that he would draw blood and partly from the spike of her arousal that the sense of danger caused.

What was wrong with her that this sort of thing turned her on?

As Negal lavished the same attention on her other nipple, Margo turned into a quivering mass of need. The pulsing in her core quickened with every swipe of his tongue, every pull of his mouth, and every gentle graze of his fangs until she thought that she could climax just from the foreplay, which had never happened to her before.

Heck, she'd never climaxed with a man before, period. Not during the foreplay stage and not during intercourse. Would today be the first time it happened?

Her musing ended abruptly when Negal's mouth left her nipple, and then he dropped to his knees in front of her.

"What are you doing?"

He grinned up at her. "Worshiping my goddess." He pressed a kiss to the apex of her thighs over her lacy panties, and then he gripped the strings connecting the two triangles and tugged them apart. "Sorry about that." He tossed the destroyed panties aside, not looking sorry at all.

Leaning lower, he kissed her naked mound with such gentleness and reverence that her knees buckled from the emotional impact, but then his hands were spanning her bottom and holding her up for his ministrations.

It dawned on her that he was still fully dressed, but she was too dazed to comment on it. Instead, she pushed her fingers into his thick hair and held on for dear life as he licked over the bundle of nerves at the top of her slit.

Margo was already so close that if Negal kept going for a few more seconds, she was going to detonate.

He dug his fingers into the soft flesh of her bottom and then swiped his tongue over that sensitive bundle of nerves, once, twice, three times, and then he growled and whipped his tongue over the same spot one more time.

"Negal!" Margo gasped his name as the coil sprang, and the explosion was like nothing she had ever experienced before.

With his hands on her bottom, keeping her from collapsing, he kept licking and growling until the last tremors rocking her body subsided.

47

NEGAL

As Margo shuddered from her orgasm, immense satisfaction filled Negal. Lapping at the fountain of her pleasure, he felt intoxicated, and he also had no more doubts about her being a Dormant. No human had ever tasted so delicious.

"Negal," she breathed, her fingers slackening their hold on his hair. "Thank you."

With one last kiss to her puffed petals, he lifted his head and smiled at her. "I'm the one who's grateful." He licked his lips.

Margo chuckled, but he detected a note of nervousness in her expression. "You look like a satisfied cat who has just finished licking a bowl of cream."

"That's precisely how I feel." He rose to his feet, wrapped his arms around her, and kissed her.

Margo sagged into him, but she wasn't as boneless as he'd hoped her climax would leave her. The muscles in her back felt tight, and even with the overwhelming scent of her desire filling the room, he could scent a slight undertone of apprehension.

When he let her come up for air, Margo pushed her hands under his t-shirt. "You are a little overdressed for the occasion."

She didn't sound as confident as he would have liked, but she sounded determined, and that was good enough for him.

Margo wanted this. Still, he needed to do everything he could to allow her to feel safe and comfortable. To let her be in charge.

Whipping his t-shirt over his head and tossing it on the floor, he let her explore his chest for a few moments and then wrapped his arms around her and lifted her. Turning them both around so he was with his back to the bed, Negal bent his knees and leaped backward, landing on the bed with Margo on top of him.

"Oof," she exhaled. "You could have warned me."

He smiled up at her. "What would have been the fun in that?"

Removing his arms from her was hard, but to implement his plan, he had to let her be in complete control of what came next.

Hopefully, it wouldn't backfire.

Some females did not enjoy sex unless their partner took the lead, and he had a feeling that Margo belonged to that group, but she'd also had some bad experiences in her past that had made her wary of males, which necessitated relinquishing control to her, at least initially.

He lifted his arms and tucked his hands under his head. "I'm yours to do with as you please."

Margo's eyes widened. Bracing her hands on his chest, she leaned up and back and regarded him with a shy smile.

He had a hard time keeping his eyes on hers and not dipping them to look at her perky breasts. She might not have minded, but it would have made staying on his back with his hands tucked under his head much more difficult.

He was a god, but he was no saint.

"I didn't expect this," Margo said.

"I want you to feel in complete control of our joining."

If Margo didn't like his idea, she could tell him that she didn't want to be in control, but she responded as he had expected, scooting back and going for his zipper.

Negal held his breath as she lowered it, and so did she. He had boxer shorts on, so the reveal would come in stages, which was also part of his plan.

Slow seduction.

With her eyes trained on his bulge, Margo pushed his jeans down, and as he lifted to help her take them off him, she pulled them all the way down and tossed them aside. When she came back, she hesitated before feathering her fingers over his erection, which was mostly covered by the soft cotton of his boxer shorts but not completely. It had elongated so much that the head was peeking over the waistband.

"Don't be afraid to touch it." He smiled with partially elongated fangs. "I promise that my one-eyed trouser snake doesn't bite."

She chuckled. "No, it doesn't. That's the danger from the other end."

The smile slid off his face. "Does it scare you?"

"No," she whispered, her eyes still glued to his shaft.

"I mean the bite, the fangs, the venom."

Finally, she tore her eyes from his erection. "No, your fangs don't scare me."

"Then what does?"

Margo swallowed. "Nothing. I want this."

She reached into his boxers, and as she wrapped her hand around his shaft, Negal hissed.

Her grip immediately loosened. "Did I hurt you?"

He laughed. "Yeah, but not in the way you think. I love the feel of your hand on my…male organ."

Most young humans had no problem with the words dick or cock, but Margo was more reserved, and she might find those two objectionable, or worse, they could turn her off.

MARGO

ale organ?

Not wanting to offend Negal, Margo stifled a laugh. His pose and awkward choice of words both helped to boost her confidence and perhaps that had been his intention.

On the other hand, Negal was an alien, so perhaps he didn't know what words to use in reference to his erection—a very long, thick erection that pulsed against her palm and tempted her to do things that she usually didn't like doing.

Fisting it, Margo gently tugged on the velvety skin, gliding her palm from base to tip and back.

Negal groaned, but she was sure that this time it was with pleasure.

As she licked her lips, tasting herself from his kiss, it wasn't bad. In fact, it was quite arousing.

Dipping her head, she swept her tongue over the tip, and Negal's bottom lifted, pushing his shaft past her lips before she was ready to take it.

"Sorry about that." He dropped his bottom back on the mattress. "You are in charge, Nesha. Not me."

Nesha? What did that mean?

Was it an endearment term in Anumatian?

She would have asked if her mouth wasn't wrapped around Negal's pleasure stick.

Yeah, that was what she was going to call it from now on. Then again, he might take offense to the word stick, so maybe rod would be more appropriate.

Except, a rod had a painful connotation in her mind, and Margo didn't want anything negative to be associated with Negal.

Gripping his shaft, she pumped it with her hand in tandem with her mouth while letting her thoughts meander in strange directions.

Pleasure baton? Pleasure tool?

"Margo," he hissed. "If you keep going like this, I'm going to come in your mouth, and that's not going to benefit your transition."

He was right, of course. It was time to woman up and welcome this magnificent male into her body.

All they had done so far had been incredibly intimate, but this was the ultimate act and the one she'd always had the most trouble with.

His shaft still gripped in her hand, Margo lifted to her knees and positioned her entrance over the tip.

Looking into Negal's glowing eyes, she lowered herself until the tip breached her entrance and then stopped to let her body get accustomed to the sensation of being invaded.

Except, she wasn't being invaded. Not this time. She was welcoming him into her, controlling how deep and how fast she would take him, and it made all the difference.

"Margo," he whispered her name. "You are killing me, but I couldn't have asked for a better way to die."

This time, she didn't stop the chuckle bubbling up her chest. "You are immortal. I can't kill you even if I tried." She lowered herself two more inches over his shaft and stopped.

Negal's hands were still trapped under his head, but the bunching of his biceps indicated how hard he was struggling to keep them there.

Should she tell him it was okay to release them?

Margo wanted him to grip her thighs or her ass, but not just yet. First, she wanted to finish what she had started. She lifted up and then glided back down, up and back down, and each time, she managed to get more of him inside of her.

Negal's forehead was covered in a sheen of sweat, no doubt from the effort to keep from taking over.

She was grateful for his restraint, for his willingness to relinquish control to her so she wouldn't get over-whelmed—so she would be comfortable with their joining.

And she was.

Somehow, he had made it so that she didn't feel any of the awful awkwardness of getting naked with a man for the first time, of letting him inside of her as if they belonged together.

Too many people didn't realize that sex shouldn't be a casual thing, that such intimacy required a level of connection that could only come after a long period of courtship—that it should be the final step to cement a relationship and not the first.

Except, she was a hypocrite because she was doing exactly what she was preaching against.

She was taking a male she barely knew into her body. But the truth was that even though she didn't know much about Negal's past, she knew his soul and the kind of person he was, and that was enough.

When he was as deep inside her as he could go, she leaned over him and kissed him.

Understanding her silent communication, Negal released his hands from their makeshift prison and gripped her thighs.

As he took charge, flipping them around so she was under him, his hold on her was firm but not bruising, and as he found his rhythm, the coil inside of her began winding tighter and tighter.

Everything had been wonderful so far, but having him in control of the joining and letting go was so much more pleasurable that it took mere moments for another orgasm to gather momentum in her belly, and as she felt the coil springing, she instinctively tilted her head to the side, exposing her neck for his bite.

He hissed, and as she climaxed, she felt his seed jet into her, and he struck with his fangs.

The pain was blinding in its intensity, but it only lasted a split second, and then a wave of euphoria washed over her, and she was climaxing again, and again, and again until her body could not take any more, and then she felt as if her soul had left her body, and she was soaring above the clouds.

49

NEGAL

After the storm had subsided and Margo drifted off on the wings of euphoria, Negal retracted his fangs and licked the puncture wounds closed.

Bracing on his forearms, he buried his nose in her silky hair and breathed her in. The connection that had been forming between them even before they had met had solidified with their joining, and the feeling of no longer being alone was incredible.

There was no more just Negal. From now on, it was Negal and Margo.

The two were one, a unit.

"I love you," he murmured against her upturned lips.

The soft, blissed-out expression on her face made her look angelic.

"My angel," he whispered before kissing her lightly and withdrawing gently.

As he padded to the bathroom to clean up, Negal wondered what Margo was seeing in her euphoric dream. Was she continuing the story they had started earlier? Was she lost in the Scottish Highlands, her mind continuing to weave the tale of him as a werewolf lord and her as the adventurous American? Or had their own story taken center stage, their real-life romance more captivating than the fictional narrative?

Stepping into the shower, Negal considered their future together. The cruise was drawing to a close, but their journey as a couple was only beginning, and even though he had to concede that nothing was guaranteed, he felt optimistic about the future.

Margo would transition, he was sure of that, and the only question was when.

Frankie and Gabi had both started transitioning after the first or second bite and so did Karen, so he hoped Margo would be the same despite what he had heard about other Dormants' transitions that had taken weeks and many bites.

He and Margo did not have weeks.

They had days.

Returning to the bedroom, Negal slipped beneath the covers, careful not to disturb her even though there was no chance she would wake up, even if he purposely tried to rouse her.

She was knocked out, and given his experience with human females, she would keep soaring on the clouds of euphoria for many more hours. If he could quiet his mind, he might be able to catch a few hours of sleep before she woke up.

As Negal gathered Margo into his arms, he relished the feel of her soft skin against his and the way her body molded perfectly to his own.

Holding her close, he allowed himself to dream of a shared life, where they embarked on missions together with Aru and Gabi, Frankie and Dagor.

He was excited by the prospect, but he would have preferred to have more time alone with Margo so they could enjoy more moments like this—quiet, intimate, and in a comfortable bed. But life was full of compromises, and he would take being with Margo just about anywhere over being without her surrounded by luxury.

Pressing a gentle kiss to her forehead, Negal whispered once more, "I love you, my sweet angel."

50

MARGO

The morning light filtered through the curtains, casting a soft glow over Negal's handsome face. He looked so peaceful in repose, almost boyish if not for the dark blond shadow over his jaw.

Margo wanted to cup that stubble-covered cheek and kiss those firm lips, but she also wanted a few more moments of just basking in his perfection and thinking about the night they had shared before she woke him up.

Negal's chest was still rising and falling with the same rhythm as it had when Margo had first opened her eyes, but she had a feeling that he had sensed the moment she had awakened and was pretending to sleep for some reason.

Maybe he was afraid that in the light of day she would freak out about last night?

That wasn't going to happen. The toughest part, which was garnering the courage to get intimate with a male she'd met only two days ago, was over, and it hadn't even been all that tough.

In fact, it had been almost easy.

The storytelling, the shared laughter, and then their fictional tale intertwining with reality—it had all led to their joining and culminated in Negal's bite.

Frankie was right, no drug could ever compare to the intensity, the sheer exhilaration of the venom bite, let alone what had followed. The memory sent a shiver of longing through Margo. She wondered if Negal would bite her every time they made love.

The bliss was indescribable, but she couldn't black out again and be out of commission for hours.

Frankie and Mia had warned her about that, but she'd thought they had been exaggerating.

If she awakened him right now, made love to him again, and he bit her, she would be out for half of the day, and as much as she craved Negal's body, she also didn't want to lose time just talking with him.

A smile curved her lips as she imagined them continuing the story they had started creating last night. She hadn't expected Negal to be such an imaginative storyteller.

It dawned on her then that he tended to undervalue himself. Negal identified as a god of humble origins, a trooper in the interstellar fleet, and a nothing-special guy.

There was so much more to him than he realized, and if the Fates smiled upon them and she transitioned, Margo would make it her mission to explore all of Negal's hidden talents and abilities.

It wasn't about trying to change him or make him strive for more than he was comfortable with. That was totally up to him. It was about self-discovery and not putting limits on himself, and if the newfound confidence led to different choices, they would be Negal's, not hers. Being aware of a talent for story-telling didn't mean that he should become a writer if he had no patience or passion for it.

Margo had watched Mia work for months on one short children's book, and she knew she would never have had the patience to work on one project for so long and then do all the revisions that the publisher had demanded, especially given that success wasn't guaranteed.

At least in advertising, things happened quickly. Usually, it took a few days to develop the concept, get approval, and then a few weeks until the campaign was ready to launch.

Despite working on the fringes of the process and not having much say in the creative part, Margo loved the fast pace and the immediate results, provided that they were good. No one liked failure, but thankfully the agency she worked for had rarely produced a campaign that flopped.

Hopefully, though, that part of her life was over, and she would get to do what she loved in Perfect Match.

But why was she thinking about the advertising campaigns when she was lying next to a naked god?

Well, she knew why. Work was simple, and thinking about it was a distraction, a way to avoid thinking about the big L-word that was pushing up from her heart and demanding to be heard.

The rational part of her screamed that it was too soon, and even though the circumstances were unlike any she had faced before, she shouldn't let herself fall in love with Negal, at least until she transitioned.

To fall in love and to be made to forget about it was too terrible to even think about. Her mind might be forced to forget Negal, but the ache in her heart would remind her that she was missing a vital part of her life, and not knowing what it was would drive her insane.

The problem was that Margo had a feeling that she had already lost the battle and just hadn't admitted it to herself yet.

Her feelings for Negal couldn't be boxed into a time-line, and they couldn't be compared to any of her past experiences or even to Frankie's or Mia's, which were similar and yet as vastly different as the three of them were different from each other.

It was like stepping into a Perfect Match adventure, where everything was condensed into a few hours but felt as if it had lasted weeks or even months.

Negal stirred, and as his eyes fluttered open to meet hers, a smile bloomed on his face. "Hello, beautiful." He lifted his hand and cupped her cheek.

She leaned into it and covered his hand with hers. "Good morning."

"How are you feeling?" he asked.

She laughed softly. "Like I've returned from the best and most restful vacation in heaven. I can't even describe the things I saw after shooting up to the sky."

His grin broadened. "It's something else, isn't it?"

"Have you ever experienced a venom bite?"

He nodded. "Getting bitten during a fight is not the same as being bitten during sex, but the effects of the venom are similar enough. I was loopy the rest of the day."

Margo pursed her lips. "I'm not loopy at all. In fact, I'm incredibly clear and feel on top of the world."

"I'm glad." He let go of her cheek and wrapped his arms around her. "No regrets about last night?"

"None." She leaned in and kissed him on the lips. "I would love to stay and cuddle, but I need to visit the bathroom quite urgently."

Margo had more than cuddling in mind, but only if Negal could refrain from biting her. She didn't want to spend the next several hours passed out in bed.

Reluctantly, he released her from the cage of his arms. "Go, but come back quickly."

"I will."

She got out from under the covers, unconcerned about her nudity as she sauntered to the bathroom, giving Negal a great view of her ass.

The hiss he emitted was followed by a groan, and both were deeply satisfying.

In the bathroom, Margo took care of the most urgent need first, and as she washed her hands, the reflection staring back at her was that of a happy woman. She had experienced many happy moments during her life, but she'd never looked so vibrant.

NEGAL

As Margo ducked into the bathroom, Negal closed his eyes and let out a relieved breath. During the night, or rather the early morning hours, he had remained mostly awake, checking up on Margo to make sure she was doing okay and only dozing off and on for a few minutes here and there.

Even though he hadn't encountered a human female who had a negative reaction to the venom, and none of the immortals had warned him that it could be potentially harmful, it only made sense that not everyone would tolerate the venom well.

Humans were so fragile.

He'd read about a young woman who was allergic to peanuts and died after kissing her boyfriend, who had eaten peanuts beforehand. So, if an allergic reaction could be so deadly, he wasn't taking chances.

To be frank, he hadn't been as concerned about the women he had been with before meeting Margo, not because he hadn't cared but because it hadn't occurred to him before that they might have an adverse reaction to his venom.

Come to think of it, allergy was just one potential health risk. What if a human had a weak heart that couldn't survive so much stimulation?

Had he thought about all those potential risks before making love to Margo, he would have insisted she get a thorough physical from the clan's doctor before taking her to bed.

Margo projected such a tough-girl persona that at first, he'd been fooled by it, but when he'd gotten to know her better, he'd realized that underneath the façade she was hiding a vulnerability.

Last night, he had done everything he could to make the experience as wonderful for her as it was for him, which meant a lot of restraint on his part, but it hadn't diminished the experience. It still had been the best he'd ever had, probably because it had been more than just sex.

It was the coming together of not just their bodies but also their souls.

Negal chuckled. Had he just graduated from making up romance stories to composing poetry?

Who would have thought that he had it in him?

When the door opened, and Margo stepped out of the bathroom, he lifted the blanket and motioned for her to duck in.

For some reason, her cheeks were rosy, and she had a sheepish expression on her face, but he couldn't smell her arousal, so it couldn't be that she was planning another round of lovemaking.

"You're cold." He wrapped his arms around her and drew her against his body.

She wiggled, rubbing against his erection. "And you are hard."

He chuckled. "I'm always hard around you, and in case your friends failed to mention it, gods' and immortals' stamina far exceeds that of human males. We don't need much time to recuperate. We can go many times in a row."

"Oh, wow." The rosy hue of her cheeks deepened, and as a delicate whiff of feminine arousal reached his nose, he smoothed his hands down her back and squeezed her bottom.

She put her hands on his chest. "I have a question."

"Ask, and I shall answer."

"Do you have to bite your partner every time you climax?"

"That's a good question, and the answer is no. My venom doesn't get replenished nearly as fast as my seed. I can probably provide two bites a day."

"Oh." Her face fell, and she lowered her eyes to his chest.

"Hey." He hooked a finger under her chin and lifted her head so that she had to look at him. "If you are craving another bite, I'm more than capable of providing it."

"I do crave it, but not now." She worried her lower lip. "As incredible as it is, I don't want to be out for hours. I want to enjoy your company."

So that was what Margo was worried about. They were docked in the port of Mazatlan, and she wanted to go sightseeing. She didn't want to spend the rest of the day in bed.

Besides, perhaps it would be for the best if they didn't make love now anyway. The goal was to induce her transition, which required his venom and his seed to be concentrated and not diluted by overindulgence.

"You are absolutely right." He dipped his head and kissed the top of her nose. "We should get off the ship and go exploring. But first, I'll make you breakfast." He smiled. "You need to replenish your energy after the vigorous activities of last night."

Margo scrunched her nose. "So, no morning hanky-panky?"

Negal laughed. "Who are you, and what have you done with my cautious and reserved Margo?"

She rolled her eyes. "Gone, hopefully, never to be seen again. I like the new me much better."

"I loved the old you, I love the new you, and I will love every new facet of you."

Her eyes widened. "You love me?"

He tightened his arms around her. "I do, and I don't expect you to feel the same about me so soon after we've met, but I will woo you until you have no choice but to love me back."

"Silly Negal." She cupped his cheek. "Isn't it obvious that I love you too?"

He made a doubtful face even though she was right. He knew. "I don't want to assume anything. I still need to hear the words."

"How could I not love you?" she whispered. "You are as beautiful on the inside as you are on the outside, and you treat me with more care and respect than anyone ever has. You didn't belittle my insecurities about intimacy or try to bulldoze over them as most men would have tried to do. You've been attentive, considerate, and patient, but you still managed to convey at every turn how much you desired me. I don't know anyone who would have been capable of navigating the convoluted maze of my psyche as well as you have."

Negal's heart swelled in response to her praise, and he felt more manly than he ever had because he had done right by the female he loved.

"Thank you." He pressed his forehead to hers. "I just wanted you to feel safe and comfortable with me." He chuckled. "Usually, though, females are aroused by danger, not by those who offer them safety."

"You are danger and safety and everything in between wrapped into one hell of a sexy package. I don't know any woman who wouldn't have been wildly attracted to you, and I'm so grateful that you are mine." She looked into his eyes with an expectant expression on her beautiful face.

Did she need confirmation? Or did she want him to say the same things to her?

Negal tightened his arms around his female. "You are strength, vulnerability, and everything in between wrapped into the most alluring, beautiful, and sexy gift from the Fates. I am yours, Margo, for as long as you will have me, which I hope is forever."

"Oh, Negal." Her eyes misted with tears. "I pray that you will be mine forever, too, and I feel greedy for wanting so much for myself. What have I done to deserve you?"

He laughed. "I'm not the saint you think I am, and I'm definitely no prize. Perhaps you have done something bad, and I'm your punishment?"

"No way." She slapped his chest playfully. "You need to stop deprecating yourself."

"Aha, so I do have faults."

She rolled her eyes. "No one is perfect. But as long as the plusses outweigh the minuses, it's a win, and in your case, the scale dips heavily on the plus side, making you a big win."

"I can live with that."

52

MARGO

Margo sat on the barstool next to the counter, feeling stupidly happy but also terrified that her happiness would be temporary.

She was in love with Negal, and he was in love with her, but if she didn't transition, it would all be lost because Kian would demand the removal of all her memories regarding the secret world of gods and immortals, including her and Negal's love for each other.

Negal didn't need to obey Kian's orders, though. He wasn't a member of Kian's community, and he could do as he pleased. Well, he answered to Aru, but she had a feeling that Aru was more flexible than Kian.

Would Aru allow her to retain her memories and tag along with them to Tibet even if she was just a plain human?

Would Negal?

If he really loved her, he would.

"What are you frowning about?" Negal pulled a skillet out of the cabinet.

She leaned her elbows on the counter and braced her chin on her fist. "Would you keep me with you if I didn't transition?"

He froze with the skillet midair above the stovetop. "You are transitioning. I have no doubt about it."

Margo rolled her eyes. "I love your optimism. But what if I don't? Will you let Kian erase my memories of you and try to forget about me?"

Negal's eyes blazed with inner light. "I won't," he hissed. "I can't. I love you too much to let you go." He shuddered. "But if you don't transition, nature will eventually take you from me." He shook his head. "Let's stop with the depressing hypotheticals because, one way or another, you are going to transition."

Margo chuckled. "Is there another way? Other than the fun way?"

"My people can probably turn anyone immortal, but I don't have access to their biotech. One day, in the not-too-distant future, human science will catch up, though."

"It's possible." She sighed. "But I doubt it will happen during my lifetime, and even if it does, it wouldn't be widely available to anyone who wants it. As much as immortality appeals to me, I'm terrified of what it would do to my world. The consequences can be catastrophic."

Negal put the pan on the heating element. "Two things would have to happen simultaneously with turning all humans immortal. Birth rates would have to plummet, and interstellar travel with colonizing capabilities would have to be developed and deployed. Otherwise, you are right. The consequences would be disastrous."

Margo sighed. "And to think that I was so happy only moments ago." She looked at the skillet and searched her mind for a different topic to talk about. "We could get breakfast in the dining hall, or we could go up to the Lido deck and get a drink."

Negal huffed. "This early in the morning? No way. You need to eat something healthy to replenish your energy."

It was sweet how much he wanted to take care of her, but given his cooking skills, she would have preferred to eat elsewhere. Then again, he would be offended if she said so, so maybe she should pretend like she loved whatever he made.

Was that the right thing to do, though?

Partners, lovers, shouldn't lie to each other, not even little white lies said out of love and not malice, but the truth should always be wrapped in a lot of love to mitigate the sting.

"Why?" Negal lifted a brow. "You don't like my cooking?"

She smiled. "I love everything about you, and I know that you will be amazing at anything you put your mind to. Therefore, I'm more than willing to be the taster of your culinary experiments."

Shaking his head, Negal rubbed a hand over the back of his neck. "I stopped listening after you said that you loved everything about me and that I would be amazing at anything I do."

Margo laughed. "You heard the rest. Don't pretend that you did not." She leaned over the counter. "Did I offend you with the remark about your culinary skills?"

"Not really. I appreciate your honesty."

"Good." She gave him a bright smile. "If I don't criticize anything, you won't believe my praise when it's actually deserved."

His eyes glinted with amusement. "True that." He opened the refrigerator, and pulled out a stick of butter, a carton of eggs, and a pack of sliced bread. "So, let's hear that praise."

Margo knew what kind of praise he meant, but she pretended innocence. "You are a great storyteller." She tried hard not to laugh at his disappointed expression.

But then he shrugged and dropped some butter into the hot skillet.

"The story we came up with last night could make a great addition to the Perfect Match virtual adventures. It has romance, mystery, and supernatural elements. Naturally, we would have to change the names, but other than that, it's good to go."

Margo huffed out a breath. "I didn't even get the job offer yet. Everything is in a state of flux. I want to transition and have a long and happy life with you, but I would be lying if I said that I was excited about trekking through Tibet or any other remote place in search of the missing pods. I would much rather sit in an air-conditioned space and brainstorm ideas for new Perfect Match adventures with Frankie and Mia, participate in test runs, and then come home to you in the evenings. But we can't have all that we want, right?"

For a long moment, the only sound in the living room was the sizzling of butter in the skillet.

"I'm sorry," Negal eventually said. "I wish I could join you in the immortals' village, but that's not possible even if I didn't have to leave on the mission."

"Why not?"

"It's complicated." He turned around and broke two eggs over the skillet and then two more.

"Is it a secret?" Margo asked.

"Not from you." He scrambled the eggs with a fork. "My people don't know about the immortals. They are not supposed to exist. Aru, Dagor and I can be tracked by the patrol ship, and we don't want to lead anyone to the immortals' village."

Margo frowned. "How are you being tracked?"

"Implants." Negal pulled out two plates and put them on the table. "The clan's doctors might be able to remove them, but then our commander would assume that we are dead, and that's not something we want or can do at the moment. In the future, though, that might be an option."

She nodded. "As long as there is a way out, the situation is not hopeless, right?"

"True." He put half of the scrambled eggs on her plate and half on his. "After we find the pods, we might be able to stage our deaths and get free, but it's also possible that the trackers can't be removed. We won't know until we get scanned, and even then, I wouldn't trust the crude equipment they have here. Our technology is so advanced compared to what humans have that even the best scanners might not locate our trackers."

"Is it possible that trying to remove the implants would cause them to explode or harm you in any way?" When Negal looked surprised by her suggestion, Margo rolled her eyes. "Don't tell me that's never occurred to you."

"It hasn't, but the truth is that I haven't given removing the trackers much thought before I met you."

He didn't sound like it was something he wanted to do, and she couldn't blame him. Negal and his friends had family on Anumati and its colonies, and they didn't want to be forever cut off from them, which would happen if they faked their deaths. The only transportation method that could get them back home was the Anumati patrol ship, which was due to pick them up in five hundred years or so.

It was so far in the future that she shouldn't worry about it, but she still felt a tightening in her chest at the thought of being separated from Negal.

"I'm going crazy." She pushed her fingers through her hair. "This is only our third day together, and I'm already so in love with you that I'm worried about us separating half a millennium from now." Provided that she transitioned and got to live that long; she decided against adding the qualifier.

There was no reason to upset Negal. He was so convinced that she would transition that he got angry every time she mentioned the possibility that she wouldn't.

He leaned over the counter and took her hands. "You are not crazy, Margo. I feel the same about you, and you know why?"

"Why?"

"Because we are fated for each other. That's how it works when you meet the person the Fates have chosen for you, and last night solidified our bond.

That's why I'm convinced that you will start transitioning soon and that you will do so successfully."

Margo swallowed. "I hope you are right."

Negal's confidence in her impending transition was infectious, and Margo wanted to believe that he was right, but she couldn't ignore the odds that were stacked against her. She had no paranormal abilities, and the supposed affinity immortals felt for Dormants wasn't something she could quantify or rely on as proof of her genetics. She hadn't mingled extensively outside her immediate circle. Aside from the time spent with Negal, Frankie, Mia, and Jasmine, she hadn't even attempted to make new connections.

There was the undeniable bond with Negal, but was that enough to prove that she was a Dormant?

"I know I am," Negal said. "And speaking of transitioning, would you mind if we stopped by the clinic to check on Karen before going ashore?"

Margo wasn't sure that she wanted to get off the ship and endure the humidity and heat of the streets of Mazatlan, but she was curious about Karen's progress.

"I would love to visit Karen. I want to know how she's doing."

53

ANNANI

"Hello, Mother." Kian kissed Annani's cheek. "I thought we were going to talk about yesterday's revelations," he whispered next to her ear.

She smiled. "I cannot invite you and your family for brunch without inviting your sisters and their families," she whispered back. "They would think that I am playing favorites. If you wish, you can stay after everyone leaves."

Annani wished she could share her conversations with the queen of Anumati with all of her children. It did not feel right to keep it from her daughters, but unless she lied and claimed to have established the communication herself, she could not. It would be repaying Aru's kindness and sacrifice with betrayal.

She was the reason he would not get picked up by the patrol ship on its way back to Anumati. The queen had arranged for him to stay so he could be her liaison to

Earth. His telepathic connection with his sister would be his only contact with home, and since their parents did not know about their connection, Aria could not even keep them updated on his well-being.

In a way, though, it was for the best.

Their parents would not be happy to learn that their son had a hybrid mate, whom he could never bring home and introduce to them.

Perhaps in the distant future, when Annani took over the Anumatian throne, she would change those archaic prohibitions and re-establish communications and travel to Earth. Aru's parents could come for a visit, and perhaps by then, he would be able to present them with a grandchild.

"What's that smile about?" Alena asked, pulling Annani out of her reveries.

"I am imagining a better future."

Amanda snorted. "Please, share your vision. We all need a dose of optimism these days."

The world was indeed entering another dark period, just as Syssi had foreseen. Wars were raging in several hotspots around the globe, and drug cartels were so powerful and pervasive that they controlled entire countries, with their governments either helpless to do anything or worse—willingly cooperating with the cartels. Those criminal organizations were not only responsible for the loss of countless lives to overdosing and other drug-related deaths, but several of them were also run by terrorist organizations that were using drug money to finance their deadly operations.

There was so much chaos going on around the world, but Annani still hoped that this time, it would not last as long as it had previously. It was a vicious cycle of good times followed by bad times and then the good times returned only to be followed by bad times again.

The cycles were becoming shorter, though.

While epochs in the distant past had lasted thousands of years and then hundreds, they had shrunk to decades and even less in modern times. The duration followed advancements in technology, and since there had never been a leap as vast as the advent of artificial intelligence, perhaps this time around things would get back to normal faster than ever.

"Technology will usher in a better future," Annani said at last. "Despite the fears of technology displacing workers, it has always improved lives, and it will continue doing so in the future. Most diseases will be eradicated, most of the work will be done by robots, and people will have to work fewer hours a week to make a living. They will have plenty of time to enjoy their children and pursue hobbies."

"Utopia," Kian snorted, "does not exist. They have technology aplenty on Anumati and no diseases. Yet, according to Aru and his teammates, it is far from the paradise you are describing."

Annani smiled indulgently. "I did not describe a paradise. People are people, and there will always be strife, competition, and jealousy. But if the great evils are eliminated or reduced, everyone's lives will be better. I will be satisfied when there are no more deadly diseases, wars, terror attacks, hunger, exploitation, illicit drugs, human trafficking, and other evils that currently plague humanity."

Sari sighed. "I would be happy with that list accomplished as well, but I don't hold my breath for it happening anytime soon. I don't know what, if anything, can end all those evils. It's just not possible."

"The Eternal King managed to do all that," Kian said. "It's not that I'm justifying his methods, especially since he had no qualms about killing his own children, but I have to admit that what he achieved was extraordinary."

Annani tensed. Would her daughters catch Kian's slip-up?

"What do you mean he killed his own children?" Amanda asked.

"I meant that the Eternal King wanted to kill the rebels, including Ahn, his legitimate heir, and Ahn's half-siblings Ekin and Athor. He would have succeeded if Mortdh had not beaten him to it."

Satisfied with his answer, Amanda leaned back in her chair. "In this case, the intent is incriminating enough. No sane person sends assassins after his own son."

"It's happened many times throughout human history," Annani said. "To gain or keep a throne, sons have murdered their fathers, and fathers have murdered their sons. Power is a corruptive force."

"Maybe it's the other way around," Alena said. People who ascend to positions of power are corrupt or sociopaths to start with, and many times, this trait is inherited by their offspring."

Annani let out an indignant huff. "My father was not a sociopath. He was ruthless at times, but he had feelings, and he cared deeply for my mother and me."

"Navuh cares for Areana," Sari said. "But he's still a sociopath. He would have killed Kalugal if he had discovered that his son was a strong enough compeller to usurp him."

"Perhaps," Annani said. "We will never know."

In the same way, they would never know whether Mortdh had dropped the bomb on the assembly or if someone shot his plane down, causing the weapon to explode.

Regrettably, she could not entertain the same doubts about Khiann's death. The three witnesses who had testified against Mortdh had given almost the same exact description with slight variations, even though they had given their testimonies separately. They might have told a coordinated lie, but why would they have done so? And if they had, her father would have known they had lied, wouldn't he?

Then again, her father had wanted Mortdh to be found guilty of the murder, so perhaps he had compelled those males to testify against Mortdh?

The thought had never occurred to her before, and Annani wondered why it had not. She had idolized her father, but she had been aware of how ruthless he was. Her father had promised her hand in marriage to Mortdh, knowing that the god would never love her. He had done so to secure peace. But when it had become clear to him that securing peace through marriage would not work, perhaps he had thought of another way to get rid of Mortdh and the threat he represented.

Could her father have ordered Khiann's murder to pin it on Mortdh?

No, she would never believe Ahn capable of that. But she could definitely believe he was capable of using the murder to his advantage.

The implications were so profound that Annani felt her chest constrict, and she had to excuse herself to go out on the terrace for some fresh air.

"I will go with you." Alena started to rise.

"No, stay." Annani put a hand on her shoulder. "I need a few moments alone."

Everyone's worried eyes followed her as she grabbed her sunglasses and stepped out onto the balcony, but she could not explain why she needed a few minutes of solitude.

She could not tell her children and their mates that she had only just now realized that her father might have compelled the witnesses who had testified against Mortdh. It had taken her over five thousand years to start doubting what she had seen and heard with her own eyes and ears, when she should have done so during the testimony.

She was so young back then and addled with grief, but she had never been naive. She had grown up in the palace, had witnessed the machinations of court, and had known that things were not always the way they seemed.

Annani took a deep breath.

Most times, though, things were exactly like they seemed. She was probably working herself up for nothing. The witnesses might have told the truth, and Mortdh had beheaded Khiann.

At least now, she had a sliver of hope that things had not happened the way the witnesses had testified, and if Khiann still had his head attached to his neck, he might have survived and was buried somewhere in the desert, in stasis and waiting for her to revive him.

PETER

Peter turned on his side, propped his elbow on the mattress, his head on his fist, and looked at Marina.

The midmorning sun filtered through the curtains, casting its rays on her blue hair, her pale, freckled skin, and her lips that were slightly parted.

She seemed so peaceful, her chest rising and falling in a steady rhythm. The nervous energy that emanated from her when she was awake was gone, and he wondered if it was because he had pleasured her so thoroughly last night or because of the venom-induced dreams that she was experiencing.

The poor girl had been exhausted when he'd picked her up from the kitchen after she and the rest of the staff finished cleaning up. When he'd offered to carry her out of the elevator, she hadn't even tried to object.

Resting her head on his chest, she'd closed her eyes and had fallen asleep on the way. He'd drawn her a bath, stripped her, and washed the smell of the kitchen out of her hair and skin before carrying her to his bed.

Marina had woken up then, and they had made gentle, sweet love because she was in no state to do anything strenuous.

He liked taking care of her.

There was something about Marina that drew him in. They had similar sexual proclivities, which was a big plus, but that wasn't all. He simply liked being with her and making her life a little easier and a little brighter. It provided him with satisfaction.

He could almost hear Kagra's disparaging voice in his head; *you enjoy playing the savior, Peter.*

"Screw that," he murmured quietly.

Kagra was a typical Kra-ell female warrior, who didn't believe in love or in exclusive relationships, and who valued her independence above all.

He should forget all the things she had told him and not let them get to him time and again, like some parasite crawling under his skin. The fact that she couldn't understand emotional attachment didn't mean that it was not worthy of pursuit.

Irritated, he slid out of bed and ducked into the bathroom.

After a shower and a shave, he felt like a new male and decided to cook breakfast for Marina and serve it to her in bed.

She'd worked so hard for the past two days that she deserved a little pampering. Today, she was only working on the cleanup after lunch, so she could laze in bed for a long time.

As he moved around the kitchenette, gathering ingredients, he deliberated whether he should make something for Jay and decided against it.

His roommate hadn't awoken yet, and when he did, Peter hoped he would go to the dining room and give them privacy.

He would make a simple meal because that was all he knew how to do, with eggs, bread, some sliced cheese, fruit, and coffee, of course.

No breakfast was complete without a cup of java.

As he whisked the eggs, added a dash of salt, and buttered the bread, he found himself humming a tune.

When he was done, Peter plated the food with care, arranging the slices of toast and the scrambled eggs with a side of fresh fruit.

Satisfied with the presentation, he was about to carry the tray to the bedroom when he heard the rustling of bedding, and a moment later Marina appeared at the doorway, rubbing sleep from her eyes.

"What are you doing?" A look of confusion gave way to delight as she took in the scene before her. "Are you bringing me breakfast in bed?"

"That was the plan." He met her gaze, his heart swelling at the sight of her, tousled hair and all. "But since you are already up, we can eat here." He put the tray on the table.

"No way. I'm not passing this up. No one has ever served me breakfast in bed." She lifted a finger. "Give me five minutes to clean up in the bathroom, and then you can bring the tray in."

Marina looked so happy, so excited, that Peter promised himself that he would serve her breakfast in bed every morning from now until the end of the cruise.

It was a damn shame that the voyage was almost over.

55

MARINA

After waking up to the aroma of breakfast cooking, Marina had rushed to the living room to see what was going on, and now she regretted it.

It would have been so much nicer to have Peter surprise her with breakfast in bed. No one had ever done something like that for her. Then again, she would have needed to excuse herself to visit the bathroom and brush her teeth, so maybe it was better this way.

At least now, when Peter brought the tray in, her hair wouldn't look like a bird's nest, and her breath would not stink.

Getting back in bed, she arranged a stack of pillows at her back, pulled the blanket up to her chin, and waited for Peter to arrive.

When he entered, the laden tray carefully balanced in his hand, the sight stirred a well of emotions that threatened to overwhelm her, and as he placed the tray across her lap, Marina felt her eyes misting with tears.

She was so touched by the gesture, the care it implied, her importance to him, the feelings he had for her. Perhaps he had meant it when he'd said he didn't want to let her go?

Or was she reading too much into it?

Peter frowned. "Why are you crying?"

"I'm not crying." She lifted a hooked finger and rubbed it under her eye to make sure. "I'm just still sleepy so my eyes get misty."

Looking doubtful, he lifted one of the mugs off the tray and handed it to her. "The coffee will wake you up."

"Thank you." She took it and cradled the warm mug between her palms before taking a sip. "Oh, wow. You made it just as I like it." Her voice quivered, and she sniffled.

He canted his head. "What's going on, Marina? I thought you would like a little pampering."

"I love it." She sniffled again. "It's just that this is such a sweet gesture, and I'm a little overwhelmed."

Peter smiled. "You've done sweet things for me, and now I'm repaying the favor."

Did he mean the sex?

No, that wasn't it.

"What sweet things?"

He chuckled. "Have you forgotten the lunch you made for me when I was on guard duty?"

"It was nothing. Just a couple of sandwiches."

"And this is just scrambled eggs with toast, cheese, and fruit. Not a big deal either." He leaned over the tray and planted a gentle kiss on her lips. "I like doing nice things for you."

Emboldened by his actions and his words, or perhaps just tired of keeping her desires bottled up inside of her, Marina found the words spilling out of her, "Take me with you to your village." When his eyes widened, she rushed to add, "I won't be a burden. There are plenty of things I can do to earn my keep. I can clean houses, cook, or babysit. And I could be your girlfriend just for as long as you want me. I don't expect a commitment. I know that it's not possible between us."

Marina waited, her heart beating a frantic rhythm and her breath frozen in her throat, readying herself for the rejection that she was sure would come, and yet hoping that it wouldn't, that by some miracle Peter would say that he couldn't live without her and would take whatever years she could give him.

Watching him absorb her confession, she saw his expression change from surprise to concern, and then to regret.

Her heart sank to the pit of her gut like it was made from lead. She could practically hear the splash as it landed and disturbed the acid in her stomach, sending it up to her throat.

She was going to be sick, and she couldn't move because the damn tray was on her lap.

"Marina," Peter said as he reached for her hand. "I would have loved it, but the longer we stay together, the harder it will be to part. I care for you deeply, and I enjoy being with you more than I have with any woman, but the reality is that you will age, and I will not, and it's not something we can ignore." He smiled sadly. "I know that humans do not like to think about their mortality, and even less so about the mortality of their loved ones, and I totally understand that, but in this case, you need to remove your blinders and look far into the future. You won't like what you see."

Marina appreciated Peter's honesty, but his words cut her, nonetheless.

What did he think, that she was stupid? Ignorant? That she wasn't aware of her mortality and his immortality?

As if there was anything else she could think about.

"Nothing you've said is news to me," she said in a much steadier voice than she felt. "I'm not asking for forever, Peter. I'm asking for now. I need to get away from Safe Haven for a while to heal."

He arched a brow. "Heal from what?"

Marina swallowed. "My former boyfriend dumped me for someone he met in college. It hurt, but it wasn't so bad while he was gone most of the time. Then he finished his studies and came back with her to Safe Haven, and seeing them together every day, kissing, touching, exchanging loving looks, is just painful." She closed her eyes. "I thought we would get married, have kids, all the silly dreams girls have. Seeing him with her is a constant reminder of that lost dream." She opened her eyes and looked into Peter's. "It's not that I still love him. I don't think I ever truly loved him, but I loved the dream, and Nicolai carelessly shattered it. So, I lick my wounds and mourn the dream, and I need to be away from him and his new girlfriend to heal. That's why I want to move with you to your village."

Everything she'd said was the truth, but not the entire truth. She had also fallen for Peter and wanted him to love her back, but evidently his feelings for her didn't run as deep.

Was there something wrong with her that no one wanted to commit to her?

Whatever.

If Peter cared for her even a little, he would not deny her. It wasn't as if she was asking him to mend her broken pieces or to commit to a future that both of them knew was impossible. She was asking for a reprieve and a chance to find joy in the present without the shadows of her past looming over her.

Was it really so much to ask?

Gazing into Peter's eyes, she searched for understanding and acceptance, but all she saw was a conflict that was peppered with sadness and sweetened with affection.

56

PETER

In a way, Marina's story echoed Peter's. They had both been dumped by their partners and then had to see them too often for comfort.

No wonder they had been so drawn to each other. Still were. It wasn't just about the incredible physical attraction and shared kink. It was about the invisible wounds they were both still licking.

"I understand your predicament because I'm in the same boat." He chuckled. "And I don't mean this ship. Thankfully, the Kra-ell stayed behind to guard the village, so I didn't have to see Kagra during the cruise." He lifted his eyes to the ceiling. "Thank the merciful Fates."

Marina tilted her head. "I remember you mentioning dating her, but I didn't realize it was that serious."

Peter chuckled, the sound more bitter than he'd intended. "It was serious for me but not for Kagra.

She's a true Kra-ell, and she doesn't do relationships. I was a passing curiosity to her."

"Yeah, she's a badass. I would have never imagined you with someone like her. How did it even work between you? Did you take turns topping each other?"

Peter laughed. "You guessed it. She wanted to try something different, a gentler approach to lovemaking, and I was curious about being with a female who could easily dominate me. It was fun to experiment, but in the end, she must have realized that gentle didn't do it for her and that she preferred the Kra-ell's brutal sex games to my much milder ones."

Marina shivered. "Don't remind me."

Damn, he was such an ass. He'd forgotten that Marina had been a victim, forced to service the Kra-ell males. Mostly, it had been hybrids who weren't as bad as the purebloods, but still, she'd had to say yes more than no or suffer unpleasant consequences.

"I'm sorry." He squeezed her hand. "It was insensitive of me to bring that up. You probably want to forget about that part of your life."

"No, that's okay. I have no problem talking about it. I'd only been with hybrids, and most were careful with humans. They didn't want to break us. I shivered, thinking of the way it was between the purebloods. With the males and females being almost equally strong, their fight for dominance was ferocious."

He quirked a brow. "Did you witness it?"

"I wasn't in the room with them, but I heard the snarls, the growls, and the thrashing. I also saw them emerge from the chamber, bloodied, shredded, and either satisfied or humiliated. It was rough."

If a pureblooded Kra-ell male failed to subdue a pureblooded female, she would kick him out, and subsequently no other female would invite him to her bed. It was survival of the fittest, and only the strongest and most ruthless got to father children.

Still, Jade had chosen Phinas as her mate, and they seemed to be happy together despite those differences. Peter had hoped that the same would hold true for him and Kagra, but she hadn't felt for him what Jade felt for Phinas.

"I've always been adventurous," he admitted. "Maybe that was what attracted me to Kagra. She was different."

"Do you still care for her?" Marina asked in a near whisper.

He nodded. "I will always care for her as a friend. It wasn't her fault that I had unrealistic expectations." Kagra had said some things that had been unkind, but in retrospect, Peter realized that she wasn't being malicious. She'd been trying to help him get over the rejection. "The only one I should be angry at is myself. Kagra told me from the very start that she wasn't interested in anything serious, but my stupidly prideful mind was convinced that I would make her change her mind." He smiled. "My heart recovered from the breakup quickly, but my pride suffered a serious blow and took longer to get over itself."

Marina nodded. "I first noticed you in the dining room because you looked so defeated whenever you thought no one was looking your way."

Ouch. He'd hoped that she'd noticed him because he was so irresistibly handsome, charming, debonair. Not because he'd seemed beaten down.

Was that why she'd approached him in the first place?

"So that was my appeal?" Peter asked. "I was an easy target?"

Marina blushed. "It made you seem more approachable. After Nicolai, I couldn't handle another guy who was full of himself and believed I should worship at his feet because he graced me with his marvelous dick."

Peter couldn't stifle the laugh that bubbled up from his chest. "I think all males are guilty of thinking that their dicks are worthy of worship, myself included." He plucked a grape off the vine and lifted it to Marina's mouth. "And I have to say, you do that so reverently."

Remembering Marina on her knees, pleasuring him with her mouth and taking him deep, had his shaft turn into a club.

Wrapping her lips around the grape, she sucked it into her mouth while somehow managing to smile while doing it.

"You have such a talented mouth, Marina."

"Talented enough to get me an entrance into your village?"

Peter's smile wilted. He didn't like thinking that she was with him to gain entrance to the village. She could do that on her own without having to do any favors for him or anyone else.

"You don't need to do anything of the sort to come live in the village. You just have to get Kian's approval, and I don't see why he would deny it. A few of the former human occupants of Igor's compound decided to move to the village, and Kian okayed it."

She lifted her fingers. "Only two requests were granted, but I don't know how many applied."

"I don't know either. But since Kian offered anyone who wanted to come live in the village the option, there is no reason for him to refuse you. He wouldn't want you traveling back and forth for security reasons, but if you want to move permanently, he won't object. There are plenty of jobs you can get in the village. In fact, people will be fighting over you."

Her eyes shone with excitement. "Really? Like what?"

"All the ones you mentioned before, and more. The village café is always understaffed, Callie could use another server in her restaurant, and Atzil is looking for barmen and barmaids."

"That's awesome. I even know who to talk to about it."

Peter arched a brow. "Me?"

"Well, yes, but also Amanda. She's Kian's sister, and she seems to like me."

Warring emotions washed over Peter. On the one hand, he was glad that Marina now knew how to get what she wanted without his help, so if she stayed with him, it would be just because she wanted him and not what he could get for her. On the other hand, though, he was afraid that she would leave.

It was pathetic that he wanted her regardless of her motives, but he needed to at least know where her heart was.

Choosing a ripe strawberry, he lifted it to her mouth. "Open wide."

Marina chuckled. "Are you going to feed me the entire breakfast?"

"That's the plan." As he pushed the strawberry past her lips, he couldn't help imagining something else breaching the seal of her mouth. "When do you need to show up for your lunch shift?"

She finished chewing and swallowed. "I have time. You can finish feeding me breakfast and then feed me dessert."

Her gaze shifted downward to where his erection was pressing against the zipper of his pants, and as she licked her lips, he almost sagged with relief.

Marina wanted him just for him, regardless of any ulterior motives.

57

ONEGUS

"Hey, you're early," Onegus greeted Connor, a smile breaking across his face as he reached out for a friendly clap on his former roommate's shoulder. "Thanks for coming to help."

Connor had always been there for him during his bachelor days, making sure that he'd eaten, that his suits had been collected from the dry cleaners, and that his socks matched. As much as Onegus loved Cassandra, she was too busy with her own career to do those things for him, and he missed having Connor around.

"I knew you would be lost without me." Connor walked into the cabin and scanned it with a knowing look. "And I was right."

Onegus tried to see the place through Connor's eyes, but he couldn't find fault with anything.

There was plenty of whiskey, enough glasses for all the groomsmen, a box of great cigars courtesy of Kian, bowls filled with nuts and pretzels, and two large trays of cold cuts and crackers.

"What am I missing?"

"Decorations, of course." Connor smiled.

Onegus rubbed a hand over the back of his head. "I didn't bring any, and I don't think the guys will notice their absence. As long as the alcohol is flowing, no one is going to complain about the lack of decorations."

Connor shrugged. "Straights are so boringly predictable."

Onegus laughed, shaking his head. "True. But to be honest, even my Cassandra lacks your touch. You have no idea how often I come home to a cold house and think of how you always welcomed me with a home-cooked meal."

Connor's hand went to his chest. "You miss me."

"I do, but don't tell Cassandra. She will feel guilty, and she shouldn't. We both have demanding careers, and I'm just as much at fault as she is for the lack of homey feeling at our place."

Connor sighed. "Unlike you and Cassandra, I spend most of my days at home, and cooking relaxes me when I need a break from practicing or composing." He started rearranging the bottles to make the counter more presentable.

"No new love interests, then?"

There was a moment's hesitation, a flicker of something passing through Connor's eyes before he shrugged. "Actually, I'm seeing someone, but it's all very hush-hush. His friends don't know about his proclivities, and he's not ready to come out."

"One of the former Doomers?" Onegus guessed.

Connor confirmed with a nod. "We met at the café, and we started talking about my music, and one thing led to another, and yeah…that's all I can say at the moment."

"Are you happy?" Onegus asked.

Connor chuckled. "Ask me in three months. Right now, it's too new and stressful. We come from different worlds."

The former Doomers had left the Brotherhood a long time ago, and nearly a century was long enough to forget Mortdh's teaching and adopt more enlightened attitudes. By now, Connor's guy should have been okay to admit his preferences, but Onegus chose not to say anything.

"If he mistreats you, let me know." Onegus bared his fangs. "I'll take care of him."

Smiling, Connor clapped him on the back. "Thanks. I'll let him know you said that. And if…"

The buzzing sound of Onegus's phone interrupted their conversation, and as he pulled it out and looked at the screen, he saw that it was a message from Kri.

"Hold that thought." Onegus lifted his hand. "It's Kri, and she's asking if she can skip my bachelor party. I need to call her."

"Go ahead." Connor waved a dismissive hand. "In the meantime, I'll make everything look prettier."

Onegus started to type a response to Kri but then decided to call her and stepped into the bedroom. After closing the door, he called the head Guardian. "Enjoying your married bliss, Kri?"

"I am. Michael wants me all to himself today, but I feel bad about bailing on you after you made him full Guardian yesterday. Did I thank you for that already?"

"You don't need to thank me. Michael earned the promotion all on his own."

"He did, but the timing is a little suspicious. You must have cut corners to welcome him into the force on his wedding day."

"I did not. Bhathian approached me before the cruise to tell me that he thought Michael was ready. I just needed a little time to go over his test scores and evaluations from all his teachers. I didn't talk to you because I wanted it to be a surprise."

"Fine," she relented. "I'm not complaining. Michael always dreamt about being a full-fledged Guardian when he and I stood in front of the Clan Mother. You made his dream a reality, and I owe you for that, so if you want me to come to your bachelor party, I will."

"It's okay. You don't have to come if you want to spend the day with your new husband. All the other head Guardians are going to be here, though."

He could have invited Michael and solved the problem that way, but there were so many males who would feel offended for not getting invited that he had to keep it to a very specific group. All the head Guardians, Kian, Toven, Shai, and Connor.

Kri sighed. "I know that you all want to make me feel included, but the truth is that I don't feel comfortable attending the bachelor parties. I'm not one of the dudes, even though I can fight with the best of them." She chuckled. "After all, I showed up at the altar in a white dress, not a white tux, although I really wanted to."

"You looked beautiful."

"Yeah, yeah. I looked like a pro wrestler stuffed into a dress, but it is what it is, right? We play the hand we are dealt ."

Onegus chuckled. "You didn't look like a wrestler. You are a beautiful female, Kri. Beauty is not the exclusive domain of the petite and dainty. My Cassandra is neither, and to me, she's beauty personified."

Kri sighed. "Cassandra has style and attitude. I have shoulders and attitude. Not the same, but I accept your compliment. Thank you."

"You are welcome. You are coming to the wedding, right?"

"I wouldn't miss it for anything. Even I am curious about Cassandra's dress, and I normally couldn't care less."

"You and me both. She didn't let me see it. I'll see you tonight, Kri."

Ending the call, Onegus opened the door and walked into the transformed living room of his cabin.

"How did you do all this?" He turned in a circle.

"Magic." Connor waved a hand around the decorations. "And Amanda. I called her and told her about the sorry state of your cabin, and she sent Onidu with a bunch of stuff."

Onegus frowned. "How long have I been on the call with Kri that you managed to do all that?"

"Not long. Onidu helped." Connor shook his head. "The guy is fast. He was like a blur. I only had to point, and it was done before I lowered my finger. I would really love to have an Odu. Wouldn't it be great if every house in the village had one?"

"Yeah, it would."

Connor's wish was getting closer by the day to becoming a reality, but it was classified information that Onegus couldn't share with his former roommate.

MARINA

M arina wiped her hands on a dish towel and glanced at the new bin of dirty plates someone had rolled up to her scraping and sorting station by the sink.

"I thought I was done," she muttered under her breath.
"That's the last one," Dimitri said. "After you are done with it, you can go."

"Thanks." Marina let out a breath.

Her friends were being super nice about her and Larissa leaving early so they could get ready for the wedding tonight. Dimitri and Chester had volunteered to finish loading the dishwashers and put everything away on the racks once they were clean. The two had at least another hour of work before the kitchen switched gears and started preparations for the wedding tonight, but they were willing to do that for her and Larissa.

The only thing missing was the dress that Amanda had promised to bring, and Marina feared that she had forgotten about it and wasn't coming.

Poor Larissa would need to somehow squeeze herself into one of the dresses that Peter had borrowed for Marina from his relatives, and asking Amanda about getting into the village would have to wait for another opportunity.

She was almost done with the bin when she heard the doors to the kitchen swish open and then the clicking of high-heeled shoes, announcing the arrival of the female she'd been waiting for.

"Hello, Amanda." Marina turned around and glanced at the dress draped over the brunette's arm. "I see that you found something for Larissa."

"It was more difficult than I expected." Amanda lifted the hanger with the dress. "What do you think? Will it fit her?" She looked around the busy kitchen. "Where is she?"

"Larissa went to get a shower." Marina admired the shimmery purple fabric but didn't reach for it. "It's loose, so it should work." She reached for the dish towel to dry her hands. "Thank you so much." She took the dress. "I need to hang it somewhere safe until I'm done."

"Go," Mila said. "You are done."

"Thank you." She blew the head cook an air kiss and turned back to Amanda. "Would you like to come to my cabin and see how the dress fits Larissa?"

Amanda lifted her hand and glanced at her watch. "I guess I have time for a short visit."

"That's awesome." Marina cast her an appreciative smile before heading out of the kitchen.

When they were out in the corridor, she headed for the stairs instead of taking the elevator. She needed a few minutes of Amanda's time before they got to the cabin and the conversation shifted to Larissa and her dress.

"I want to ask you for another favor if that's okay." She cast Amanda a sidelong glance.

"Shoes?" Amanda asked. "I'm afraid that you are on your own in that department."

Marina chuckled. "No, not shoes. I would like to move to the village, and I was wondering who I should talk to about approving it."

Amanda canted her head. "Does this have to do with Peter? Because if it does, he could make a request on your behalf."

"Well, it does, and it doesn't. I like Peter a lot, and I hope we can be together for a little while, but I know that it won't work in the long term. I'm not happy at Safe Haven at the moment, and I need a change of scenery. I was told that there are plenty of positions in the village I could fill."

As they exited the stairwell and headed down the long corridor of staff cabins, Amanda's heels clacked and clicked on the hardwood flooring.

"The best way to approach this is to ask either Eleanor or Emmett to arrange a transfer. They will ask for approval, and if it's granted, you can pack your bags and accompany the Guardians who are heading home at the end of their tour of duty at Safe Haven. I think that they have two-week rotations there."

Marina's heart sank.

She'd hoped Amanda would intervene on her behalf, which would have guaranteed her request's approval, but she'd miscalculated. The princess either didn't have the sway Marina thought she had, or she didn't want to get involved in the lives of the humans.

"You should talk to Atzil," Amanda said as they stopped in front of Marina's door. "He's the guy who looks like an army drill sergeant and follows Ingrid around. The interior designer."

"I know who Ingrid is, and I know the guy you are talking about. Peter said that he's looking for barmaids for his bar."

Amanda flashed her a brilliant smile. "That's the one. Talk to him, tell him that you are interested in the position, and ask if he could send a request to Eleanor to arrange a transfer for you."

Marina frowned. "Doesn't your brother need to approve the request?"

"He does, but after Atzil and Eleanor ask on your behalf, it's going to be rubber-stamped."

Marina wasn't sure what a rubber stamp meant, but she guessed it meant that Kian would approve her transfer without putting up any roadblocks.

What Amanda suggested made a lot of sense, but it would take time to go through the official channels, and Marina knew that she would miss Peter terribly in the meantime. It was better that way, though. He hadn't been overjoyed at her suggestion of moving in with him, and it seemed like he intended to end things between them or keep them casual.

In either case, she should be glad to have an option that didn't involve him.

Except, she wasn't. Her heart ached, and the rejection stung.

Plastering a smile on her face, she looked up at Amanda. "Thank you for the great advice. I'll try to talk to Atzil about working at his bar during the wedding tonight."

59

CASSANDRA

"Oh, Mom. This is amazing." Cassandra turned in a circle in her mother's cabin. "You and Darlene have outdone yourselves."

The space was transformed, adorned with beautiful decorations that sparkled and shimmered, making the cabin look festive. Fancy little appetizers that had been prepared by the staff were spread out on tables that her mother and sister must have gotten from other cabins in addition to the one that had come with it.

"I'm glad you like it." Her mother pulled her into a warm hug while her sister waited her turn, standing to the side and smiling.

"Come here." Cassandra reached for Darlene's hand, pulling her into a group hug. "Thank you for doing this for me."

"It was my pleasure." Darlene untangled herself from the hug. "I got to see your dress and all the bridesmaids' dresses that you've been hiding from us."

Cassandra cast her a mock glare. "I wanted the reveal to be the highlight of my bachelorette party. You know, in the absence of strippers."

As her bridesmaids began to arrive, the cabin filled with laughter and excited chatter, each guest bringing their own unique energy to the gathering. Alena, Sylvia, Callie, Wonder, Mey, Jin, Eva, and Mia—each held a special place in Cassandra's heart, and having them there to celebrate with her meant the world to her.

She had never had so many friends. For most of her life, it had been her mother and her, living almost in hiding, and now they had a whole clan as their family.

Despite the hardships they had suffered, they had been extremely lucky to end up in this amazing community, and Cassandra thanked the Fates, the stars, and every supernatural force out there for the blessing she had been given.

Once the party was in full swing, Cassandra could feel the anticipation in the room rising. Her bridesmaids were casting glances at the closed door to her mother's bedroom and whispering conspiratorially about pretending to need to visit the bathroom so they could take a peek at her wedding dress and their bridesmaids' dresses.

She had kept the details under wraps, wanting to surprise everyone at her bachelorette party and adding an element of excitement to the celebration.

"Okay, okay." Cassandra lifted her hands in the air, scanning the eager faces of her friends. "I know you've all been dying to see what I picked out for tonight, and I promised that I would reveal the dresses at my party. Please follow me." She led them to the bedroom, where the dresses hung on a mobile rack, hidden beneath silk covers to add to the mystery and grandeur of the reveal.

Turning to her bridesmaids, she announced, "First, your dresses." With a dramatic flourish, she pulled back the covers, unveiling the array of bridesmaid dresses she had chosen.

They weren't custom made, but then that wasn't her mode of operation. Cassandra was an expert at finding spectacular designer stuff that was ready to wear with just a few alterations.

The bridesmaid dresses were the creation of Ursula Bemonir, an up-and-coming designer who was still trying to find her way to the top. They were elegant and modern, each tailored to flatter the individual wearer while maintaining a cohesive look for the group. The fabric was a soft, shimmering gold, designed in a sophisticated, floor-length sheath style. Each dress had a unique touch, with a subtle variation in necklines, sleeves, or straps, allowing each brides-maid to shine in her own way.

"They are all stunning." Alena smoothed a hand over her protruding belly. "Which one is mine?"

Cassandra removed it from the rack and handed it to her. "It's not a maternity dress, but it's loose enough to fit your cute little belly."

Alena chuckled. "I think my belly passed the cute and little stage a month ago, but I'll take the compliment."

"I wanted you all to feel stunning and yet comfortable." Cassandra removed the dresses one at a time from the rack and handed them to their owners. "Would you like to change into them now?"

Darlene shook her head. "You have to show us your gown first."

Her sister had already seen it, but she was saying that for the benefit of the others.

"Very well."

The room fell into an expectant silence as Cassandra moved towards the last covered garment, and as she pulled down the zipper, she couldn't hear anyone breathing.

The gown was breathtaking in its simplicity. Delicate spaghetti straps set the stage for a graceful, cowled neckline, while the bias-cut design and soft satin fabric elegantly draped the silhouette. The voluminous train and alluring low back added a daring touch to the otherwise reserved dress.

"Wow, Cassandra, it's gorgeous," Mia breathed. "You are going to look stunning in it."

"Put it on," her mother said. "I want to see you in it."

It was still several hours until the wedding, but the dress was such a simple garment that it was no problem to put it on and then take it off.

"As you wish."

A round of applause followed her acquiescence, and when she put it on along with the matching shoes, her friends ahhed and oohed.

Amanda shook her head. "I don't know how you do it, Cassandra, but you find hidden gems in places I wouldn't even think to look."

"Thank you." Cassandra beamed. "Now it's your turn, ladies. Put on your dresses, and if any last-minute alterations are needed, my mother will whip out her sewing kit."

60

MARINA

A sea of dresses was spread over Marina and Larissa's beds. Some were from Frankie and Mia, others were from Peter's relatives, and one was from Amanda, or rather the person she borrowed it from.

Amanda refused to disclose the information for some reason. Perhaps the lady who had donated the dress was embarrassed about letting someone else wear it, or maybe she was just the shy type who didn't want Larissa to thank her.

"So, what's the verdict?" Marina asked.

Lace and chiffon, silk and brocade, they came in all shapes, fabrics, and colors, and the one she had on now was red, had a tight bodice, and was short in the front and long in the back.

Larissa regarded her with a hand on her hips and pursed lips. "It's hard to decide. They all look so good on you, but this one is a little too much."

"I agree." Marina lowered the zipper in the back and peeled off the dress.

Thankfully, the dress Amanda had brought for Larissa fit her with the help of a travel sewing kit and some creative adjustments. Amanda hadn't stayed to see the transformation, leaving moments after arriving, saying that she needed to make an appearance at the bachelorette party for tonight's bride.

It was so weird that they were celebrating the bachelor and bachelorette parties on the same day as the weddings, but maybe it was the immortals' tradition.

"Since you are wearing purple, I'll go with black." Marina draped the red dress over the bed and lifted the one that was the most flattering on her. "I can't do red with my blue hair, and the gold one is a bit too much, so black it is."

Larissa nodded. "Black is always a safe bet." She patted the curlers on top of her head. "Will you help me with my hair and makeup?"

"Of course." Marina pulled on a t-shirt and motioned for Larissa to sit on the only desk chair in the cabin.

"Just not too much foundation," Larissa warned. "I don't want to look like I have plaster on my face."

The prospect of being Jay's date for tonight excited her roommate, but it also made her a little jittery, which wasn't surprising. It was the first wedding that Larissa was attending as a guest. It wasn't Marina's first, but she was even more nervous tonight than she was the first time.

She'd lowered her guard this morning and blurted to Peter that she'd noticed him because he'd looked defeated. The guarded look in his eyes had said it all.

He was a smart guy, and he'd put two and two together, realizing that she thought him easy prey. She'd managed to salvage the situation with some clever wording that hadn't been a lie, but in retrospect, it would have been better to come clean.

The weight of the deceit pressed down on her.

She was in love with Peter, and with that came the fear of losing him if he learned the truth. But the flip side was that keeping it from him was not healthy in the long run.

Yeah, as if there was a long run.

There was no future for them, and even though Peter might have feelings for her, he wouldn't allow himself to fall in love with her because that would be plain stupid.

Marina finished removing the hair rollers and brushed out Larissa's locks with her fingers. "I think it looks perfect the way it is." Her voice wobbled a little, and her friend noticed.

Looking at her through the mirror, Larissa frowned. "What's wrong? You've been moody the entire day."

Marina had thought that she'd done a good job of hiding her inner turmoil, but apparently, Larissa knew her too well to be fooled by her fake smiles.

Her friend's earnestly concerned expression broke the dam, and Marina found herself wanting to confess everything. "I've fallen into my own snare," she said after telling Larissa her plan. "I love Peter, and he cares about me, but not the same way I care about him."

Larissa's eyes were soft as she regarded Marina in the mirror. "You need to tell Peter the truth and get it off your chest. Honesty is scary, but it's liberating. If what you have with Peter is real, he'll understand that you were desperate, and he will forgive you. If not, then he's not worthy of your love, and it's better to find that out sooner rather than later."

Larissa was a simple girl, but what she'd said made perfect sense, her words echoing the thoughts that had been circling in Marina's mind.

The fear of Peter's reaction had held her back, but she couldn't allow their relationship, as fleeting and short as it might be, to be built on a foundation of lies and omissions.

No matter how terrifying the prospect, she owed Peter the truth.

61

MARGO

"I'm so relieved," Negal said as he held the clinic door open for Margo. "Karen is doing amazingly well."

"She is," Margo agreed. "Even the doctor seems surprised that Karen woke up so quickly from her coma."

Bridget had murmured something about Karen's transition being unusual because she'd been unconscious for nearly twenty-four hours and then woke up as if nothing had happened. No relapses. Not even sleepiness.

Karen was chatting with her family and her visitors as if she was recuperating from a light cold, not a complete overhaul of her body. She still looked a little tired, but the fine lines around her eyes were nearly gone.

"Thank the merciful Fates, she's okay," Negal said, sounding a little smug as if he had something to do with Karen's rapid recovery.

It must be her imagination.

He was simply happy that Karen was doing well. So what if it was strange that he showed so much interest in a woman who was a mother of five and in a loving relationship with the father of three of those children? He'd told her that he was friends with Karen's partner but observing them interacting hadn't convinced Margo of that.

There was more to this story than he was letting on. Perhaps the number of children Karen had was what fascinated him about the woman.

Where Negal came from, people counted themselves lucky if they had one child, and given the scarcity of children on the cruise, the immortals were facing the same problem.

Margo's gut twisted. Would she and Negal ever be blessed with a child? Would he want children with her?

It was one of the many things they needed to talk about, but maybe not today. It was too soon to have that kind of talk.

Had Frankie and Dagor discussed children already?

Mia and Toven had, but they had been together for a while, and Toven already had at least two children he knew of, and there could potentially be more. Mia had told her that Toven had been convinced that he was infertile, and since he had been around for seven thousand years, that meant a hell of a lot of women he had been with, and as it turned out, when gods took humans as partners, their chances of creating offspring increased dramatically. The guy could have hundreds of children he didn't know about.

As they entered the elevator, Negal wrapped his arm around her waist. "Do you want to go shopping or sightseeing in Mazatlán? We still have a few hours before the wedding."

Margo scrunched her nose. "I would rather go up to the Lido deck and have a drink. But if you want to see the town, I'll come with you."

"I'm okay with skipping it." He pressed the button for the top deck. "But I'm surprised that you don't want a shore excursion."

She didn't want Negal to buy more things for her, and given their prior experience in Puerto Vallarta, he would insist, and she would cave, and then she would owe him even more money that he would refuse to accept.

"It's too hot and humid." She smiled sweetly at him. "And besides, there is so much we still need to talk about, and I'd rather do that over drinks."

"Like what?"

She rolled her eyes. "Did you forget already? You promised to tell me more about your life."

He made a face. "Unless you want to hear about count-less missions, most of them boring, there isn't really much to tell."

"Are you kidding me? There is so much I want to know that has nothing to do with your missions. Tell me about your parents, what they do for a living, the kind of people they are, and whether they were strict or lenient with you when you were growing up. Who was your first crush? What happened to her?"

Shaking his head, Negal chuckled and led her out of the elevator and onto the Lido deck. "Slow down, my love. I can only answer one question at a time."

He called her his love, and her heart fluttered like it had wings. The happiness bubbling inside her made her feel as if she were walking on air rather than the solid deck of the ship.

Leaning against the railing, Negal turned to look at her with amusement in his eyes. "What's that smile about? Did I say something funny?"

"You called me your love," she said, her eyes locking with his. "I like the sound of it."

Negal's expression softened. "I love you."

She batted her eyelashes. "Say it again. I love the way it sounds."

"I love you." He smiled. "Now say it back to me."

She lifted her hand and cupped his cheek. "I love you, and I don't care how absurd it is for me to feel that way after knowing you for three days." She stretched on her tiptoes and kissed his lips.

When he wrapped his arms around her and pressed her to his chest, her unanswered questions and the uncertainties of their future faded away.

62

KIAN

Yamanu draped his arm over Onegus's shoulders. "I hope Cassandra doesn't blow up anything during the wedding."

The Guardian had been drinking nonstop since the start of Onegus's bachelor party and was now a little unsteady on his feet. The others were only in slightly better shape, with the exceptions being Onegus and Kian.

Onegus because the chief was always on alert, and Kian for the same reason.

Trouble seemed to follow them no matter how hard they tried to stay away from it.

Anandur laughed. "We should be fine as long as we keep her away from the punchbowl."

When Cassandra had first joined the clan, she'd started training to learn how to control her strange power, but Kian knew that she hadn't been doing that nearly as intensively as she should have. Lately, she'd been busy revamping the entire style of advertising for the cosmetics company she worked for and had halted her training altogether.

Regrettably, she loved her job and had no intention of quitting. Her only concession to the secretive nature of the clan had been to do some of her work from home.

Onegus grimaced. "Cassy hasn't accidentally blown anything up in a long while, so don't even think of teasing her about it."

Anandur lifted his hands in the air. "I wouldn't dare."

Everyone laughed, including Kian, probably because each of them had been privy to one of her chilly looks at one time or another.

Nothing and no one intimidated Cassandra, which was what made her such a perfect mate for Onegus. The chief only appeared to be easygoing because of his innate charm, but he wouldn't have risen to his position if he was lenient or overly accommodating.

When Onegus's phone buzzed with a message, Kian assumed it was his bride checking up on him, but as the chief pulled out the device and read the text, his deep frown indicated otherwise.

Kian was not the only one who noticed, and the change in Onegus's demeanor had a chilling effect on everyone present.

As they all fell silent, the jazz music playing in the background suddenly sounded too loud, and Connor did everyone a service by turning it off.

Noticing the sudden quiet, Onegus shifted his gaze away from the screen and looked at Kian. "The guys watching the surveillance feed from Modana's estate report that Carlos Modana has arrived with two individuals, who they strongly suspect are Doomers."

Kian's blood chilled in his veins. "This is bad news. If they manage to break through Kalugal's compulsion and thralling, they could uncover the truth about Julio's religious awakening." He pulled out his phone and called his cousin.

When Kalugal finally answered, the shrill sound of a baby crying in the background made Kian grimace. "Hello, Kian. Can I call you later?"

"I'm sorry, but this cannot wait. Carlos Modana showed up at the estate with two individuals who could be Doomers. Is there a chance they can break through what you've done to Julio?"

"Hold on," Kalugal said.

The baby's crying stopped abruptly, probably because Kalugal walked into another room and closed the door.

"They can't break through my compulsion and thralling unless they have a compeller stronger than me among them, and we know that they don't. The Brotherhood's only powerful compeller is my father, and he never leaves the island, so the only way they can have another one is if Lokan is not as well informed as he thinks he is, and the Brotherhood has gained one in recent years."

The possibility of a young Doomer developing an extraordinary compulsion ability was almost nonexistent, and even if that had somehow happened, Navuh would have done away with the guy. He didn't want anyone around him to have the power to usurp him.

Kian let out a breath. "I know it's not a good time, but I need you to meet me in the control room. I want you to take a look at those suspected Doomers."

"I'll head out there in a few minutes."

"Thank you. I'll see you there." Kian ended the call.

When Onegus followed Kian to the door, he stopped him with a hand on his arm. "Stay. This is your bachelor party, and I can handle this without you."

Onegus shook his head. "Duty always comes before pleasure for me, Kian. I'm coming with you."

63

NEGAL

After sitting down and ordering drinks, Negal took Margo's hand and asked the question that had been bothering him ever since Margo had admitted her difficulties with intimacy.

After last night, he knew that there was nothing wrong with her. She was sexy, passionate, and responsive, so the only thing he could think of was some creep in her past had left a bad impression.

"I want to ask you something that might be upsetting to you, so if you don't want to answer, that's fine."

She frowned. "After such a preamble, I'm scared of what you want to ask me."

Had she guessed what he had on his mind, or was she imagining something worse?

"Did something happen to you to make you afraid of intimacy? Did you have a bad experience?"

Margo seemed relieved, so she must have imagined a worse question, although he could not think of what it could be.

"Only two really bad things have happened to me. One was Mia almost dying and then having her legs amputated. I forced myself to remain strong for her sake and for Frankie's, but I was terrified and devastated. The second bad thing was getting drugged and kidnapped by Alberto and delivered to his boss."

Her intimacy problems had started long before her latest ordeal, so that wasn't the cause. Could there be a connection to what had happened to Mia?

"Were you afraid to get close to anyone because you feared losing them like you almost lost Mia?"

Margo shook her head. "It has nothing to do with that. It was the pedophiles who ogled me when I was too young for such attention. It repulsed and scared me, but I wasn't molested, if that's what you are thinking." She grimaced. "There were a few instances of that almost happening, one of them with my uncle, but I was always cautious, so it never came to that."

He bared his fangs. "Is that uncle still around?"

"Yeah, but he lives in Europe now. I had an active imagination when I was a teenager, and it's possible that he really had no nefarious intentions when he wanted me to go with him into a dark corner of the park, so, sheathe those fangs and forget that I ever told you that."

Could it be that there had been more to it than Margo remembered? Sometimes, people repressed memories to protect themselves from pain. Only a trained therapist could help her process that, but perhaps Negal could help in some other way.

Reaching for her other hand, he held both and looked into her eyes. "No one will dare to ogle you while I'm around," he vowed.

It didn't have the impact he'd hoped for.

Margo laughed, a burst of genuine amusement that lightened the moment. "They'll just do it behind your back."

He bared his fangs. "Let them try."

"That's sweet." She lifted one of their conjoined hands and kissed his knuckles. "But I'm a grown woman now, and ogling me does not merit being torn apart, so please, retract your fangs and don't bite anyone's head off."

"Yes, ma'am." Negal commanded his fangs to recede.

"Wow, that's impressive control. How did you make them shrink so fast?"

He chuckled. "First of all, the word shrink has a very negative connotation when applied to any part of my male anatomy, which includes my fangs. And secondly, control comes with age and lots of practice."

"There's so much about you I don't know," she said, looking up at him with eyes filled with wonder. "I don't even know how old you are."

He'd walked into a trap of his own making. Why had he mentioned age? What if she had a problem with how old he was compared to her?

Negal took a deep breath. "Brace yourself for a shock," he warned.

Margo's brow furrowed. "That old?" she asked, her tone laced with a hint of humor.

Perhaps he was overthinking it, and she didn't care how old he was.

He nodded, the truth finally spilling out. "I'm afraid so. Not counting the time I spent in stasis, I'm five hundred and twenty-two years old. But, since I've served in the fleet for a very long time, I've logged in thousands of years of stasis."

Negal braced himself for a look of shock, but to his astonishment, Margo shrugged. "Toven is over seven thousand years old," she said casually as if discussing the weather. "Numbers are irrelevant, but all the experiences you've had during your service must be fascinating. I bet there are thousands of stories you can tell me from missions all over the galaxy."

He looked into her sparkling eyes and saw only excited curiosity. She really didn't care that he was ancient compared to her.

"Let me see." He rubbed a hand over his jaw. "Where should I start?"

"Anywhere you want. You can just pick one." She leaned closer. "The dragon world should be exciting. Tell me about that."

He laughed. "If fear of being torched alive is exciting, then yes. But honestly, I'm not a thrill-seeker, and I didn't enjoy that. Despite what you might think, I'm not indestructible."

"But you're a god. You should be impervious to dragon fire."

Negal shook his head. "Even if I was, which I'm not, it would have been painful in the extreme. My body can heal fast, but not fast enough to remake itself from ash."

Margo swallowed. "Suddenly, I'm no longer interested in hearing about dragons. I don't want to think about you being in mortal danger." She sucked in a breath. "What else can kill a god?"

"Many things. No one can survive without a head or a heart, so if either is removed or explodes, it is death for a god."

Margo grimaced. "Let's not talk about that. Tell me about your world."

That was much easier because he'd spent a lot of time thinking about Anumati's injustices.

"Our society has a class system that distinguishes the royals from the commoners. Royals glow, and commoners do not. Royals can suppress their glow and pretend to be commoners if they want to, but commoners can't pretend to be royal. Within the royals, there are degrees of luminosity, and those who shine the brightest are the elite. Each class attends different schools, which dictate the universities they move on to, creating a system that favors the elite and is nearly impossible to break into for someone like me, Dagor, and Aru. The ironic part is that we are all supposed to be equal because, supposedly, we have equal rights under the law, but that's the biggest lie of all. The vast majority of Anumatian citizens are considered superfluous, and only the elites who support the Eternal King have a voice. The rest of us have very limited options. Every move we make is monitored, evaluated, and judged, and we have to obey orders without question."

"You are a soldier. So, of course, you have to obey."

Negal shook his head. "It's true for all commoners, and that's why the resistance was born. People are fed up with the system, the lies, the lack of say in how they live their lives."

Eyes full of understanding, Margo squeezed his hand. "It's not as bad here in the West, at least not yet, but things are rapidly heading in that direction. I hoped that the gods would be more enlightened. I hoped that they'd created a better world."

Negal smiled. "One day we will, but for that to happen, the current system needs to be abolished, and the Eternal King's reign needs to come to an end."

64

KIAN

In the control room, Kian, Onegus, and Kalugal huddled around the screen showing Modana's office as captured by the surveillance cameras Julio had installed there.

The idea to hack into the existing surveillance network was brilliant, especially since the cameras they had been able to procure in Puerto Vallarta hadn't been the kind that were easy to hide. Still, Kian didn't like to rely only on that, and they had installed backup listening devices in case Modana disconnected his own cameras, or someone sabotaged his network.

The Modana brothers had just left, probably to continue shouting at each other out of their guests' earshot, and as the two males switched to talking in their own language, the guttural sounds proved beyond a shadow of a doubt who they were.

Kian strained to catch familiar words or phrases, but his knowledge of the Doomer language was limited.

They talked fast, and with too many words meaningless to him, their conversation was a frustrating puzzle he couldn't solve, but that was in part why he had asked Kalugal to join him.

His cousin should still be fluent in it.

"They've figured it out," Kalugal said after a moment. "They suspect that Julio Modana was thralled or compelled."

A cold shiver ran down Kian's spine. "How?"

Kalugal listened for a few more moments. "It seems that Carlos told them about his brother's sudden religious awakening, and it didn't take a genius to connect the dots to the immortals they suspected of eliminating their team in Acapulco."

Kian motioned for Reuben to pause the replay before turning back to Kalugal. "Did they say that, or are you extrapolating?"

"They said it. They came along with Carlos to investigate who was behind Julio's transformation, and if they could, to undo it." Kalugal smirked. "Obviously, they can't, and that's why Julio and Carlos are at each other's throats."

Onegus leaned away and crossed his arms over his chest. "Are you absolutely sure that they can't break through your thralling? I know that they can't override your compulsion, but thralling is simpler to detect and undo."

Kalugal shook his head. "No, they can't break through my thralling because I reinforced it with compulsion, but they might try to introduce a different thrall to lead Julio away from the path we've set him on. I don't think they will be successful, but they might try."

Onegus shook his head. "I wish I had your confidence. Why do you think they will not succeed in thralling him into going back to the way he was?"

Kalugal regarded the chief with his trademark smirk that conveyed how much smarter he believed himself to be. Not that his belief was unfounded, but it wouldn't have hurt Kalugal to have some humility.

"My compulsion and thralling were strong because they were not applied in a vacuum. Julio was raised religiously, but as a young man, he believed himself to be invincible and above the law. As he got older, though, he started to be concerned with the fate of his eternal soul, and he was convinced that he was going to hell for all the evil he had done."

Kian chuckled. "If there is a hell, he would sure go there."

Kalugal gave him one of those condescending smiles. "You don't know for a fact whether there is no hell or there is. No one does."

"True," Kian conceded. "No one has come back from beyond the veil to enlighten us either way."

Kalugal nodded. "Many humans believe in them, though, and Julio is one of them. I reinforced his belief in his

God's endless capacity for forgiveness. I also made him believe that the Mother of God spoke to him, telling him that his redemption must start on the earthly plane. His good deeds have to equal his evil deeds for his soul to stand a chance at the end-of-life trial that he will face. Julio grabbed on to that chance with both hands. He won't let go unless someone much more powerful than I am forces him to do it, and even then, there is a higher chance he will go insane than go back to the way he was."

Kalugal's lengthy explanation eased some of Kian's concern, but Julio resuming his evil ways was not the only thing to be worried about in regard to the Doomers' presence.

Kian was glad that the ship was currently at sea and that the Doomers didn't know where the immortals who had annihilated their Acapulco team and their cohorts were, where they had come from, and how they had found out about the Modana brothers' connection to the atrocities committed in Acapulco.

"Let's hear the rest of it," Kalugal said. "Maybe there was more said that could clue us in to what they are planning."

Kian motioned for the Guardian to un-pause the replay.

As it started from the exact point at which it had been stopped, one sentence that Kian understood without Kalugal's translation raised his hackles.

"Is it all about the woman?" one of the Doomers asked. "The one the tour guide said his clients were picking up in Cabo San Lucas? Or maybe the other one, the actress that Julio was obsessed with?"

The other Doomer shrugged. "The actress is a nobody that he wanted to fuck, but I don't know what part the other one plays in the story. The goddess's corrupt and immoral female descendants might be fighting along with their males, so maybe that Margo woman is one of them, and she was sent to the hotel to spy on us."

"The actress could be a plant, too," the first Doomer said.

Kian signaled for the Guardian to pause the replay. "I think I understood what they were saying, but I want to be sure."

When Kalugal translated, Kian nodded. "Yeah, I was afraid of that. If they find out about Margo, they can find out about Frankie and Mia too. They've been friends since they were little girls, and their families know each other. It will be very easy for the Doomers to find the connection. We can keep Mia's grandparents in the village, but Frankie has a huge family. How the hell are we going to protect them all?"

Kalugal lifted his hand. "Let's hear the rest of it first. Maybe they didn't follow the thread."

Kian waved a hand, and the replay continued.

The first Doomer shook his head. "Margo's background was checked, and her human connections were real, not the fabricated kind to make her look human."

"She could be working with the clan," the second Doomer said. "Her parents think that she's in a witness protection program. We use humans to do our dirty work for us all the time. The enemy could be doing the same thing."

The first Doomer huffed out a breath. "They pretend to be such do-gooders, when, in fact, they are rotten to the core. They not only allow their women to be morally loose but encourage it."

When Kalugal was done translating, the eyes of everyone in the room were glowing with rage.

Onegus shook his head. "Their disconnect from reality is infuriating. Do they really think that denying their own females immortality, forcing them into prostitution, and turning them into breeders for the cause is morally superior?"

"They do," Kalugal said. "They believe that a female's only value is her womb and that it belongs to the males of her family to do with as they please, all in the name of Mortdh's cause."

As the two Doomers continued spouting Navuh's malicious propaganda against the clan, Kian signaled to Reuben to stop the replay.

"That's sick," Reuben murmured. "I wish we could wipe the Brotherhood off the face of the Earth." He smiled apologetically at Kalugal. "No offense to you, sir. You are no longer a member."

"None was taken, but you need to remember that they are what they are being preached to believe and act upon day in and day out for millennia, and that preaching is constantly reinforced by my father's compulsion. And to start with, people are rather easily brainwashed, humans and immortals alike, and males in particular are easily incited to violence, although females are not much better." Kalugal smiled sadly. "That still doesn't excuse the evils the Doomers commit, but the Brotherhood is not the only evil organization in the world."

Kian grimaced. "We can't even take the Doomers out. There are too few of us. The only way for us to change the world is the way my mother envisioned, by spreading the right ideas. The problem is that one step forward is usually followed by two steps back, and right now, we are on a backward trajectory."

65

ONEGUS

Onegus let out a breath. "We need to ignore their hateful propaganda. These paragons of morality believe that rape is justified as punishment of female disobedience, and so is beheading those who dare to voice opposition, even in the most trivial way, to the way things are run."

He let out another breath, breathed in, then out, repeating the process a few times until his fangs stopped itching and his venom glands stopped pulsating.

The enemy was not here for him to attack, and fueling his own anger served no one.

"I apologize." He turned to Kian. "We need to focus on Margo's family, and perhaps Frankie's and Mia's as well. Mia's grandparents are at their Arcadia home during the cruise, which leaves them exposed."

Kalugal looked at his phone's screen and winced. "Jacki and I are invited to Lokan and Carol's cabin, so if you can continue without me, I should be going."

"Go." Kian clapped him on his back. "Thanks for the help. I might call you later, though, to ask your and Lokan's advice."

"No problem." Kalugal said his goodbyes to the others and hurried out of the control room.

As Kian and Onegus stepped outside, Onegus turned to Kian. "I wonder what made Margo's family think that she was in the witness protection program. She couldn't call them with the phone she was given, and her friends were warned not to let her use theirs. But maybe she asked one of them to call her family for her and tell them the story."

Kian nodded. "I was wondering the same thing and reached the same conclusion, and I'm not happy about it. They should have known better. If Margo's parents didn't know anything, they would have been in less danger."

"Not really." Onegus started toward the elevator. "Margo's future sister-in-law raised the alarm, calling the police and notifying them that Margo was missing. They would have been worried sick about her and would have probably booked a flight to Cabo to search for her. The witness protection story was actually not a bad idea."

"I'm not sure about that. Our problem now is how to protect Margo's family while our entire force is here. I could lift the lockdown and ask Jade to organize a team to watch over them, but the last thing I want is for the Doomers to discover the Kra-ell's existence."

They stopped in front of the elevators, and Onegus pressed the button. "I guess it's Turner to the rescue once more."

"I guess so." Kian pulled out his phone and texted the strategist.

His phone rang a moment later, just as the elevator doors opened.

"What's up, Kian?" Turner asked.

"Can you come to my cabin?"

"When do you need me?"

"Right now." Kian leaned against the wall. "We have a situation."

Turner chuckled. "A new one?"

"It's still the same shit, just with a different flavor."

Turner laughed. "Give me five minutes." He ended the call.

Kian turned to Onegus. "Go back to your party. There isn't much you can help with now, and your guests are waiting for you."

Everything inside Onegus rebelled against the dismissal. He was the chief Guardian, and it was his duty to be on top of things, even if someone else was managing a part of the mission.

It was a matter of principle.

Ever since Turner had joined the clan, Kian had been entrusting him with handling all their hired human teams, and with all of the Guardians stuck on the ship, there really wasn't much Onegus could do for Margo's family.

Still, that wasn't the reason he was willing to acquiesce. Today was a special day in his life, and for once, he should dedicate himself to celebrating with his friends and letting someone else be in charge.

Being a Guardian meant always being on duty, always vigilant, and moments of happiness were all the more precious for their rarity and shouldn't be squandered.

"Call me if you need anything." Onegus pressed the button for his deck.

"You know I will. Try to enjoy what's left of your day."

As he made his way back to the party, Onegus deliberated whether to tell his friends about the Doomers and the threat to Margo's family.

Most of his guests were head Guardians, and he would need to tell them at some point even though there was nothing any of them could do.

Perhaps he could wait with the upsetting news and not ruin the party.

Toven was there as well, and he should know about the threat to Mia's grandparents, even though Onegus considered that a very remote risk. If the Doomers found the connection, they would disregard Margo's obviously human childhood friends. In fact, their friendship might protect Margo as well. Nothing in her history connected her to immortals.

66

KIAN

As Kian opened the door to his cabin, he found Syssi standing in the tiny foyer with Allegra in her arms. Their daughter was dressed in an adorable little swimming suit adorned with a pink tutu, indicating they were on their way to the pool.

"Hello, my lovelies." He kissed Syssi's cheek and then Allegra's. "Are you going swimming with Mommy?"

Allegra patted her tutu.

"It's very pretty." Kian smiled.

"What happened?" Syssi adjusted Allegra in her arms. "Why aren't you at Onegus's bachelor party?"

"I'll tell you in a moment. First, I need a hug from my daughter." He took Allegra from her and peppered her face with tiny kisses, eliciting adorable giggles.

His heart was so full of love that it could burst from happiness, and for a moment, he allowed himself to enjoy it and forget about the latest gathering storm.

"Don't keep me in suspense," Syssi said. "What happened?"

"Carlos Modana arrived at his brother's mansion with two Doomers," he said softly, not to upset Allegra. "They found out about Margo and suspect that she's somehow connected to us."

Syssi's eyes widened. "What are you going to do?"

Kian sighed, shifting Allegra to one arm while wrapping the other one around Syssi's shoulders. "Turner is on his way. I want to ask him to station some of his people to watch over Margo's family and possibly Frankie's and Mia's as well. The Doomers might dig deeper for information about Margo, and if they do, they will find out about her two best friends."

Syssi nodded. "It's a good idea to cover all the bases. Mia's grandparents are in their Arcadia home, and we can't tell them to go to the village because it's on lockdown, and even if we could lift the lockdown, we shouldn't because they might already be watched."

"My thoughts exactly."

"Nana." Allegra pointed at the door.

"We are going, sweetie." Syssi shifted her gaze back to Kian. "I'm meeting my parents and Andrew and Nathalie at the pool, so you will have the place to yourself to strategize with Turner for as long as you need to." She lifted on her toes and kissed his cheek. "Poor baby. You never get a break."

He chuckled. "I object to being called a baby, and it's all fine as long as I can come home to you and Allegra at the end of the day." He planted a soft kiss on top of their daughter's head before giving her back to her mother. "Enjoy the pool, my loves."

As Kian opened the door for them, he found Turner standing outside. The guy's severe expression softened when he saw Allegra. "Hello, little lady. You look absolutely adorable in this bathing suit. Are you going swimming?"

"Nana," Allegra said with a satisfied smile.

"We are going to meet Grandma at the pool," Syssi said. "By the way, how is your grandson?"

Turner's face split in a grin. "Big. That boy is going to be even taller than Douglas."

"I would love to see his pictures if you got them," Syssi said. "But perhaps some other time. Allegra is impatient, and you have a new emergency to deal with."

"Right." Turner's smile morphed into a frown. "I still don't know what this latest one is about."

"Come in, and I'll tell you." Kian ushered him inside and waved goodbye to his family.

Turner walked over to the bar and pulled out a bar stool. "Do I need a shot of whiskey to hear your news?"

"No, but you can get one anyway." Kian poured them both a drink from one of his finest bottles and told Turner about Carlos and the Doomers, as well as his concern about Margo's family.

"You need to call Margo and tell her what's going on," was the first thing Turner said.

"I know, but I need to know what to tell her. Can you arrange for someone to watch over her family?"

"Of course." Turner pulled out his phone. "I'm texting my assistant to find out who is available in Los Angeles for immediate deployment."

"Does your assistant work on a Saturday?"

"She's not in the office, but she knows she must always be on call."

Turner's mode of operation was to keep a skeleton office staff, and subcontract operations to a select group of former Special Ops who had exchanged their uniforms for civilian clothing and continued doing what they had done before but for better pay.

When Turner was done texting, he shifted his gaze to Kian. "Are you calling Margo?"

"I'm waiting for your assistant to tell us if anyone is available to send to her parents' house."

"Just ask Margo to come here and don't tell her why. By the time she arrives, I'll have an answer regarding availability, and I will need to know where to send the team. The fastest way to get all the information I need is to talk to Margo."

MARGO

Margo's head was spinning with all that Negal had told her about his home world, the colonies, and the many missions he had completed. If she had Mia's talent for storytelling, she could have written a science fiction series based on Negal's adventures alone.

"Your life has been so exciting." She gave his hand a light squeeze before reaching for the chilled cucumber water Bob had served her. "You must be bored out of your mind here on Earth."

Negal laughed. "I've condensed centuries of existence and told you only the highlights. What do you think happened the rest of the time?"

She lifted one eyebrow. "Boring stuff?"

"A lot of it." He frowned. "Your phone is ringing."

"It is?" She bent over, lifted her purse off the floor, and pulled out her phone. "Apparently it is." She looked at the screen, expecting to see Mia or Frankie's name. Instead, Kian's name flashed brightly, causing her eyes to widen in surprise.

"Why is he calling me?" she murmured as she accepted the call. "Hello, Kian?"

"Hi. I'm sorry to disturb whatever you're doing, but I need you to come to my cabin. I'll text you the number. My cabin is at the top residential deck."

"I know where it is."

"Good. Please, don't delay."

"I won't. I'll be there in a few moments," she said, her mind racing with possible explanations for why Kian wanted to see her so urgently.

When he ended the call without giving her the opportunity to ask why he needed to see her, she turned to Negal. "That was unexpected. Why do you think he wants to see me? Could it be about the job offer?"

Negal's expression was doubtful. "It wouldn't be Kian calling you about that," he said. "It would be someone else. It must be about a different issue."

"Like what?" Margo asked, her worry deepening. She hadn't considered other reasons for the call, her mind fixated on the potential job.

"I don't know," Negal said. "But I can come with you if you want me to."

She wanted him with her, needing the support and reassurance his presence provided. But what if Kian wouldn't be okay with it?

"I don't know if that's okay," she admitted, biting her lip. "I didn't ask Kian if I could bring you along, and I'm not about to call him back and ask."

Negal leaned toward her, his eyes glowing brightly even in the middle of the day. "If he doesn't want me there, he can just tell me to leave, right?"

Margo swallowed. "I guess."

"Don't worry about it." Negal rose to his feet. "Kian doesn't scare me."

She took his offered hand. "That makes one of us."

He chuckled. "You said that he wasn't as scary as everyone said he was."

"I expected worse and was surprised that he was courteous with me, but he's an intense guy. I hope he will still want to play nice for the benefit of the poor human."

As they made their way to Kian's cabin, Margo tried to come up with possible reasons for the summons, but each one she thought of was more absurd than the last.

What if he wanted to ask her if she and Negal had started working on her induction? That was too private, and she hoped he wouldn't be that uncouth, but according to the rumors, Kian often disregarded social conventions, so he might ask that. Or what if he wanted to tell her she had to choose one of the immortals to be her initiator because she couldn't join the village otherwise?

When they were finally standing in front of Kian's door and Negal rang the bell, Margo's heart lodged in her throat, and her mouth got so dry that she feared being unable to talk.

The door was opened by a guy she assumed was Kian's butler.

"Good afternoon, Mistress Margo, Master Negal. Please, come in. Master Kian and Master Turner are waiting for you."

Who was Turner?

Margo didn't remember being introduced to him.

"Thanks for coming so quickly," Kian didn't waste time on pleasantries. "Please, sit down." He motioned to the chairs the butler had pulled out for Margo and then for Negal.

"Hello." Margo offered her hand to Turner. "Have we been introduced?"

He took her hand and shook it lightly. "Not officially, but I've seen you at the weddings. Victor Turner at your service, but everyone calls me Turner."

That still didn't explain why he was there and why Kian wanted her to meet the guy. Hopefully, he wasn't one of the immortal males Kian wanted her to hook up with.

Perhaps she should save them time and tell him that she was in love with Negal and wouldn't accept anyone else as her inducer.

"So, here is the situation," Kian said. "You know we hacked into Modana's security feed, right?"

Negal nodded, and so did Margo, even though she didn't remember anyone telling her about it. So much had happened in such a short time that much of it was a blur in her mind.

"Carlos Modana showed up at his brother's mansion with two men," Kian continued. "The Guardians monitoring the feed called me to watch a conversation that occurred in Modana's office. Long story short, they mentioned you by name and also that your family is under the impression you are in the witness protection program."

A chill ran down Margo's spine as she realized the potential danger to her family.

Kian was still glaring at her with his intense eyes. "Why would your family think that? Did you disobey my orders and call them from someone else's phone?"

Swallowing, she shook her head. "I didn't."

Kian lifted a brow. "So, how did they arrive at that conclusion?"

She tried to think of something that wouldn't implicate Frankie, but then Frankie hadn't broken the rules. She hadn't given Margo her phone or called Margo's parents for her. She'd sent a messenger, which was very clever.

"I asked Frankie to help me," Margo said. "She called her cousin Angelica, who knows my parents, and she went in person to relay the message to them, ensuring there was no digital footprint to trace."

"That was clever." Turner nodded in approval. "No one can trace that."

Kian, who had initially looked angry, seemed to accept Turner's opinion because his expression changed from menacing to approving.

"What do you think Carlos and his goons will do?" Margo asked. "What do they know about me?"

68

KIAN

"Do you think the Doomers will go after Margo's family?" Negal asked before Kian could formulate his answer to Margo.

He didn't know how much she'd been told about what had happened in Acapulco and whether she knew about the involvement of the clan's enemies.

On the one hand, it would be difficult to explain the danger to her family without giving her context, but on the other hand, it wasn't advisable to give her substantial additional information that would need to be erased if she failed to transition.

"It's possible," Kian answered Negal's question first and then turned to Margo, deciding that telling her the truth about the situation was the decent thing to do.

When he was done recounting the events, sparing Margo only the most gruesome details, her cheeks were stained with tears, and her eyes blazed with fury.

"I hope they are all dead," she hissed. "And I hope that they died in agony."

Kian's smile was cold. "Those who actively participated are, but the leaders who either ordered the massacre or allowed it remain at large, and I intend to rectify the situation."

Going after the Brotherhood leaders, those responsible for what had happened in Acapulco and countless drug-related deaths, hadn't occurred to him until that moment.

Kian didn't command the manpower to attack the Brotherhood's base and take out Navuh and his entire mercenary army. He also couldn't just nuke the island because he would kill thousands of the Brotherhood's victims along with their abductors and jailers. But he could target the leaders when they were away from the island.

Before, the Brotherhood's upper-level commanders had rarely left their stronghold, but now that they had shifted to financing their operation with drug and trafficking money, they needed to oversee the human scum in their employ, and the mid-level commanders were out in the world for extended periods of time.

Regrettably, the upper echelon of the Brotherhood's leadership hardly ever left the island, but he could start taking out the mid-level operators one by one.

Come to think of it, Losham had been operating in California for years now, but going after Navuh's adopted sons would be an open declaration of war, and Kian wasn't ready for that.

The mid-level scum would have to do for now.

It wouldn't be easy, and he would need much better intelligence than he had now, but it was doable.

As the decision solidified in his mind, it settled the burning ache that had taken residence in his chest the day he'd learned of the massacre. Vengeance would not bring those lives back, but it might deter the evildoers from striking with such brutality again, and that was priceless.

In addition, it just might disrupt and slow down the drug supply and human trafficking superhighway, which would also save countless lives.

First, though, he needed to take care of Margo and her family, who had been inadvertently dragged into his world and the war he'd been waging his entire life against the Brotherhood and other devil-spawned evildoers.

Feeling his fangs grow in his mouth, Kian commanded them to retract, and when that didn't work, he closed his eyes and thought of Allegra's slobbery kisses, which never failed to do the trick.

"Did anyone check on my family to see if they are okay?" Margo asked.

"Not yet," Turner admitted. "If you can give me their phone numbers, I'll have my assistant call them pretending to be a telemarketer."

Margo grimaced. "They will end the call before your assistant can ask them anything."

Turner smiled. "But we will know that they haven't been kidnapped. Are they usually home on the weekend? Or do they go shopping or out to eat?"

"My parents are most likely home, but my brother and his fiancée are probably out and about."

Kian and Turner exchanged glances.

"Your brother's fiancée was the one who called the police and filed a missing person's report, so you are right about them being in danger as well."

Margo reached into her purse and pulled out a notepad and a pen. "I'm writing down all four cell numbers. My parents still have a landline but rarely answer calls since most are from telemarketers." She tore out the page from her notepad and handed it to Turner.

"I'll text my assistant the information right away," he said.

Margo shifted in her chair and turned her gaze to Kian. "If all of your Guardians are on this ship, who will you send to protect my family?"

"Turner has human subcontractors he works with. They are all highly trained former Special Ops people. They know what they are about."

Margo's expression turned skeptical. "What good are humans against immortals who can thrall and compel?"

"Most immortals can't compel, but thralling is usually more than enough to get humans to cooperate with them. Given the circumstances, I wish we had a better solution, but that's the best we can do. I hope that the Doomers didn't get to them yet and that we can whisk them away somewhere safe." He looked at Turner. "We can use the cabin again."

"Good idea," the guy answered without pausing his rapid typing on the phone's screen.

Kian shifted his gaze back to Margo. "We have a very nice cabin in the mountains where we can house your family until we are convinced that the coast is clear and they can return home."

69

MARGO

"They are going to hate the disruption to their lives." Margo focused her gaze on Turner. "And what will your men tell them? I assume they don't even know about immortal goons who can thrall my parents and anyone assigned to protect them."

She just hoped that they weren't too late.

"The cartel threat is enough of an excuse," Kian said. "We can tell your parents that they are going into the witness protection program like you did. They already believe that you witnessed a crime committed by a drug lord, so we will ride that wave."

Casting another glance at Turner, Margo surmised that he hadn't gotten an answer from his assistant yet.

"That could work. They will not make too much of a fuss about being moved when their lives are in danger, although knowing Lynda, she will complain anyway."

She would bitch and complain, but whoever Turner sent to guard her would deal with that. Former Special Forces operators would not be intimidated by a thirty-two-year-old valley girl with a superiority complex.

"How long will they need to stay in hiding?" Margo asked.

"It depends on whether anyone actually comes looking for them." Kian turned to Turner. "What do you think? Would one week be enough?"

"Two is better," the guy said. "If no one comes for them over the next two weeks, then they probably won't come at all." He shifted his gaze to Margo. "My people will install surveillance cameras in both homes to monitor suspicious activity."

"What about their workplaces?" Negal asked.

"There is very little chance the Doomers will try to abduct or harm your family members in front of other people. I'm not worried about them being taken from their prospective workplaces."

That made one of them.

Margo was definitely worried about that, but Turner was supposedly an expert, so she should trust his risk assessment. The problem was that Margo didn't trust anyone implicitly. Everyone made errors in judgment and needed to be monitored, even if they were supposed to know more than she did.

Still, if her family was hidden in some remote mountain cabin, it didn't matter if someone came looking for them where they worked. They wouldn't be there anyway.

"Can I talk with my parents and brother?" she asked. "They are probably worried sick about me, and hearing from me might alleviate their fears.

"Not now. When Turner's people are in position, they can give your family members a secure phone, and then you can call them and explain."

That made sense.

Margo looked at Turner. "Any news yet?"

He checked his phone. "My assistant is typing a message. Hold on."

It took forever, or at least that was how it felt to Margo before Turner lifted his eyes from the screen and smiled.

"Good news. They all answered, and your brother and his fiancée were home. My assistant located a contractor who was available to take the case on, and he's deploying two teams to collect your family. Their estimated time of arrival is two hours."

Margo's heart fluttered, and not in a good way. "Two hours is a long time. They might be taken while your guys are on the way. Call the police. Report a burglary or some suspicious activity. That might keep the goons away until your people arrive."

Turner smiled. "This is not the movies, Margo, and things don't happen in an instant. The Doomers don't even know how you are connected to us and if you are connected at all. They will likely decide that you were taken along with Jasmine for the Modanas' nefarious reasons, which is true. Then again, the fact that neither you nor Jasmine are with the cartel bosses is suspicious to them, and they might want to investigate it, but it would be a very low priority for them."

"Speaking of Jasmine," Negal said. "Shouldn't we protect her family as well?"

Kian winced. "The bigger problem is that we can't just drop her at home as planned. She can't go home." He shifted his gaze to Margo. "Neither can you, but that's less of a problem." He cast a quick glance at Negal. "What's your progress with the induction?"

Margo felt her cheeks catch fire. How could Kian be so uncouth?

Negal squeezed her hand. "We are working on it, and I'm confident that Margo will start transitioning before the cruise is over. That means that she will need to stay in your clinic, either the one downtown or in your village. Once she's okay to travel, she will accompany me on the search expedition."

Pulling her hand out of Negal's, she glared at him. "She is right here, so don't talk about me like I am not. Besides, it's not guaranteed that I will transition, and even if I do, I'm not sure what I want to do after that."

She turned to look at Kian. "I really want that Perfect Match beta tester job."

Margo knew that if she transitioned, she would follow Negal, but she was angry at him for discussing their sex life and their future with Kian as if she wasn't there, and in front of Turner.

Negal's eyes widened. "We talked about all of that. I thought that was what we agreed on."

"We talked about it, but we didn't finalize anything. Besides, we can't make decisive plans when the most important step is still pending. It all depends on whether I transition."

70

KIAN

Kian stifled a chuckle.

Negal was still a rookie when it came to relationships, and he had a lot to learn about what triggered women.

"I'm sorry if I offended you and made premature assumptions," Negal said. "Can we at least agree that if you transition by the end of the cruise, the plan we discussed is the one we will follow?"

As apologies went, Negal's was so-so, but Margo seemed like a down-to-earth kind of girl who didn't usually blow things out of proportion. Perhaps if she weren't so worried about her family, she would have let Negal's offense slide.

Margo let out a breath. "You are lucky that I love you too much to let you go, or I would have sent you to Tibet alone. I hope my transition starts and ends soon so I can accompany you without causing additional delays."

Kian's heart swelled with emotion, but he kept his expression schooled. Perhaps Syssi was right, and he was a romantic at heart, because Margo's grumpy but heartfelt response touched him.

Negal lifted Margo's hand to his lips and kissed her knuckles. "I am incredibly fortunate, and I thank the Fates daily for you."

She cast a sidelong glance at Kian. "How long will the job offer hold? Is there a chance I will still get it after Negal's mission is done?"

Kian didn't have the heart to tell her that it might take centuries for Negal and his team to locate all the missing Kra-ell pods. "I'm not in charge of the Perfect Match studios, but Syssi and Toven are, and I'm sure they will find a spot for you upon your return. I expect the company to grow exponentially over the next decade, so there will be plenty of job openings at any given time."

"Thank you." Margo put a hand over her chest. "It's good to know that I will have a job waiting for me no matter when I return."

Turner cleared his throat. "Congratulations on your newly formed bond with Negal, and best of luck on your transition. Now, let's get back to the issue of Jasmine and her family." He trained his gaze on Margo. "Do you know where they live?"

Margo canted her head. "I think she told me that her father and stepmom live in New York, or maybe it was New Jersey. I don't remember. She's not close to them or her stepbrothers, though, and she rarely sees them."

"Any siblings other than the stepbrothers?" Kian asked.

"Jasmine didn't mention any, so I assume there aren't. Her mother died when she was five, and her father married a woman who had two sons."

"I don't think that we have anything to worry about with regard to Jasmine's family, but I will send Kri to talk to her." Kian pulled out his phone.

Turner lifted his hand. "Perhaps send someone else. Kri deserves a day off after her wedding."

Shamefully, Kian had already forgotten that Kri had gotten married the day before. "You are right. I'll send someone else."

Typically, he would have called Onegus and asked him to send a Guardian to question Jasmine, but he didn't want to interrupt the chief's bachelor's party again.

"We can talk to her," Negal offered. "We can explain what's going on and why we need information about her family, without mentioning immortals and Doomers. We can then send the details to Turner so he can inform his people."

"If I allow you to do that, you need to come up with a good cover story. I don't want her to know more than she already does just from being exposed to the rescued women."

"At the end of the cruise, you are going to thrall her memories away anyway, so I don't know why it's important to keep things from Jasmine," Negal said. "But if you tell us what we can say to her and what not to, we will make sure to follow your instructions."

Kian sighed. "This particular story will leave an impression that will haunt her in her dreams, but you are right. In the end, it doesn't really matter."

"Was Jasmine tested for immunity?" Turner asked. "We need to make sure that she's susceptible to thralling before we let her know too much."

Kian nodded. "Kri tested Jasmine, and according to her, the woman was easy to thrall."

"Jasmine might be a Dormant," Margo blurted. "Frankie and Mia think so. She has two indicators. One is her uncanny ability with card games, and the other is how quickly I took a liking to her, and that doesn't happen to me often. In fact, it's very rare. I don't connect with most people. And it's not only me. Mia and Frankie also felt an affinity with her." She chuckled. "It's kind of ironic that I am considered a potential Dormant just because I'm friends with Mia and Frankie. I don't have any paranormal talents, and Jasmine has that and the friendliness factor."

"My sister and wife reported similar experiences with her." Kian cast a glance at Turner. "Maybe we should send some of the unmated guardians to talk to Jasmine."

"Have you seen her?" Negal asked.

"Just a peek or two through the surveillance feed. She seems confident and outgoing. Quite charming, I must say."

The feed had shown him a woman who moved with ease and confidence, smiled a lot, and laughed with ease.

"She is a beautiful woman who knows how to use her looks to her advantage," Negal noted.

The comment intrigued Kian, not because Negal thought Jasmine was beautiful but because he'd noticed that she used her looks to her advantage. "Perhaps I should visit Jasmine myself."

Personal observation could provide him with valuable insights that surveillance and secondhand reports could not. If there was more to Jasmine than met the eye, he needed to know what it was.

71

NEGAL

As soon as Negal closed Kian's cabin door behind them, Margo's shoulders slumped and she leaned against the wall, closing her eyes.

She'd been so resilient through all the life-altering events that had happened to her in the last several days, whether good or bad. But everyone had their breaking point, and evidently, Margo had reached hers when her family was threatened. The strength she had mustered in front of Kian evaporated, leaving her shaken and distraught.

"I'm so scared for my family. I hope Turner's people move fast," she whispered. "Two hours are an eternity."

He wanted to comfort her, to provide some solace in the storm, but he knew platitudes would offer little reassurance. "Do you want to get a drink before we talk to Jasmine? If she sees you like this, she will panic."

Margo opened her eyes and gave him a feeble smile. "We could make up a story for her that will be partly true and partly fiction like we did last night. That was so much fun."

He cupped her cheek. "Yes, it was. But we will not use our own names this time."

The idea had been to make her smile again, but she shook her head.

"For this story to be relevant to her situation, it can't be fun. It has to relay that her family might be in danger."

"We don't have to go," Negal said softly. "Kian will send someone to collect the information from Jasmine anyway, or maybe he will go himself. Besides, I don't think they will go after her parents."

Margo nodded. "It's a stretch. We are not sure they will come after my parents either."

"Absolutely. Kian is just being overly cautious, which is commendable, but you don't need to worry too much about this." Negal was glad that Margo was willing to listen to reason. "I suggest we go back to the Lido deck and try to relax with a drink. We could also go to your cabin. Which option do you prefer?"

"I'm too upset for the Lido. Let's go back to the cabin." She sighed. "I hope Frankie is there. Talking to my besties always helps."

It occurred to Negal that her friends' families might also be in danger, but he'd managed to get Margo's panic down a notch, and he didn't want to get it up again. The first chance he got, though, he was going to text Kian and remind him to check on the other two families.

Negal hated feeling helpless. He could go ashore, get a taxi to the airport, catch the first flight back to Los Angeles, and safeguard Margo's family himself, but it would take too long. He wouldn't get there before Turner's people, who would arrive in less than two hours, and hopefully they would make it in time.

When they entered the cabin, Margo sighed with relief when she saw Frankie sitting on the couch, and her next move was to abandon Negal by the door and rush to embrace her friend while releasing a great shuddering sob.

"What's wrong?" Frankie caressed Margo's back. "What happened?"

As the words tumbled from Margo in a rush, Negal offered a clarification here and there, but mostly, he remained silent. He would never admit it, but he was a little jealous that Margo was seeking solace in her friend's arms and not his.

He was her mate, and it was his job to comfort her. But then she'd known Frankie for most of her life, and she'd met him only a few days ago. In time, he would become the one she ran to, but he couldn't expect it to happen overnight.

Frankie patted Margo's back. "Kian and Turner know what they are doing. I know it's scary, and not knowing is the worst, but you need to have faith in them."

Margo's chuckle sounded more like a hiccup. "You know me. I'm a cynic. Even the most capable people make mistakes, and when it's the lives of my loved ones on the line, I need to stay vigilant and on top of things. But I might start transitioning, and then what?" Margo's gaze flicked to Negal. "Who will ensure that my family is being taken care of?"

His heart swelled with pride that she was looking to him for help. "No matter what happens, I will make sure that your family is safe. You have my word. But even if you start transitioning, I don't expect you to be completely out of commission." He pushed to his feet, sat on Margo's other side, and took her hand. "I fully expect you to issue commands and run the show from your hospital bed in the clinic."

72

MARGO

Margo smiled and cupped Negal's cheek. "I appreciate your confidence in me, but I doubt I will be as lucky as Frankie. I will probably pass out like Karen."

"You will not, but even if you do, Karen was out for less than a day."

It was so sweet of him to believe in her, but he was being overly optimistic. "Let's just hope that I start transitioning and that it happens after my parents and my brother are safe in that mountain cabin that Kian talked about." She turned to Frankie. "You don't happen to know where it is, do you?"

Frankie shook her head. "No clue."

Suddenly, a wave of dizziness washed over Margo, and when she closed her eyes, it got even worse. "I don't feel so good." She put a hand on her upper chest.

The ship was swaying slightly, so some of the dizziness could be attributed to that, but she was also feeling faint, which was probably because of the anxiety and worry coursing through her veins.

Negal regarded her with concern in his eyes. "What's wrong?"

"It must be the stress." She looked at Frankie. "Can I bother you for a cup of coffee?"

"Sure thing." Frankie rose, pushed her feet into her platform slides, and walked into the kitchen. "Did you eat anything today?"

Margo frowned. "I had eggs and toast for breakfast and munched on some pretzels on the Lido deck, but that was it."

Frankie cast her a knowing look. "The pretzels were no doubt served with a side of alcohol."

Margo chuckled. "Of course."

"I made the same mistake the day I met Dagor." She cast her mate a loving look. "I didn't eat, and I had a couple of drinks, and then I saw the goddess that night, and when she introduced Dagor as a god, the shock was so great that I fainted." Frankie popped a pod into the coffee maker.

It sounded like what was happening to Margo, but the difference was that she'd had a proper breakfast and skipping lunch had never affected her like that before.

"It's the worry," Margo said. "I wish I had Turner's phone number so I could call him to see if he's deployed people to safeguard my parents. I can't call them, and I can't ask you or Mia to call them either because it will only expose them to greater risk."

"I can send Angelica again," Frankie offered. "She doesn't live far from your parents, so it's really no bother." She removed the cup from the coffee maker, added cream and sugar, and brought the cup to Margo. "Do you want me to call her?"

Margo looked at Negal. "What do you think?"

"It's not a bad idea. Frankie's cousin visiting would probably be less scary than some big military-looking guys showing up on their doorstep, and she can prepare them for the arrival of the military types. I can ask Aru to get me Turner's number and suggest to him that he use Angelica as his undercover agent."

Frankie laughed. "She will love that."

"She will," Margo confirmed. "Angelica is so feisty that I'm worried she'll get herself in trouble, but desperate times call for desperate measures." She looked at Negal. "Call Aru, please."

"Yes, ma'am." He pulled out his phone and placed the call. "Hi, Aru, I hope I'm not interrupting anything. I need a small favor."

He proceeded to explain what the new concern was in fewer words than Margo could have ever managed to cram all the information into, but that was probably thanks to his military training. Succinctly conveying information was crucial in combat situations.

"I'll get you the number," Aru said. "Is it okay if Gabi and I join you and Margo?"

Negal glanced at Margo to get her approval.

"Of course, it is," she said. "The more heads we put together, the better."

"You heard the lady," Negal said. "We are waiting for you." He ended the call.

Margo sipped on the coffee, but it wasn't helping as much as she'd hoped. She was still feeling dizzy from all the stress, and her stomach was starting to feel uneasy, too. Perhaps Frankie was right, and the two drinks she'd had on the Lido deck and no real food since breakfast were to blame.

"I need to lie down." She kicked her shoes off and turned to lie down with her feet propped on Negal's lap.

"I'll get you a pillow from the bed," Negal said, starting to move her feet off his lap.

"No, don't move. Just give me one of the throw pillows."

He did that and tucked it under her head. "Better?"

"Yes." She forced a smile. "I guess I'm getting too old to handle what I could with ease only a couple of years ago."

Frankie chuckled. "You can stop worrying about that. Now that you and Negal have finally started working on your transition, you will be immortal in no time."

Margo's cheeks heated up with embarrassment. She'd thought they were being discreet, but she should have known that Frankie would guess they hadn't slept on the couch in the living room the entire night.

"Fates willing." Negal took her hand and kissed the back of it.

"I'm texting Mia." Frankie lifted her phone. "We need to assemble the bestie war council." Her small fingers raced over the phone's screen. "And then I'm ordering food from the kitchen. You need to eat more than pretzels and popcorn."

"I didn't eat popcorn."

"I know, but that's all we have left here. We need to restock."

73

NEGAL

The thought that began forming in Negal's mind excited and scared him at the same time. Could Margo's sudden dizziness and nausea be the first signs of transition?

Bridget had said that every Dormant's transformation was unique, but there were some commonalities. Most developed fever and body aches, and Margo hadn't complained about either.

That didn't mean those were absent, though, only that she wasn't aware of them yet because they were just beginning to manifest.

Negal wanted to lean over and press his lips to her forehead to check her body's temperature, but with her feet propped on his lap his movements were somewhat restricted, and he couldn't do that without telegraphing his intentions.

In case he was wrong, he didn't want to raise her hopes for nothing. It was too early for her to start transitioning. They'd only had sex once, and it had been last night.

The vain part of him wanted to believe that his venom and seed were so incredibly potent that they had triggered her transition, or that his and Margo's connection was so powerful because it was fated, and therefore his venom worked its magic in record time.

But the rational and pragmatic part of his brain doubted both.

Aru and Dagor were also gods, neither of them inferior or superior to him, and as far as he knew, neither of their mates had transitioned after a single venom bite.

Then again, Karen was transitioning after he had bitten her only once, but her symptoms hadn't manifested immediately, and it had taken four days for the first signs of transition to appear.

Still, it proved that sometimes one bite was enough.

Closing his eyes, Negal sent a silent prayer to the Fates. *Please, make my mate immortal because I can't live without her. She's my one and only.*

Only fated mates could fall in love so quickly and deeply in such an incredibly short time, and it was clear to him that Margo was his. He wasn't a young man with his first crush, believing that no other male had ever loved a female as much as he loved his. He'd been around long enough to recognize how different his feelings for Margo were from any feelings he'd ever had for any female.

It was like in the stories about fated mates that he used to think were fables. The love was all-consuming, all-encompassing, and, like the universe, ever-expanding.

Surely, the Fates saw that too, and would bless Margo and him with an eternal union.

"What are you thinking about so intently?" Margo asked.

Negal smoothed a hand over the silky strands of her hair, tucking a stray strand behind her ear. "I was praying to the Fates."

She chuckled. "I'm not dying, Negal. You don't need to pray for me."

Hadn't she guessed what he was praying for?

Margo was brilliant, so there was no way she hadn't. She was just too afraid to hope.

As the doorbell rang, Frankie pushed to her feet. "That must be Aru and Gabi."

When she opened the door though, a different couple entered.

Toven's mate zipped toward Margo, stopping her wheelchair a hair away from colliding with the furniture. "Frankie said you nearly fainted. Did anyone call

Bridget?" She put her hand on Margo's forehead. "You feel a little warm."

Negal's breath caught in his throat.

"I'm fine," Margo waved a dismissive hand. "The stress finally got to me, and I just fell apart." She smiled at Negal. "Thanks for catching me."

"Any day." He reached out his hand and put it on her forehead, but she didn't feel warm to him. On the contrary, she was a bit too cool. "You don't have a fever."

Toven sat down on the armrest and trained his eyes on Negal. "So, what's going on that is stressing Margo so much?"

"Her family might be in danger." Negal continued to tell Toven and Mia what Kian had told them.

The royal frowned at Negal. "Why didn't Kian tell me? You and I ought to hop on a plane to Los Angeles and take care of those Doomers if they show up."

Margo looked like she was fighting back tears. "Thank you, Toven."

"The same idea occurred to me," Negal said. "But Turner's team will beat us to it. There is no way we can get there before them."

"True." Toven rubbed the back of his neck. "But perhaps we should go just in case things go south and the Doomers overpower Turner's operatives."

Negal nodded. "There is merit to what you are saying."

"Of course, there is." Toven pulled out his phone. "I'm calling Kian."

MARGO

Margo tried to listen to Toven's conversation with Kian, but her mind was racing, her stomach was roiling, and she had trouble following what was being said.

Lying on the couch with her head nestled on the throw pillow, she fought to keep the dizziness at bay as her thoughts spun faster than the ship's propeller.

Everything felt surreal, like a nightmare she couldn't wake up from.

Her family was in danger, but instead of rushing to them, she was stuck here, feeling weak, helpless, and useless. Not that she could have done anything to protect them from immortals with mind-manipulation abilities, but she might have made it in time to get them out before the Doomers got to them.

"Time is of the essence," Toven said, ending the call. "Kian is on his way," he announced.

Everyone else in the room had probably heard both sides of the conversation thanks to their freakish immortal hearing, but Margo was still human, and she'd only heard Toven's side, and not all of it, mostly because her mind was frazzled, but also because Gabi and Aru had arrived while he'd been on the line, and she'd gotten even more distracted.

"What did Kian say?" Margo asked.

Toven put the phone in his trouser pocket. "Let's wait for him to get here. He was already on his way while we talked."

The doorbell rang a moment later, and when Dagor opened the door, Kian walked in.

Looking around the room, he smiled. "It looks like a god convention in here."

Margo couldn't help the half-hysterical laughter that bubbled up from her queasy-feeling belly. It wasn't even all that funny, but she was at her wits' end, and those ends were completely frayed.

"I was on my way to visit Jasmine." Kian glared at Toven. "But then you called with all kinds of suggestions, so I had to make a stop here to convince you not to get involved. You are too valuable to risk for such a minor operation."

Toven's expression turned thunderous. "Mia's grandparents are in their Arcadia home, exposed, and I don't need your permission to go ashore and fly home to check on them."

Kian didn't back down. "Turner's people are going to take care of them and Frankie's parents." He looked at Negal. "You, Dagor, and Aru can volunteer, though. In fact, you should check flight availability and book seats just in case. I hope there will be no need for you to go, but if something goes wrong and we need to rescue family members, your thralling ability over immortals will be helpful."

Toven pulled out his phone. "I'm checking available flights for the four of us."

"I need you here, Toven. To secure the ship," Kian added.

"No, you don't. You have Kalugal and your mother. Between the two of them, they can thwart any Doomer attack. Stop coddling Annani. You are doing her a disservice."

For a long moment, Kian gaped at the god as if he couldn't believe anyone dared to talk to him like that, but then he shook his head and turned to Frankie. "We don't think your parents are in danger, but we sent a team to sit outside their house just in case." He shifted his gaze to Mia. "The same is true for your grand-parents."

Frankie's eyes widened. "I should call them."

Kian raised a hand. "Don't. You will just scare them, and if the Doomers are monitoring them, their phones are being tapped, and your call will alert them that we are onto them."

"I can call my cousin and have her go over to my parents' house, pick them up, take them for a ride, and tell them what's going on in the car."

"You could do that," Kian agreed. "But I suggest waiting for the teams to arrive at their designated locations and reporting to us before doing anything that could potentially sabotage them." He glanced at his watch. "Their ETA is less than an hour." He lifted his head and looked at Margo. "I'm positive they will arrive in time to get your family out and relocate them to the cabin. You have nothing to worry about."

When someone told Margo that she had nothing to worry about, her response was usually the opposite, which was what was happening now.

"A lot can happen in an hour." Margo swallowed the bile rising in her throat. "And in the meantime, they're sitting ducks. I don't want to wait that long. Frankie's cousin Angelica lives less than a fifteen-minute drive from my parents. She can get to them before Turner's people. I should have asked Frankie to call her as soon as you told me about the Doomers."

Kian shook his head. "I didn't want to worry you with hypothetical scenarios, but the Doomers might already be in your parents' or your brother's house, waiting for your return so they can interrogate you about us. If Frankie sends her cousin, they will apprehend her as well and have one more hostage to negotiate with."

Margo hadn't thought about that scenario, but now that Kian had painted that picture for her, it was the only one she could see. She wanted to scream, but instead, she bit her tongue until she tasted blood.

This was her fault. She had poked her nose in where it hadn't belonged, got herself kidnapped by a drug lord, and brought this danger to her family's doorstep.

The guilt was suffocating in its intensity, and suddenly, she couldn't breathe or see through the dark spots multiplying in her field of vision. The world tilted and spun as the voices around her faded into a distant buzz.

Dimly, Margo heard someone call her name but couldn't answer because she was spiraling into a black abyss.

Awareness returned in sluggish increments. First, there was touch, Negal's fingers brushing against her cheek. Then sound, the low murmur of concerned voices. Finally, after a gargantuan effort, Margo managed to crack her eyes open just a sliver and squinted against the too-bright lights.

"There you are," Negal breathed. As his handsome face swam into focus, the relief and love shining in his eyes made her heart twinge. "You scared me, Nesha," he whispered.

"Sorry," she croaked, wincing at the dry rasp of her throat. "How long was I out?

Negal helped her sit up just enough to sip from a glass of water. "A couple of minutes, but it felt like an eternity."

Margo glanced around at the worried faces of her friends and their mates, but Kian was gone.

"Where is Kian?" she asked.

"He called Bridget to come check on you and then went to see Jasmine." Negal smoothed her hair with such tender fingers that tears pricked her eyes. "He said that as soon as Turner's people check in, he will let us know."

Margo wished she could close her eyes, and when she opened them again, everyone she loved would be safe.

NEGAL

Negal cradled Margo against his chest and thought of ways to get his hands on a syringe. He needed to administer a transfusion of his blood as soon as possible, regardless of whether Margo was transitioning or there was something else wrong with her.

His blood could fix whatever needed fixing.

Seeing her like that, looking sickly and defeated, was slaying him. He needed his vibrant and assertive mate back.

How did humans deal with the mortality of their loved ones? It was intolerable.

Where was the doctor? Why was it taking her so long to get to Margo?

It felt like an eternity until the doorbell finally rang.

When Dagor opened the door, Bridget strode in with her medical bag in hand.

"Here is my patient." She sat on the coffee table, put her doctor's bag beside her, and gripped Margo's wrist.

"I think Margo is transitioning," Negal said in a near whisper.

"I'm not," Margo murmured. "It's just the stress and anxiety. It got to be too much, and I fell apart. I'm sorry they dragged you here for nothing, Doctor Bridget."

"Nothing to be sorry about." The doctor let go of her wrist. "Your pulse is all over the place, which can be the result of intense emotions."

Negal shook his head. "You've been kidnapped and drugged. You were terrified of becoming a monster's plaything, rescued, and then faced with the existence of gods and immortals, yet you handled it all with your head held high and in good spirits. Your reaction was never this extreme."

"Not true." Margo smiled at him. "I fainted when I first saw you." She lifted her hand and cupped his cheek. "My angel." She gave him a look so full of love and adoration that his heart turned to goo.

Bending down, he pressed a kiss to her forehead, which, regrettably, still felt cool to him. "That was different. You fainted because of the drugs and the alcohol and being in the sun for too long. Something else is going on with you now."

A ghost of a smile played on Margo's lips. "When it was just me in danger, I could handle it. But when it's my family, it's so much worse." Her voice broke, and she swallowed thickly. "I feel responsible for dragging them into this mess."

"None of this is your fault, my warrior mate." Negal brought her hand to his lips and brushed his lips over her knuckles. "I love how fiercely protective you are of those you love, but falsely blaming yourself is not helping anyone."

Bridget cleared her throat, reminding them that they were not alone. "Since you suspect Margo is transitioning, I assume you have started the induction process."

As Negal nodded, Margo tensed in his arms.

"When did you start?" she asked.

"Last night," Negal said.

As a deep blush tinted Margo's cheeks, she pinched his thigh in a warning.

He took her other hand to prevent her from pinching him again. "You have nothing to feel embarrassed or ashamed about, my love, and certainly not when the information is medically relevant."

The doctor nodded and looked at Margo. "It's not likely that you are transitioning so soon after your first venom infusion, but I can't rule anything out. I need to check what's going on with you, but I suggest we move to the bedroom for the examination so you will have some privacy."

Margo's fingers tightened around Negal's. "Can Negal come with me?"

Bridget's expression softened. "Of course. I know better than to keep the mate of a transitioning Dormant away, not unless they are uncomfortable about being examined in front of their lovers."

Negal looked into Margo's eyes, and when she smiled and nodded, he gathered her into his arms once more, cradling her like the precious treasure she was, and carried her to the bedroom.

She relaxed against him, tucking her face into the crook of his neck. "I'm not transitioning."

He chuckled. "I see that you haven't lost your stubbornness."

"I'm not stubborn," she insisted as he laid her on the bed. "I'm just being realistic. Even Bridget says that no one transitions after one venom bite."

"I didn't say that," Bridget said as she closed the door. "I said that it's not likely, not that it's impossible."

76

MARGO

B ridget's touch was gentle but professional and firm as she checked Margo's vitals. "Can you describe your symptoms for me?" she asked, wrapping a blood pressure cuff around Margo's arm.

Margo took a slow, steadying breath. "I feel dizzy, like the world is spinning, even when I'm lying down. And I'm weak like my limbs are made of lead." She swallowed against the dryness in her throat.

"Sore throat? Runny nose?" Bridget asked after recording the blood pressure test results.

Margo shook her head. "Just dry."

"What about aches and pains?"

"Only my head," Margo said. "It has just started pounding."

She glanced at Negal, who was standing by the door, a concerned expression on his handsome face. She missed the warmth and strength of his hand but felt silly about reaching for him and kept her hands loose at her sides.

Bridget's forehead furrowed as she jotted notes on her tablet. "Your temperature is slightly elevated but within the normal range, and your blood pressure is a little low, which could explain the dizziness and fainting. Usually, the transition is accompanied by elevated blood pressure, not low, but I still think that you are transitioning."

Margo wished it was true, but nothing the doctor had said should have led to that conclusion. "Why do you think that I'm transitioning if my symptoms don't align with how it usually happens?"

The doctor put her tablet on the nightstand. "None of the humans on the ship are sick, so you couldn't have caught a virus from them, and the fact that you just started working on the transition last night, and developed symptoms today cannot be dismissed as coincidental. Besides, we've seen transitions play out in so many different ways that it's difficult to say anything is unusual. Kri's mate, Michael, started growing venom glands before we realized that he was transitioning."

"Are you sure?" Margo's throat felt even dryer. "Has it ever happened to anyone so quickly?"

Bridget pursed her lips. "Well, we do have an instance where a Dormant was induced by one bite from a powerful immortal during a random hookup, and the symptoms of her transition were so mild that she just thought she had the flu. That immortal is what we call 'close to the source.' As is Kian, who performed the induction of my mate. Just the one bite and Victor didn't even wake up until his transition was complete."

She glanced between them. "Still, I would have expected at least twenty-four hours to pass before any symptoms manifested, but Negal is a god, so he has extra mojo that mere immortals do not have."

Margo's mind spun with the implications. If this wasn't the start of her transition, then what was wrong with her? A cold tendril of fear slithered down her spine. "What else can it be?"

Bridget shrugged. "It might be the overload of stress, as you have suspected. The mind-body connection is very powerful, and intense anxiety and prolonged stress can have an adverse effect."

"So, what do we do now?" Negal asked. "Should Margo move to the clinic for observation?"

Bridget shook her head. "I don't think that's necessary at this stage. Karen is still there. She's stable, and if needed, I can release her earlier than I intended, but there is no reason to rush." She fixed Negal with a stern look. "Just keep an eye on Margo, and if her symptoms worsen, call me."

They were talking about her as if she wasn't there, but this time Margo had no energy to remind them that she was listening. Besides, the doctor was giving Negal instructions on how to care for her, so it was all good.

Negal nodded. "Of course. I won't leave her side."

Satisfied with his response, Bridget started packing up her equipment. When she was done, she smiled at Margo. "Rest, stay hydrated, and don't hesitate to call me if anything feels off. Your body is going through a lot right now, whether it's the start of transition or a reaction to stress."

"Thank you," Margo said.

"You are most welcome." The doctor smiled before walking toward the door, and as she opened it, the aroma of food reached Margo's nostrils, but then Bridget closed the door behind her, and the smell faded.

"I smell food." Margo put a hand on her belly. "Am I imagining it because I'm hungry?"

"You're not imagining it." Negal sat down on the bed. "The delivery from the kitchen must have arrived. But I thought that you were feeling nauseous."

"I am. And I'm hungry at the same time. Isn't that strange?"

"I guess so. I've never felt both at the same time."

Margo wondered if Negal had ever felt nauseous at all. "Can you help me up?" She lifted her arm.

"Wouldn't it be better if I carry you?"

"I can walk." She swung her legs over the side of the bed and sat up at the same time, which caused her head to spin.

"Slow down." Negal took her hand. "You are so damn stubborn." He helped her to her feet, keeping a secure arm around her waist as they made their way back to the living room.

The scene that greeted them was almost bizarrely normal given the circumstances, with their friends gathered around the table, digging into the food Frankie had ordered from the kitchen.

The scent of ginger and spices turned Margo's stomach, and she swallowed hard against a surge of nausea. Negal guided her to the couch, settling her against the cushions like she was made of spun glass.

"I'll bring you a plate," he offered.

"I've lost my appetite. I'm no longer hungry."

Toven paused in the middle of typing on his phone. "I'm making plane reservations to LA." He looked at Negal. "Are you coming with us?"

Negal looked at Margo, Toven, and then back to Margo. "Bridget said that I need to keep an eye on you."

"Negal needs to stay here." Dagor looked at Toven. "Aru and I will accompany you."

Margo opened her mouth to protest, to insist that Negal should go, that her family needed him more than she did, but the words felt false even in her own mind and then died on her tongue as a wave of dizziness crashed over her.

Negal was there in an instant, gathering her into his arms. "Breathe, Nesha," he soothed, his lips pressing a cool kiss to her temple. "I'm not going anywhere. I'm staying right here with you."

"What does Nesha mean?" she asked.

"Soul," he whispered. "You are my soul."

77

NEGAL

As Negal held Margo close, he watched warring emotions flicker across her eyes. She was relieved and grateful that he was staying with her, but she also felt guilty about keeping him from aiding her family.

That was life, though. Nothing ever was easy, and everything had a price. To him, though, there was nothing more important than Margo, and he wasn't going to leave her side until she transitioned.

She and Bridget might still be doubtful about the cause of her symptoms, but he wasn't. The Fates had answered his prayers, making his mate immortal so she could be with him forever.

Catching Dagor's eye over Margo's head, he conveyed his thanks for his friend's intervention with a nod and a smile, and Dagor responded in the same way before going back to shoveling noodles into his mouth.

"I want you to eat something." Negal stroked Margo's hair.

"I can't, but you should eat."

"Not without you."

She smiled up at him. "That's blackmail, but fine. If you get me a piece of toast, I'll munch on it while you eat lunch."

"Your body needs more than toast to combat whatever is going on."

Her blue eyes were full of challenge as she looked at him. "That's the deal I'm willing to make. Take it or leave it."

He laughed. "Given that you are back to being stubborn, I think you are starting to feel better." He rose to his feet and walked over to the table.

Gabi handed him a plate. "I'll make toast for Margo while you pile food on your plate," Gabi said.

As he got busy collecting samples from all the different dishes, Negal thought of a way to sneak out for a few minutes to get a syringe so he could give Margo a blood transfusion.

Glancing at Dagor, he suddenly remembered that his friend had stolen a whole stack of them.

Come to think of it, he should have given Margo a transfusion in preparation for the transition, but things had moved faster than he'd expected, and he hadn't been prepared. He'd been caught off guard by how swiftly Margo had welcomed him into her bed.

Negal was almost done loading his plate when the doorbell rang. Since he was the only one standing, he walked over to open the door.

"Kian," he said in surprise. "Did you hear from Turner's people?"

"Not yet." The guy walked in and stopped in front of Toven. "You can't go. It's too big of a risk. We can't let the Doomers learn of your existence."

Toven opened his mouth to argue, but Kian cut him off with a raised hand. "Orion can go in your stead. He's also a powerful compeller, and more than capable of handling a few low-ranking Doomers."

Toven shook his head. "Orion just got married. To your sister. And they are enjoying their honeymoon. The only other compeller that you will be okay with going is Kalugal, and it's even more risky for him to get recognized by his former so-called brothers."

Kian was about to answer when he suddenly noticed Margo on the couch. "How are you feeling?"

"I'm okay, more or less." Margo shifted, so she sat propped against the pillow. "Did you talk to Jasmine about her family?"

Kian shook his head. "Not yet. I was on my way to see her when I decided that talking some sense into Toven was more important."

"There is nothing to talk about," Toven grumbled. "As you said, some low-ranking Doomers are no match for me. It'll be child's play."

Just then, Kian's phone rang, and everyone in the room tensed.

"Talk to me," he barked into the phone as he walked out the door and closed it behind him.

Afraid that the stress of waiting for Kian to deliver the news might cause Margo to faint again, Negal put the plate on the table and rushed to her side.

Thankfully, the door opened a moment later, and Kian entered the room with a very different expression on his face than the one he had sported when he'd left. "Turner's teams reached Margo's parents, brother, and sister-in-law, and they are safe and packing their things as we speak."

"They are okay," Margo breathed. "But they need to hurry. If the Doomers get to them while they are still home, Turner's men will be defenseless against them."

"They are okay, love." Negal cupped her cheek. "If the Doomers hadn't got to them yet, they won't now."

"Can I talk to them?" she asked Kian.

"Not yet," he said apologetically. "We don't want them to delay their departure. Let's wait until they're en route to the safe house."

Margo nodded. "You are right. I wasn't thinking."

Negal pressed a kiss to her hair, breathing in her scent and letting it soothe his own ragged edges.

For now, they could all breathe a little easier.

MARGO

M argo clutched the phone to her ear, tears of relief streaming down her face as she listened to her parents' voices. They were scared, confused, angry, but safe.

"I don't understand," her mother said, her tone wavering between fear and indignation. "Why do we have to hide? We didn't see any crime committed, and we can't testify about anything, so why do we need to be in the witness protection program?"

"It's just a precaution, Mom. The people handling the case were afraid that the cartel would kidnap you to blackmail me so I wouldn't testify against them."

It wasn't a complete fabrication because the fear was that the Doomers planned to use her family as a negotiation chip, just not for the reasons she had told her parents.

"I see." There was a long moment of silence. "How long do we need to stay away? Rob's wedding is in three weeks, and so much still needs to be done. Lynda is going to be hysterical."

Margo closed her eyes. She'd forgotten about that.

Everything was already paid for, and all the invitations had been sent months ago. They couldn't postpone the wedding now.

"Two weeks max, Mom. I know it's terrible timing, but what can we do?"

Her father's calm voice came on the line. "We know it's not your fault, Margo. I'm just grateful that you're okay and that we have people looking out for us." He paused, and she could almost see him running a hand through his sparse hair. "Are you safe, though? Are they taking good care of you at the place they are hiding you in?"

A watery chuckle bubbled up in her throat. "I couldn't be safer locked up in Fort Knox. I have a lot of people taking care of me." Her gaze drifted to Negal, Kian, her best friends, and their mates. "I'm surrounded by wonderful people."

After a few more assurances and tearful I love you's, Margo ended the call.

As the adrenaline that had been fueling her during the call drained away, leaving behind bone-deep exhaustion, a wave of dizziness swept over her, and she leaned against Negal's chest. "I'm so glad this is over," she whispered. "Well, almost." She looked at Kian. "Two weeks, right?"

He nodded. "Turner's people planted hidden cameras around both homes. Let's hope no one suspicious shows up over the next two weeks."

"I sincerely hope not. If they have to stay in hiding longer than that, my future sister-in-law is going to assassinate me." Margo let out a shuddering breath and burrowed deeper into Negal's embrace.

Sweeping her gaze over her friends' faces, old and new, she felt a rush of gratitude for all they had done for her.

Toven, a god, a royal god, had been ready to drop everything and fly to her family's rescue.

"Thank you," she said, her voice thick with unshed tears as she met Toven's gaze. "For being willing to put yourself at risk for me and mine. I can't even begin to express what that means to me."

Toven smiled. "There's no need to thank me, Margo. We're family now. Besides, I would have been in no danger, and I'm not saying that to boast."

"I don't know about that." She chuckled. "I don't mean about your formidable godly powers. I'm well aware of those. I don't know if we are a family yet. That depends on whether I will turn immortal."

"You will." Kian surprised her by the conviction in his voice. "I can welcome you to the clan with full confidence that you will meet the necessary criteria, which are immortality and loyalty to the clan."

Mia heaved a sigh. "I wish Dagor, Aru, and Negal could join the clan as well so we could all be together."

Margo swallowed past the sudden tightness in her throat. She wished for that, too, but it was impossible to get everything she wanted.

"We'll make it work, Mia," she said. "If everything goes well, and I transition, Frankie and I will call you every day from the trail." She looked at Frankie. "Right?"

"For sure. We have satellite phones, and they work everywhere."

It was a bittersweet promise, and Margo's heart ached for Mia, who would be left behind. But Mia had Toven, her family, and an entire warm and tightly knit community of the clan, so it was all good.

Margo had Negal, Frankie, Dagor, Gabi, and Aru, and that was enough. She would miss her family when she trekked through Tibet or wherever else their search for the missing pods led them, but as much as she loved her parents and her brother, knowing they were well and safe would have to be enough for now. Perhaps she would be able to go for a short visit before leaving the country.

Besides, immortality meant that one day, she and her besties would get to do everything they had dreamt of doing together as little girls, including having families that would be close to each other and husbands who would be best friends.

If she transitioned, all of their shared dreams would be fulfilled, just not all at the same time.

Kian rose to his feet. "Thanks to the merciful Fates, one more crisis has been averted." He chuckled. "I hope my chat with Jasmine won't lead to the next one."

COMING UP NEXT
The Children of the Gods Book 83
DARK WITCH: ENTANGLED FATES

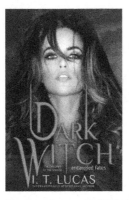

*To read the first three chapters, JOIN the VIP club at
ITLUCAS.COM.*

Jasmine's quest for her prince charming takes an
unexpected turn when she finds herself on a luxurious
cruise ship steeped in secrets. Navigating a tangled
maze of destiny, intrigue, and desire, she discovers that
the key to unlocking her future may lie in the very
cards she's been dealt.

Coming up next in the
PERFECT MATCH SERIES

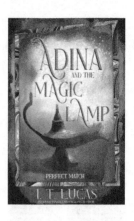

ADINA AND THE MAGIC LAMP

In this post-apocalyptic virtual reimagining of Aladdin, James, the enigmatic prince, and Adina, the fearless thief, navigate the treacherous streets of Londabad, a city that echoes London and Ahmedabad and fuses magic and technology. In the face of danger, the chemistry between them ignites, and the lines between prince and thief, royalty and commoner blur.

JOIN THE VIP CLUB
To find out what's included in your free membership,
flip to the last page.

NOTE

Dear reader,

I hope my stories have added a little joy to your day. If you have a moment to add some to mine, you can help spread the word about the Children Of The Gods series by telling your friends and penning a review. Your recommendations are the most powerful way to inspire new readers to explore the series.

Thank you,

Isabell

Also by I. T. Lucas

THE THIEF WHO LOVED ME
MY MERMAN PRINCE
THE DRAGON KING
MY WEREWOLF ROMEO
THE CHANNELER'S COMPANION
THE VALKYRIE & THE WITCH
ADINA AND THE MAGIC LAMP

TRANSLATIONS

DIE ERBEN DER GÖTTER
DARK STRANGER
1- DARK STRANGER DER TRAUM
2- DARK STRANGER DIE OFFENBARUNG
3- DARK STRANGER UNSTERBLICH

DARK ENEMY
4- DARK ENEMY ENTFÜHRT
5- DARK ENEMY GEFANGEN
6- DARK ENEMY ERLÖST

DARK WARRIOR
7- DARK WARRIOR MEINE SEHNSUCHT
8- DARK WARRIOR – DEIN VERSPRECHEN
9- Dark Warrior - Unser Schicksal
10-Dark Warrior-Unser Vermächtnis

LOS HIJOS DE LOS DIOSES

EL OSCURO DESCONOCIDO
1: EL OSCURO DESCONOCIDO EL SUEÑO
2: EL OSCURO DESCONOCIDO REVELADO
3: EL OSCURO DESCONOCIDO INMORTAL
EL OSCURO ENEMIGO
4- EL OSCURO ENEMIGO CAPTURADO
5 - EL OSCURO ENEMIGO CAUTIVO
6- EL OSCURO ENEMIGO REDIMIDO

LES ENFANTS DES DIEUX
DARK STRANGER
1- DARK STRANGER LE RÊVE
2- DARK STRANGER LA RÉVÉLATION
3- DARK STRANGER L'IMMORTELLE

THE CHILDREN OF THE GODS SERIES SETS

BOOKS 1-3: DARK STRANGER TRILOGY—INCLUDES A BONUS SHORT STORY: THE FATES TAKE A VACATION

BOOKS 4-6: DARK ENEMY TRILOGY —INCLUDES A BONUS SHORT STORY—THE FATES' POST-WEDDING CELEBRATION

Books 7-10: Dark Warrior Tetralogy

Books 11-13: Dark Guardian Trilogy

Books 14-16: Dark Angel Trilogy

Books 17-19: Dark Operative Trilogy

Books 20-22: Dark Survivor Trilogy

Books 23-25: Dark Widow Trilogy

Books 26-28: Dark Dream Trilogy

Books 29-31: Dark Prince Trilogy

Books 32-34: Dark Queen Trilogy

Books 35-37: Dark Spy Trilogy

Books 38-40: Dark Overlord Trilogy

Books 41-43: Dark Choices Trilogy

Books 44-46: Dark Secrets Trilogy

Books 47-49: Dark Haven Trilogy

Books 50-52: Dark Power Trilogy

Books 53-55: Dark Memories Trilogy

Books 56-58: Dark Hunter Trilogy

Books 59-61: Dark God Trilogy

Books 62-64: Dark Whispers Trilogy

Books 65-67: Dark Gambit Trilogy

Books 68-70: Dark Alliance Trilogy

Books 71-73: Dark Healing Trilogy

Books 74-76: Dark Encounters Trilogy

Books 77-79: Dark Voyage Trilogy

MEGA SETS

The Children of the Gods: Books 1-6

INCLUDES CHARACTER LISTS

The Children of the Gods: Books 6.5-10

CHECK OUT THE SPECIALS ON
ITLUCAS.COM
(https://itlucas.com/specials)

FOR EXCLUSIVE PEEKS AT UPCOMING RELEASES &
A FREE I. T. LUCAS COMPANION BOOK

Join my *VIP Club* and gain access to the VIP portal at itlucas.com

To Join, go to:
http://eepurl.com/blMTpD

Find out more details about what's included with your free membership on the book's last page.

TRY THE CHILDREN OF THE GODS SERIES ON
<u>AUDIBLE</u>
2 FREE audiobooks with your new Audible subscription!

FOR EXCLUSIVE PEEKS AT UPCOMING RELEASES & A FREE I. T. LUCAS COMPANION BOOK

Join my *VIP Club* and gain access to the VIP portal at itlucas.com
To Join, go to:
http://eepurl.com/blMTpD

INCLUDED IN YOUR FREE MEMBERSHIP:

YOUR VIP PORTAL

- READ PREVIEW CHAPTERS OF UPCOMING RELEASES.
- LISTEN TO GODDESS'S CHOICE NARRATION BY CHARLES LAWRENCE
- EXCLUSIVE CONTENT OFFERED ONLY TO MY VIPS.

FREE I.T. LUCAS COMPANION INCLUDES:

- GODDESS'S CHOICE PART 1
- PERFECT MATCH: VAMPIRE'S CONSORT (A STANDALONE NOVELLA)
- INTERVIEW Q & A
- CHARACTER CHARTS

IF YOU'RE ALREADY A SUBSCRIBER, AND YOU ARE NOT GETTING MY EMAILS, YOUR PROVIDER IS SENDING THEM TO YOUR JUNK FOLDER, AND YOU ARE MISSING OUT ON

IMPORTANT UPDATES, SIDE CHARACTERS' PORTRAITS, ADDITIONAL CONTENT, AND OTHER GOODIES. TO FIX THAT, ADD isabell@itlucas.com TO YOUR EMAIL CONTACTS OR YOUR EMAIL VIP LIST.

Check out the specials at
https://www.itlucas.com/specials

Made in the USA
Las Vegas, NV
13 July 2024

92269753R00246